DEATH OF A HIGHBROW

Frank Swinnerton

DEATH
OF A
HIGHBROW

DOUBLEDAY & COMPANY, INC.
GARDEN CITY, NEW YORK

Library of Congress Catalog Card Number 62-9458
Copyright © 1961 by Frank Swinnerton
All Rights Reserved
Printed in the United States of America

In becoming acquainted with people you uncover layer after layer . . . the final result may be quite unexpected. I suppose the inmost layer is the most important, but each has its importance.

ARNOLD BENNETT: *Journal*

Contents

PART ONE

Prelude

ONE

A Great Man is Dead

ALL were silent while the organist played Chopin's Funeral March; and as usual Stanhope was greatly affected by that sorrow-laden music. He felt his lips trembling. Tears filled his eyes. They rose, not from grief at Curtal's death, but from generalized emotion, charged with age and helplessness and self-pity.

He had listened with inexorable detachment to the panegyric, noting its errors and absurdities, scornfully ridiculing its evasion of Curtal's lechery, atheism, and ferocious malice, and its too fluent account of the man's early struggles and failures. The words 'this brave spirit', ' "baffled to fight better",' and 'gay laughter at defeat' had been particularly nauseating. They were a part of the yarn always spun by obituarists. Legend! Legend! Curtal's characteristic had been gross self-interest. He had responded with rage to snubs, attacks, or the occasional scathing exposure of his ignorance, shouting, vowing revenge, and sometimes giving way to hysterical illness. There had been no gay laughter. The speaker was either ignorant or scandalously dishonest.

Rising arrogance gradually kindled many-hued facets in the kaleidoscope of Stanhope's memory. He thought: 'This sonorous, fat-gilled, wind-bellied hypocrite must know he's lying before God. *De mortuis nil nisi bunkum.* They should have asked *me* to compose an epicedium. I'd have done it *de main de maître*, with superlative irony.'

When at last the trite quotation from *Hamlet* brought all to an end,

> He was a man, take him for all in all,
> I shall not look upon his like again,

11

and long-repressed coughs echoed sharply about the church, the emotions of nearly sixty years had been relived in half-an-hour. Chopin followed. Stanhope wept. He was very old.

Now the congregation was on its feet. Clergymen and ruffled choristers, their eyes downcast, their hands brought together in simulated piety, filed into the vestry. The memorial service to a famous dead man being over, everybody stared to see who, among famous living men, had dared the bitter November wind to do him honour. Knots formed, directing hungry curiosity towards perhaps a dozen emergent figures, and finally concentrating upon Stanhope as the most distinguished of them all. Whispers spread.

'Stanhope.' 'Stanhope.' 'That tall chap.'

Leaving his side pew, where he had been screened, Stanhope moved among the crowd like a noble spectre. Pride, and the old habit of calculation, had insisted that he should come today, to avert a charge of valetudinarianism or jealousy; and sick unwillingness to endure the strain now yielded to longing for release from it. Health was a private concern, something to be anxiously watched, day by day, but never discussed. As for jealousy, the suspicion would be grotesque. Nevertheless, in a world of base interpretations, inevitable.

Suspicion of suspicion set his nerves jangling. He heard again, at a distance of more than half-a-century, the dead man's rank taunts. These, erupting from fantastic egotism, betrayed anger at a rival's good fortune.

'Why *you*?' The tone and expression were savagely contemptuous.

'I suppose I was thought fit,' he had quietly answered. Oh, there was great advantage in height and the public-school training in stoicism.

'Fit. D'you imagine your wire-pulling isn't the chatter of London?'

The charge seemed to drain all blood from his heart. It did so again today. He stumbled.

Why bring such a charge? Merely because one had been commissioned to write—as one had done, with acceptance to all but a few pedants—a new biography of Stendhal. You'd have thought that inoffensive enough? Such a book was quite outside Curtal's range. Curtal, who could hardly read French, was much

too brilliantly obtuse to understand the exquisite contradic-
tions of Stendhal's temperament. The themes natural to him
were all plain; they were social, historical, and political. Well
then?

The truth was that Curtal was an arrogant cad, flattered by
toadies who swore that he could do everything on earth better
than other men. Preference for oneself became an affront to the
Master.

'What's there?' he had demanded of others. 'If you scratch
Stanhope, what comes out? Not blood; but a viscous suppura-
tion!'

The words had been faithfully reported to Stanhope by
friends.

And then one day came the furious direct attack.

'You a poet? Good God! This platitudinous drool poetry?
Southey sausaged it out by the furlong. Where's Southey now?
A poet needs guts. Not a heart of slate and the loyalty of a pole-
cat. Not the spirit of a sham who'd have sold his mother for a
bob, if his dad hadn't already killed her with boredom!'

The words were unforgotten, unforgiven. Stanhope had remembered them many times since, nine days ago, as he rested in
his darkened study after a supper of dry biscuits and a glass of
claret, he heard a quiet voice on the lowered radio, after telling
of strikes and threats and rough weather, say:

'The death is announced of Thomas Curtal. He was seventy-
eight. An appreciation of Curtal's work . . .'

Painfully shocked, Stanhope had plunged the room into
silence.

He could not now recall his immediate sensation, but only
that it was followed by extraordinary tumult, the roar of Curtal's
insults, hundreds of his own unspoken retorts; and, after long
insensibility, consciousness of the hushed clock upon his mantelpiece. Tick-tack-tick-tack-tick-tack, like the quick husky breathing of a dying cat. He was cold. The fire was no more than a
glow. His bones ached. He stared before him at the twilit wall,
where seeming movement was caused by the thumping of his
heart.

'One day I shall hear nothing at all,' he thought. 'Like
Curtal.'

For the first time, that inevitable day came credibly, suffocatingly near.

> There is no armour against Fate;
> Death lays his icy hand on Kings;
> Sceptre and crown
> Must tumble down,
> And in the dust be equal made
> With the poor crooked scythe and spade.

Curtal. Tom Curtal. Not a genius. Never a genius. Never even, in spite of his reputation, an original thinker. An utterly small, noisy man, picking up ideas—some of them one's own ideas—as a robin picks up crumbs; pouring them out, as jubilant as a thrush, but with the voice of some brassy trumpet, in books and articles, on platform and stage, with an explosive quickness that awakened dreams in men and women who prayed, no longer for heaven, but for earthly freedom.

They thought he spoke for them, for his age, for all time. He was the idol of mediocrity.

Now, braving civilization no longer, he lay silent, powerless, the immediate victim of bogus recollections of men who had never known him. This clergyman today, straining after poetic eloquence, well knew that his words, dancing mellifluously among the rafters, would be forgotten in an hour; but he had enjoyed his own performance, thinking what a wonderful impression he was making upon his hearers.

Poor fool! Oblivion was the human destiny. All men, all words, were quickly forgotten. Within one's lifetime, Curtal would be forgotten.

Within one's lifetime: the passionate hope made Stanhope breathe fast.

He was not yet familiar with the extraordinary fact of Curtal's death. A rough voice still barked in his ears; an uncouth presence, like that of some alarming animal in a small drawing-room, still caused his pulse to race. It still raced as he experienced almost frantic relief. Curtal had always cruelly penetrated the characters of other men. His brain was merciless; his pen charged with gall. But he was dead! One need no longer live in terror of pre-demise, to be followed by that inevitable exposure by lampoon! Thank God! Thank God!

So thinking, with the tears upon his cheeks, Stanhope continued through the crowd, remote, wraithlike; almost the oldest literary man now living. The carriage of his head suggested noble dignity; the exquisite melancholy of Chopin's music had obliterated every trace of bleakness in his expression. He was aware of a hush of respect, a silence in which murmured comment was lowered, in case it should disturb his sorrow, a faint bustling withdrawal to give him room. Finally, with thankfulness, of a grey sky and a searing wind.

TWO

The Stranger

THE hush, the reverie, the superbly aloof exit, were all shattered
by one intrusive voice. Alarmed, Stanhope looked down, as if
from high clouds, into the face of a dark young man, hatless, with
a sweep of black hair across his broad brow, whose bold eyes and
spiteful lips suggested a mind as self-confident as it was acute.

The face, not at once identifiable, was half-familiar; and
Stanhope thought he must at some time have seen it in a newspaper photograph. How old was its owner? Thirty-five? Anything
up to forty. Not more. Its expression held neither sympathy nor
reverence; only sceptical inquisitiveness.

'Very trying for you, sir. Your oldest colleague, I think?'

Stanhope, although he heard the mockery, had learned many
years ago to unite graciousness with caution, so that his reply was
gravely bland.

'A lifelong friend. A great writer; a greater man.'

The correction was acknowledged by a sarcastic smile.

'That's your considered opinion, is it?'

With noble courtesy undiminished, Stanhope grew warier.
This young man enjoyed that common sport of conceited youth,
senior-baiting. Youth assumed that nobody over fifty could
detect insolence, or, granted some dim perception, had the skill
to parry it. Also, that no successful man had preserved his integrity. Perhaps, too, admiring Curtal's destructiveness, the
fellow had adopted Curtal's technique.

Nevertheless, confident in his own far-ranging and hyper-
aesthetic subtlety, Stanhope remained as bland as before.

'Based on sixty years of unbroken friendship—and admiration.'

'Hm!' The sound conveyed, and was meant to convey, the
most impertinent disbelief. 'What did you think of the address?'

16

'Admirable. Admirable.' Seeking his car, and escape, Stanhope looked over all the heads and ears which were turned to catch what he said.

'You found it just? I thought it missed——'

'It was bound to miss a thousand treasured *nuances*. Did you know Curtal?'

'As a humble disciple!'

Humility was not in the man's nature. His words held only superciliousness towards a humanist, as if the speaker added: 'With an edge your soft mind can't understand!' Here was a modern type, rejoicing in its own hard insensitiveness, and above all things aggressive. The young man would have been capable of badgering Curtal on his deathbed, while shadows darkened that once powerful mind. He probably had done so.

'Like myself.'

Stanhope, turning away, smiled in pretended benignity, thankful to see, beyond innumerable levelled cameras, his last luxury, the big chauffeur-driven Daimler, drawing close to the kerb.

He did not escape, however. The bold-eyed young man reached the car first, wrenching open the door in advance of several other outstretched hands. He was quite near, the sarcastic smile unveiled, mental conceit swelling his olive cheeks. One must thank him for his officiousness.

'Thank you. Thank you.' Stanhope restrained a shiver of distaste.

'I wish you'd let me call on you, sir; and talk about Curtal. I'm sure you could tell me important things.'

Oh, God! Had brazenness no limit? This sneering patronage! This assumption that, because *he* wanted to pry, one's knowledge must be put at his disposal! An impulsive refusal must be checked. It was impossible to say, as one wished: 'No, no, no; I'm too old, ill, weary!' Or: 'I insist on my privacy!' Or: 'You shall not make a convenience of me. I have defensible rights as an individual!'

Foreboding grew very dark. Old men were mercilessly ransacked. Privacy, nowadays, was an anachronism. Heathen photographers, grinning, snapped their hideous little boxes of torment in one's very face. Tomorrow shots of this scene would be in every newspaper; tomorrow, or next week, or next year, the exchanged words, malevolently garbled, would be in print as *I talked to Graham Stanhope*. God! Disgusting! But how dangerous to refuse! 'Memorial Service Ends in Row. Stanhope Rebuffs Youth.' Malicious stories, brutal misrepresentations, even persecution, would follow. They would kill him!

Safety, however temporary, must be bought by the smooth answer which in times past had averted so many quarrels and slanders.

'I shall be charmed to talk about my old friend . . . my dear old friend.'

'Thank you, sir. That's a promise!'

Blackguard! Stanhope, still benign with effort, averted his eyes from the now burningly familiar face. A drip, impatiently wiped away with his handkerchief, tickled the end of his nose. Bystanders raised their hats. Touching his own in acknowledgment, he sank against the cushions of his car, seeking oblivion.

But the face remained before his eyes, conceited, contemptuous, determined. Every scheme to deny its owner admittance must fail. Such a hide was impenetrable; such a will too strong to be checked by an old man's feeble obstinacies. Stanhope shuddered. Chill pressed upon his heart.

THREE

An Air that Kills

NEARLY sixty years ago he, Curtal, Key, Thompson, Holmes, and Ruddock, all in their early twenties, had gathered to discuss plans for a common assault upon Fame. The scene was Thompson's dingy sitting-room over a greengrocer's shop in the Hampstead Road, where dirt made the windows agate-hued, and the shabby furniture suggested a mass bargain in Caledonian Market. A most unpromising background for idealism.

One rickety table was in the middle of the room; around it were two sagging armchairs covered in torn dark green rep, three other nondescripts, and a tall office stool. The filthy walls were spattered with reproductions of drawings, woodcuts, and watercolours, framed *passe-partout* or not at all, cut by Thompson from periodicals. Thompson thought the world of this abode, 'abode' being the word he used to describe it.

The other youngsters forgot dirt and discomfort in confused talk as they drank beer and munched ham-rolls; but Stanhope, disgusted by his first glimpse of the room, listened unrefreshed. This place was repulsively different from his own carefully nonchalant study, where undergraduate acquisitions of original paintings, china, and finely-printed books indicated the fastidiousness and classic continuity of his critical intelligence. It irked him severely.

Moreover the unbrushed reach-me-down clothes of his companions, not one of whom had employed a tailor, were distasteful. They reproached, with a mute charge of affectation, his self-consciously artistic costume of low-collared silk shirt, flowing amber tie, and fine suit of green face cloth. His impulse was to leave at once.

Fortunately he had stayed. Yes, fortunately, for this assembly proved to be of cardinal importance in his career.

19

'Cardinal. Cardinal,' repeated the tired brain; perhaps, too, the weary teeth and tongue. A traffic-block stayed the car's progress; the red omnibuses towered threateningly, as if to crush all other vehicles. He could not bear the threat, any threat. He closed his eyes again, exhausted.

Memory, nevertheless, persisted, like the drone of a circling aeroplane. . . .

Curtal, like himself, was present by Thompson's invitation. The others appeared to have met before; and Key and Ruddock, who were evidently friends, sat together. Holmes glowered from a corner, heavy as a sullen drunkard. Holmes was always the stupid member of the band; he resented his own inarticulateness, which he explained to himself in terms of profundity. 'I *think*,' Stanhope heard him say. 'I don't *talk*.' Well, he didn't talk, because he had nothing to say. He was miles behind the rest, struggling to comprehend what quicker wits than his own had said five minutes earlier. A bore. Duller at every encounter.

'One of Thompson's mistakes,' Stanhope remembered saying to Ruddock.

'Nature made it first,' was Ruddock's laughing rejoinder. Nobody was offended by anything Ruddock said: his merriment robbed it beforehand of ill-nature.

Thompson was a great letter-writer to other amateurs; and when such amateurs are young they welcome the most pompous commendations from strangers. *My dear Sir*, had been his approach to Stanhope. *Will you allow a fellow-scribe to say with what pleasure he has read your magnificent discourse anent the poet Beddoes? This macabre and too-little-appreciated genius* . . . etc. All written with a J-pen, to give a characterless script character.

'Anent'—fatuous! 'Fellow-scribe'—good heavens! Today, Stanhope would wearily have tossed the letter into the fire; then, in juvenile vanity, he scoffed, but was excited. Though the terms were absurd, the writer had evidently appreciated one's unique quality! One's unique and 'magnificent' quality! Ludicrous in retrospect.

Thompson must have addressed Curtal in similar style, probably about a ferocious attack, which Stanhope had not seen, on some lion of the day, such as Stephen Phillips. The other young men were equally ignorant of the iconoclast's doings; but

as soon as Curtal stumped into the room they reacted to a personality more vivid, because more aggressive, than their own.
There was a stir of interest. Short, broad, provincial, defiant,
roughly dressed in shabby tweeds, his face the colour of granite
and his mouth ready to blast everything gentle or circumspect,
Curtal was like thunder at a picnic.

Stanhope's instant counter-impression had been, not of
thunder, but of a starving wolf in a strange house, smelling food,
fearing a trap, growling at any outstretched hand lest it should
seize his throat. The man had entered a gathering which he
supposed to be already consolidated and therefore hostile to
himself, a stranger. Hence the first angrily scornful glance at one's
fastidious clothes.

'That's a natty bit of suiting. Your dad pays, I take it.'

One had smilingly answered:

'As a matter of fact, I pay for them myself. Dressing the little
ego, you know.'

The following handshake had been a knuckle-cracker; but
one's unwincing stoicism was rewarded. For the rest of the evening Curtal, as if appreciating quality, addressed every remark to
oneself, treating the others as bystanders.

The truth was that he had been disarmed. Knowing himself
to be ill-bred, he always assumed condescension in another; he
needed a friend of his own calibre; he unwillingly admired, and
in time respected, a man whose manner remained suave under
gauche affront. Oh, but that rasping voice! Today, fifty-six years
later, as the traffic was released, and a lorry-driver ground his
gears close behind, Stanhope shivered at an instant comparison.

'The very sound!'

Curtal's pugnacious nose, his small cloudy eyes, lacking
beauty of any kind, and a habit he had of clenching slightly
mottled teeth, which converted a smile into a snarl, were again
visible. Something within Stanhope shrank as it had done that
evening. He smelt foul pipes and stale beer; he was choked by
the sourness of dust-rotted curtains and carpet.

Yet there had been a sense, too, of mental capacity in the
gathering. Ruddock, the straw-haired, bright-eyed Saxon, was
decidedly quick, with an attractive grin of good-humour. Key's
more secret face recalled the Keats death-mask, which belies

every charge of softness and invalidism in that poet. If Key had been educated, and ambitious, he would have made his mark in any profession; but foolish idleness, and too early marriage to a girl he had picked for her looks in some street encounter, had been fatal. It was a history familiar enough in the general pattern of clever young men. He'd also had unfortunate war and post-war experience.

Thompson was always poor quality stuff. Feebleness showed in that long chin and wide indeterminate mouth, and was heard in the broken sentences of incoherent idealism. Wavy fair hair, worn long, but destined to vanish by the time he was forty, suggested the poet; but his mind was incapable of development, his verse was always meaningless, his enthusiasm, vital enough to the group's inception, ultimately became ridiculous. He admired everything, from Donne to Bernard Shaw, Beddoes to Hall Caine and even—yes, one was ready to swear it—Marie Corelli and Ralph Waldo Trine. Nonconformist ministers, Liberal politicians, and the evening lecturers from whom he drew most of his stray knowledge, were on the same plane of excellence. They were Great Minds! 'Very powerful,' he said. 'A mighty intellect.' 'A glorious effusion of song.' 'A statesman worthy to rank with Burke or Gladstone.' And so on. Much, much too grandiose!

So was his admiration of Curtal, whatever resentment he might express, in corners, of Curtal's sledge-hammer denunciation. Once, when they had both observed his open-mouthed wonder at something Curtal said, Ruddock turned with a wink.

'Good dog!' he murmured.

How like Ruddock!

Thompson's admiration of oneself had been dithyrambically expressed.

'That marvellous gift of yours for going straight to the heart of the mystery. I can't tell you how much I rejoice in it. To me, all life's a mystery, a clouded opal. To you, crystal. How you do it, I can't imagine. You're an extraordinary man!'

That was well enough. Years later, however, he confessed to feeling that one was inferior at every point to Curtal.

'Of course, I always knew you were good, old man. Very good indeed. Fine taste. Beautiful prose. Really distinguished. But . . . hm . . . well, just a trifle—how shall I put it?—I mean, I don't want to go back on that—but ever so little inclined to wait till others had given a lead. D'you know? Curtal never waited.'

'He rushed in?'

'I wouldn't say that. You do comprehend my meaning?'

Comprehend! Good God, it was one of the elaborate meaning-less words of that grotesque vocabulary! Unfortunately the hiss that damned Charles Lamb's farce drowned all the applause. In the same way, Thompson's fumbling confession was still unforgotten. Thompson!

As the meeting took shape, one had received deference as the only member of the group who, with middle-class prosperity behind him, had been to a University. Deference increased when they knew one had enough money, inherited from Grandmama, to finance a small broadsheet for half a year. Class, education, money; the money was decisive. One had felt it to be so. One had consciously been moved to a position of superiority. One had behaved, not condescendingly—no, no, no!—but with a sort of noble indulgence to those less fortunate.

The others had hitherto enjoyed no privileges. Key was on some local sheet in North London, reporting flower shows and petty thefts; Thompson in a branch of the Post Office; the rest in business. All lived from hand to mouth, the weekly wage exhausted by Thursday, and Friday's lunch rising, if they were lucky, only to a twopenny Cambridge sausage, a roll and butter, and a cup of coffee at, oddly enough, a teashop. They had ideals, and the youthful talent that fades in maturity.

Their post-fourteen-year-old schooling had been picked up, if at all, at evening classes. Only Ruddock, with a merry, intelligent mother, looked gaily towards the future. His attitude was light-hearted. Always in good spirits, he was ready to catch and reproduce types seen in the street, in bars, or, latterly (with the same derision), in superior places.

'Does Ruddock laugh at us?' Thompson suspiciously asked, one day. Holmes's sour reply was: 'He'd better not try it on with me. I'd break his jaw.'

Clever, clever Ruddock! Third-rate; but with a butterfly's touch. On the whole, the most attractive. . . .

Curtal, from the first, calculatingly used the band for his advancement.

'One man can be ignored,' he grated. 'Six men make a phalanx.'

He had counted and appropriated them!

It was Curtal who aggressively discovered one's background and the legacy from Grandmama. He brushed aside the subtlety of a reluctance to benefit from a detestable woman. It was something his coarseness couldn't appreciate. All he saw was that the money was available for his paramount aim, the success of Curtal. In the same way he proposed to turn one's family and schoolfellows to account.

'They'll all say: "Let's help darling Graham. We can spare a pound or two." And of course darling Graham has five precious friends.'

'Us!' cried Ruddock. It was as gay as a bird's song. 'Every one a "jewel".'

Curtal was not amused.

'We need punch. And a name. Something to fix attention. The Pleiad, the Lake Poets, the Oxford Group——'

'And the Cockney School!' murmured Ruddock.

'Never mind that. It's stuck for a century. Like So-and-So's Pickles. People ask for them. "Push; do you see my cap?" '

They had been impressed by his confidence. Only oneself, it appeared, shrank from the man's vulgarity. Curtal, crude, domineering, nakedly careerist, swept all before him.

As a boss, he scrutinized all their productions. 'We'll use this,' or: 'Not good enough. We must strike sparks all the time.' He meant that every decision must rest with him. His own contributions always struck sparks. The rest did not.

'No good, Thompson. Damned inflated stuff; doesn't mean a thing. What you want is guts, man; guts! Short sentences. Point blank range. Bang, bang, bang!'

Thompson stood, scarlet, with sweat round his eyes, and the expression of a boy caught stealing. You saw him gulp with emotion as the big words disappeared. Yet if he had been able to do as Curtal advised he would have learned a great deal. He could not learn. His bangs were less like pistol-shots than the windy bellowings of a cow robbed of her calf.

Curtal, to Key:

'Pretty good, Harold. Nice touches. But unimportant. You're afraid of the big theme. That's where you'll always fail.'

One saw Key smiling, tickled and unworried, sure that he knew what he was doing; but, in the end, fulfilling Curtal's prophecy. 'That's where you'll always fail.' He had failed.

As for the bovine Holmes, his productions were flung down upon the table with a violent hand.

'Bloody awful, Holmes. Dead as an exhumed mummy.'

'Too deep for you, Curtal. It's taken me three weeks of hard work to write those five hundred words.'

'Time wasted, then. You'd have done it better in half-an-hour. As I should have done.'

'That's what *you* think.'

'Well, I'm telling you.'

They had stared at each other in conflict. It was Curtal who turned away, not in defeat, but with the natural peremptoriness of a dictator.

Afterwards, Thompson fumed: 'Who does Tom Curtal think he is? I question his credentials.'

Key, amused by the pomposity, murmured ironically: 'Tom dips a skewer in other men's brains, wipes it on paper, and calls the result an original masterpiece.'

It was Holmes who vindictively grumbled: 'One day I'll kick his lordship in the belly!'

Curtal had never browbeaten Ruddock nor patronized oneself. He'd somehow been disarmed by Ruddock; and in oneself he had recognized superior culture. Such outbursts, rising from a black depth of hostility, which he had been unable to hide, occurred in private.

Another point. Curtal had always praised his friends from the platform or in the Press. Just so might Shakespeare have praised (yet did not praise) Dekker and Nashe. This gave him a reputation, with the *naif*, for generosity. In public, too, he boisterously slapped their shoulders—'Hail, fellow; well met!'—in pretended affection.

All part of an elaborately studied picture for the world to admire. He loved nobody but himself.

Today's impudent young fellow outside the church, although better educated than Curtal, proclaimed similar ruthlessness; but there was one difference between them. Whereas Curtal's bad manners arose from ebullience, perhaps from consciousness of inferior breeding, the young man's were deliberate. Respect for age had given place to ignorant scorn for it.

As the car was driven southward towards Chelsea, Stanhope longed that he might never see the fellow again, never more hear the name of Curtal or be reminded of that stormy past. The past was over; he was tired, unresilient, quite unfit to battle with a self-constituted inquisitor.

'I won't have it!' he exclaimed.

Cox, in the driving-seat beyond the glass partition, half-cocked one ear, as if he heard the cry. Otherwise, solid and square-built, he was quiet as an automaton. Absolutely steady in nerve, unaware of everything outside his animal concern with the car, horse-racing, the Pools, fornication, and what he read in the sensational Press, Cox would silently have shouldered the young man out of his path. Cox had no need to care what anybody but his employer thought of him. This job, or another, would always earn a living; the rest didn't matter. Lucky Cox!

The car's speed increased when they cleared the West End traffic; and as its springs were magnificent Stanhope had hardly any sense of movement. Though not warm, he was less cold than he had been in church, and apart from the agitations of memory and dread of the pertinacious young man would have been well content, almost happy. He drifted into reverie.

It was strange to notice the trembling of one's hands under any mental stress, and the uneasiness of one's bladder. The mind's keenness was impaired by preoccupation with physical discomfort. In this state, names became harder to recall; whole books, even Shakespeare's plays and the novels of Tolstoy, slipped into haze. He tried to say over the titles of books he had read in the past months; all were gone. Only the memory of former angers and resentments pressed close, and the exact words written or spoken of him in hostility thirty-five or forty years ago wounded him anew. They were daggers.

When the car stopped, and Cox left his seat to run round and open the door, Stanhope was at first unable to move, from faintness. It was only with Cox's help that he fumbled his way to the pavement, where he stood trembling.

'I'm . . . all right, Cox,' he panted, unconscious of the tears upon his cheeks. 'This has tried me more than I . . .'

'Hold my arm, sir,' ordered Cox. 'It's the cold wind. Too much for you.'

The cold wind. Stanhope muttered some words under his breath.

> 'Into my heart an air that kills
> From yon far country blows.'

'Pardon, sir?' asked Cox.

'Nothing, Cox; nothing. I'll have some sherry when I get indoors.'

'Brandy, sir, more like it. A day like this.'

'Don't . . . don't say anything to *them*.'

'Very good, sir. But you have a little brandy. There's nothing like it for putting heart into you.'

Brandy! He shuddered. He and Curtal had drunk brandy that night, fifty years ago, when their rivalry over Sally Raikes had been ended by news of her sudden and secret marriage to Holmes. The revived memory made him feel sick.

'Thank you, Cox. Thank you. I'm sure you . . .'

The effort to speak was too much. He staggered.

Curtal, in his violent way, as the brandy robbed him of his wits, had been ready for suicide. He had grown pale, maniacal. It had needed all, and more than all, one's strength to wrestle with him, tear away the knife he had snatched from an open drawer, and send it flying across the room. Meanwhile Curtal's gasps were tempestuous, and the smell of his brandy-laden breath was disgusting.

'I'll . . . kill myself! Kill! Kill!'

'You fool! Listen to me! Listen to me, I tell you!'

They had struggled, not only with bodily effort, but mind to drunken mind. Oneself, astounded, and with teeth clenched to suppress sobs of agony, longed that Sally might suffer equal pain; but fought with no sound except that of heavy breathing. Curtal, on the contrary, wasted strength in bull-like roarings and desperate resolve. In the end, collapsing at the knees, he fell backwards into the big armchair—it was as cold as ice—where he was held, choking, with one's knee in his stomach, until he could fight no more.

His amazed, gaping stare was still before one's eyes.

'God! God!' he had panted. 'I can't . . . breathe!'

'Listen! Can you hear me? Listen! Imagine her vanity. Her triumph. "A man killed himself for me." Not you; "a man." Do you see? Holmes's triumph. You wouldn't be here. *Holmes would!*'

No answer. No further struggle. A thought had been instilled. It was working in the drink-muddled brain. One had saved Curtal's life. That was certain. By subtlety, by the use of Holmes's name, one had pierced madness, turning a volatile intelligence from fever to scorn. Suicide had been made ignominious.

The effect was to be seen in the change of Curtal's expression from crazed stupidity to cunning, to contempt for a saviour upon such terms. This was followed by a shocking fit of hysterical laughter.

'Ha-ha-ha-ha! Bloody funny! That she should prefer Holmes!' Laughter ended. 'You're stronger than I thought.'

'Yes, I'm stronger than you thought.'

'That clod! Triumphant!'

'Triumphant.'

One had relaxed one's grip; but Curtal hadn't stirred. His ejaculations were checked by a hiccup that destroyed tragedy. The hiccup persisted for a while, until it was drowned in a snore. The would-be suicide, his first crazy impulse forgotten, slept, sprawling like a corpse in the cold armchair.

One had watched, hour after hour, until dawn, when curtains and windows could be opened to admit fresh rainy lung-filling wind. Having done this, one had inhaled the breeze, looking down into the empty street, shivering, teeth chattering as they repeated the devilish words used earlier to Curtal. They were half-credible. Anger at Sally vied with exhaustion. One had imagined her with Holmes, she already sick of her bargain and wishing that the arms which held her were one's own; knowing that one's love had been killed.

Was she capable of such premature wisdom? Was she not a wanton to be despised? The wind had become oppressively chill.

Presently Curtal, still pale, with a dark bristle upon his chin visible in the morning sunlight, stared wonderingly about him. The stare yielded to embarrassment, in which shame of overnight self-betrayal to a fellow sufferer who had betrayed nothing was joined to abysmal weariness. He was still the complete egoist. Therefore, yawning deeply, he blinked, moved his stiff shoulders, and sank into morose gloom.

It must have been twenty minutes later when he spoke.

'Full of hypocritical solicitude, I see. *Fidus Achates*. Your rôle. Not so immaculate as usual, though.'

One remembered answering:

'We can't all be as debonair as you are in the dawn.'

'Hm, sarcastic. Blast you!' The little bull-like eyes had sent poison from the awakening brain. There was blood in them. Resentful cunning passed at high speed into a scowl. 'Well, she'll bedevil him. She'd have bedevilled you, you know—thinking of me!'

Never show a wound. Never.

'She won't bedevil either of us now. It's over.'

For oneself, suffocating, that was untrue; pride alone spoke. Nobody knew of the after-collapse, illness, and long period of unproductive lethargy. One had never drunk brandy since. The smell of it was foul with sick memory. . . .

Thankful to be rid of Cox, he guided himself by the wall to his study, creeping within, and stealthily shutting the door. A coal fire made the rugs glow and the gilded book-backs glisten. The portrait of his dead, calm, heavy-lidded wife Adelaide looked down upon every weakness with disdain. He reached his chair, sank into it, closed his eyes, feeling the approach of oblivion.

FOUR

Sally Raikes

AT FIRST, waking suddenly, he could not remember where he was. The dream had been so vivid that he thought himself young again, brimming with the old quick fluency. Alas, this dream, like all dreams, thinned and faded as the room grew clear. He was slow, almost obtuse. Fluency, of course, in spite of an occasional stammer, had not crystallized. It had been called, by that dogged bore, Holmes, his worst characteristic.

Remembering when the remark was made, he laughed in scorn. That ass!

In one of the nineteen-twenties, years after Sally had deserted Holmes and disappeared from all their lives, when he was dining alone in the Wayfarers' Club, he spotted Holmes in the doorway. Checking a first ignominious impulse to duck, he looked hard at his food, praying for invisibility; but Holmes, ever blind to aversion, was relentless. He swelled, drew back a chair, gave his glum, disagreeable nod.

'Hullo, Stanhope. Don't see much of you now.'

He meant, obviously, that a successful man always shuns unprosperous friends. Also, that he refused to be shaken off by any man alive.

A dull glance from suit to suit betrayed resentful comparison of rough clothes which were never folded or cleaned with the elegance of what he would call 'Savile Row'. The glance said: 'I see you're still effeminate. I'm not. People have to take me as they find me.'

They did, indeed! Clothes. Mind. And yet, gloomy with ill-success, he fought a laboured battle for self-approval. He had failed in many forms of writing, and with various women, from drabs to virtuous spinsters, all of whom, he believed, had let him down. He had embraced, successively (passing from his

30

native Nonconformity), Romanism, Communism, Atheism, and Christian Science; and his last effort had been an incredible raking for truth among Mystics. Sooner or later, dissatisfied, he contemptuously described his teachers as 'Them', claiming once again to have been betrayed. Sally's flight was a single item in the conspiracy.

One had heard it all, yawning. Another session would be intolerable.

Too polite to leave the table immediately, however, one had replied, smiling:

'I usually dine at home.'

'With your rich wife?'

'With my rich wife.'

Holmes was never disconcerted by pleasant scorn. His wooden head defied it.

'I see your stuff everywhere. I suppose you get huge prices.'

'Fair enough. Fair enough. I forget if you still read the Bible? Something about a labourer being worthy of his hire.'

The charge was then made, while Teeks, the old head-waiter who still tottered miraculously through his duties, offered an order-tablet, and, with his incurable tic, quavered over them both.

'You don't labour. You just spill it.' Holmes took Teeks's pencil without acknowledgment, and failed to write his order. 'You never think things out.'

'Would you call that automatic writing?'

'You've always been too fluent, Stanhope. My God, when I consider the hard thinking it takes me to write a page!'

'But then you've always loaded every rift with ore.'

'I don't know about that. I aim at the guts of the matter. Giving people something to get their mental teeth into.'

'Biting hard. They must feel they're chewing the Rock of Ages.'

Some movement occurred in that solemn dulness; sarcasm had penetrated. For a moment there was no reply; but after cogitation vanity and resentment were resolved. Scowling, Holmes remarked with satisfaction:

'What I said about your superficiality went home.'

'It may have been true.'

'It *is* true, by God! You laugh, you sneer, because you don't understand.'

'I really understand very little indeed. Almost nothing. And now you must order your dinner, and I must go. I'm due at the Ruddock first night. That's why I'm not dining at home. A light snack.'

'Ruddock? He doesn't send *me* free tickets.'

'Nor me, I assure you. I'm privileged to buy them.'

'I shouldn't dream of doing that. Who's Ruddock? A damned popular dramatist.'

'He'll probably be damned tonight. Or tomorrow morning. You'll be able to see for yourself.'

Looking back from the doorway, one had seen the patient Teeks bending obsequiously, while Holmes masticated the end of a borrowed pencil.

Smiling with renewed irony at thought of that grotesque talk, Stanhope dwelt again upon Sally, imagining her before him with the slyness, pretence to fine taste, and uneasy gaiety which, he now knew, confessed her immature bewilderment. She had appreciated nothing but the delight, the tears, the exhilaration of the moment. A poor little pretty butterfly, to whom charm was a protective shield.

How had such a trifler infatuated Curtal and himself? Through lust of the eye? How clearly had she perceived her own shallowness? Probably not at all. She had thought of love as an extension of the kissings and tumblings of children's parties— Postman's Knock, where darkness made herself and little boys bold, or Consequences, with its 'in the end they . . .' No doubt 'married'.

She must have recognized that men, much older than herself, who spoke professionally of the arts and sciences, were exceptional; and was flattered by their interest, titillated by guesses at their feelings. Desire to please—to please at all times—had done the rest.

Had she, finally, taken fright at too great a responsibility?

Neither he nor Curtal could decide. In after years the gay lustre of youth must have died, and the short—oh, exquisitely endearing—flutter of mind dwindled. She had certainly come to loathe Holmes!

He brooded upon the incessant waste, through folly and vanity, of human happiness.

.   .   .   .   .

Long afterwards, his ears caught the sound of whispering;
but he did not move. Keeping his eyes closed, he peeped stealthily
under long lashes at the two women who stood watching him
with a flustered hunger for sensation. By God—as Holmes would
have said—they were anticipating his death and all the excitement that, for them, would follow it.

'Should I ring Meredith, then?' were the first intelligible words.

'Might be as well.' There was a pause. 'He's breathing, anyway. Did you see his mouth go? He's shut it again. I should wait
a bit.'

'Give me quite a turn. You know, seeing him so white.'

'Yes, I know. It's bound to happen sooner or later, at his
age. A good thing if he did slip away. Well, for him, I mean;
not us. Lose our jobs.'

'That's what Cox said. He said: "It's coming, my lady! We
shall all be in the street by the end of the month." '

'Well, they'd have to pay us our wages.'

'It was Cox's way of speaking.'

'I know.'

'Lose our jobs': the whisper was like the soft crushing of
tissue paper. Stanhope's blood, warm in the moment of waking,
seemed to freeze. 'Slip away.' 'Bound to happen.' 'It's coming.'
A shocking contraction of time was implied. Death would mean
oblivion. All his knowledge. memories, feelings, gone for ever,
as Curtal's were. He felt like a man trying to scream in a nightmare.

Now one of the women had moved back into the doorway.
She was out of sight. The other, his house-parlourmaid Martin,
remained as before, pretending, in case he looked, to smile.
False! False! Having hurried from Cox, and Cox's forbidden
talk of his collapse, she had found him asleep, jumped to a conclusion, and summoned Cook to see the corpse. What a revela-
tion of crude, avid, animal relish!

'Did you want something, Martin?' he asked, with a gentle
benevolence as false as her smile.

He believed that she blanched; but her reply had a ready
briskness.

'No, sir; just to make sure you were comfortable. After your
cold journey.'

A faint rustle beyond the door indicated Cook's withdrawal.

'Cox spreading a tale?' suggested Stanhope, roguishly.

'Oh, no, sir. He doesn't do that. He said you were a bit chilled by the wind.'

In other words, as cold as mutton! The conspirators!

This woman had been his servant for a long time; a quiet creature who pried so discreetly that she probably knew as much about his affairs as her mind could grasp. No affection worked in her heart; but interested proprietorial concern and, of course, expectation. If they stayed with an old man for longer than five years, servants always nourished hopes of a legacy.

Martin, Cook, Cox, and Miss Boothroyd, his secretary—'Jackie', as he privately called her, though never to her face—knew that he had outlived his few relations. They supposed him to be rich. What, therefore, might not fall into their open mouths? Perhaps Jackie did not think in these terms; but the others certainly did so. Why not Jackie? Only because she was young, pretty, graceful? He was the sentimentalist still.

'You can pour me out a glass of sherry, Martin. Not the dry; the rich, full, life-giving brown. I need warmth.' And when the glass was passed to him he boasted. 'Look at that steady hand, Martin! Plenty of vigour there yet.'

She pretended to admire, although in fact he had spilled a little of the sherry on two long white fingers. He did not tell her this; no doubt she saw it. Afterwards she went away, like a good servant, without sound, opening and closing the door so gently that he felt no draught. She was an inferior Sphinx. He could guess at her thoughts; he could not read them.

Did she and Cox share a bed? Upstairs, downstairs, what went on in his house? A wife—Adelaide, over there in effigy, on the wall—would have known everything with a virtuous woman's malignant instinct; but from himself all that passed beyond the door was concealed. If, as bee-keepers do, one could look through a hive window at its occupants' actions and indisciplines, one would probably discover something nauseous. Better, at eighty, to discover nothing.

He sipped; and the sherry moistened his throat and ran within, thawing the frozen blood. Presently an empty glass dropped from his hand. He relapsed into uneasy slumber.

PART TWO

The Past Relived

FIVE

Manœuvre

'AND what happened then?' persisted an inexorable voice.

Just beyond the arc of light shed by his table-lamp loomed an oppressive shadow. The shadow of that shadow, very faint in the darkness, moved beyond, obscuring the comfort of familiar gilded book-backs. A spurt of flame from one rebellious piece of coal occasionally flickered upon a polished black shoe, the signet ring ornamenting a sallow finger, the angles of a saturnine face; and when it died left the restless body more shadowy than before.

The man had a starling's uneasiness. His constant quick movements so exasperated Stanhope's already over-strained nerves that the impulse to cry: 'Stop! Keep still! I can bear no more!' was almost uncontrollable. This torture had continued for thirty minutes; half-past ten had chimed; it was the hour at which, normally, Stanhope was in bed and drowsing gently into sleep.

Had he been younger, with his old aplomb, he would have sprung up, moved to the fireplace, and by towering to full height with his back to it ended the untimely interview. But strength had gone from him. He was intimidated by the man, the theme, the subtleties of his own dread, and the sense of his visitor's inadequate imagination.

Martin could not rescue him. She had peeped once, and would now await a summons by bell. He could not reach the bell. His eyes closed in weariness.

This had no effect.

'And what happened then?'

The eyes were open again. He must on no account, whatever the provocation, fail in courtesy. Courtesy, indeed, prompted what could well strike such a man as an evasion.

'You don't smoke?'

'No.' An emperor dismissed a beggar.

37

'I'm sorry. I smoke very little, nowadays, myself. The doctors advise against it, in view of my age and the state of my heart.'

Still no effect. In Milan, *Don Giovanni* was at this moment being performed. Having planned a night of aesthetic pleasure, he had hoped, sitting very near to a lowered radio, to hear the beloved melodies and visualize the hushed theatre, the gay scenes, the traditional gestures of an unseen cast. *Don Giovanni* was his favourite opera. It gratified his ear, his irony, his sense of fitness; it did not once disturb equanimity, as Verdi's melodramas did. Lovely, lovely work!

Alas, the treat had been ruined. When Martin crept into the darkened study to whisper that a gentleman had called he had felt panic. He had sought vainly for words of repulse, and, in what he knew to be cowardice, had switched off the radio. A minute later he was waving the insensate creature to the other chair. Some perfunctory apology, he believed, had been made, and his own equally perfunctory response ignored. 'I thought I'd come at once, before you forgot.' 'Of course.' . . . Try as he might to pretend that exquisite harmonies were reaching his soul upon a celestial wavelength, he saw nothing but that contemptuous face, heard nothing but that harsh and repellent voice. It came again.

'What happened then?'

No man with such a voice could love Mozart, nor be tolerant of a poet's dreams and an old man's love of solitude. This fellow's interest lay solely in 'facts', and 'ideas' which he could 'break down' (frightful *cliché*) by analysis. Abominable science! Detestable dialectic! They were diseases of an age abandoned to mechanism. Art, taste, civilized behaviour were all dead, as Curtal was dead. Curtal had helped to destroy them.

'Get rid of the lumber!' Curtal had shouted. 'The histories of fool-kings and their wars of ambition; the bloody epics, novels and treatises that nobody wants to read. Burn all the rubbish! Build! Build! Build!'

What had he built? He'd added to the rubbish. And, having said his say in millions of unmusical words, he was dead, along with everything he had despised.

> Thou thy worldly task hast done,
> Home art gone, and ta'en thy wages.

His wages were a false eulogy, a scattering of inquisitive sightseers, this persecuting fiend's interest, and, within measureable time, oblivion.

'What happened then?'

Hark! Elvira was on the balcony; Giovanni and Leporello stood, concealed, in the shadow underneath. They were singing the trio *Ah taci, ingiusto care.* . . . Lovely! Exquisite!

'Happened? Happened?' The Elvira was unaccountably hoarse. She had forgotten the words, the beautiful Italian tongue. She sang like a crow. 'You said? I didn't hear. Oh, I forget what happened.'

What had they been discussing? Was it Sally Raikes? Pretty silly little butterfly, Sally Raikes, lost in oblivion long ago? Or that fool Holmes? Had one's thought hurried forward to later years, to literary intrigues, to the chequered history of the generations?

'Concentrate!' admonished the crow voice. And yet not a crow's voice; it was sharp, bitter. . . . 'It's so important to get this right.'

'To get everything right, I hope?'

'You were in Thompson's room. You saw the others for the first time. They drank beer, smoked pipes. You did neither, I suppose.'

Oh, they were back in Thompson's room, were they? That horrible room with the newspaper cuttings on the walls, reached by steep, very dirty, and uncarpeted stairs. An extraordinarily unpleasant memory. What was the question?

'Yes, yes. All undergraduates smoked huge pipes. I was lately an undergraduate.'

'But yours, I suppose, were carefully-chosen grain at five guineas a time? The other lads had paid a shilling apiece for theirs.'

'Had they? In those days we didn't ask. We had mutual respect.' He would have stopped, in vague dignity; but an urging 'Hm? Hm?' led him to add: 'You assume that I was rich. I was, in fact, quite poor.'

'By comparison, I suppose you were comfortably off? Living in your father's vicarage? The rest, Curtal said, were sweated clerks, earning twenty-five or thirty shillings a week; all afraid of getting the sack.'

Stanhope felt impatient of this dogmatic effort to show the past as so much worse than it was. The habitual falsification of self-righteous contemporary historians!

'That's not quite accurate. They were in good jobs. Happy. Confident. Only Curtal and Thompson weren't living at home. Curtal had come south to make his fortune. Thompson's parents —consumptive, I suppose, because he was tubercular—were dead. Books were cheap—threepence, sixpence, or a shilling a time, with grand bargains in the twopenny boxes;—you bought beer and tobacco for pennies. The only thing they lacked was education.'

'Which you had?'

'Which I had.'

'Was there, on your part, a sense of superiority?'

Impertinent fool! Fortunately one's hesitation could be attributed to an old man's fumble for truth.

'Why should there have been? I remember only the appalling stench of decay in Thompson's room. That was really quite——'

'So you said. The dust, the potatoes, the stale cabbage. Curtal told me all about them.'

'He'd noticed them, had he? That's interesting. I didn't know he'd been so much affected.'

One meant, naturally, that Curtal had a coarse nose. Coarse as his palate. Garlic, unflushed drains, garbage in the gutters after Saturday night markets, had never interrupted his garrulity. One had often stepped aside to avoid unspeakable foulness; while Curtal, tramping through it like another Dickens, grinned at one's fastidiousness, snuffing the odours as the perfumes of Nature's garden. Yet he'd told this chap about the vileness of Thompson's room. Extraordinary!

What else had he told?

What else, indeed, had he told? That was the cause of all trepidation, of the unwilling endurance of aggressive questions. Another such question was immediately fired.

'There's something about a legacy. You contributed a legacy, didn't you?'

Much lay behind the question. Recognizing this, and newly alarmed, Stanhope answered with seeming frankness.

'Yes, there was a legacy of two hundred pounds from my

grandmother. Quite a lot of money in those days. I'd forgotten it.'

'Curtal hadn't.'

'That was generous of him.'

The shadow jerked, presumably in annoyance.

'I suppose it made you feel like a noble patron?'

'You mean a sort of Chesterfield? "Seven years, my Lord, since I was repulsed from your door." I've no recollection of patronage.'

'Curtal said you never forgot it. With regard to the others, did you see them as instruments for your ambition?'

Stanhope's heart jumped at this cool affront. He thought even the voice in which it was uttered had become Curtal's. How atrocious that a whippersnapper should think himself entitled to use such insolence!

'Is that another of Curtal's stories?'

'It's an inference.'

Stanhope laughed at a betrayal of littleness.

'We were all ambitious. We pooled resources. In discussion, it appeared that they had no substantial funds—ten or twenty pounds apiece. It wasn't enough. They asked me what I had; and I remembered this legacy.'

'Reluctantly? Curtal said——'

'Did he say it was extorted? Very naughty of him. It was a gesture of good will, and something more. I mean, something more subtle. I'd loathed my grandmother. I was shocked at being left any of her money. Can you understand what I mean? I knew she would turn in her grave if she knew of what she'd think such waste. And I was desperate to get rid of it. This was the very opportunity.'

He imagined, but could not see, a sardonic smile on his guest's face. When the inevitable comment came, it was in the form of another abrupt question.

'Some guilt complex, would you say?'

'You mean, on her part? An atonement for lamented cruelty? She was too savagely "good" and self-righteous a woman for that. On mine? I once put out my tongue at her. A gesture d'escalier. Nothing worse, that I can recall.'

'Probably censored long ago. Why hate her?'

Stanhope, seeing again the old woman's inquisitive beak and

vulture's eye for his every fault, shuddered. But he would not confess his vision. Smiling, he said:

'I'm sure you don't want to hear about my childhood.'

'Well, I'm interested in that, too.'

'Not tonight. Let's stick to Curtal. That's what you're here for, isn't it? Curtal's your man. Now, we're in Thompson's room, planning ways and means—Curtal's ways and everybody else's means. Curtal merely used us, and the legacy. If there had been no legacy, he'd have raised the money elsewhere. He could always get money—and publicity. Part of his genius. By the way, I feel it would help me, in communication, if I knew a little more about *you*. Your own ambitions (for I suppose you have them, although you seemed to speak a little hardly of mine); and what you mean to do as a result of these . . . shall we call them inquiries? What, for example, did you say your name was?'

The bitter voice snapped:

'My name is White. John White. I wrote it down. There it is, beside you. My affairs are of no consequence, except to myself. What I want to do is to place Curtal in those early surroundings.'

'You're writing his biography?'

'I may do so. I don't know. If you can help me enough. Don't you see, sir, you're the only man alive who can reconstruct a particular phase of his life. Your knowledge is unique. Once you're gone, it will be lost.'

'I must learn to see myself as less a person than a repository. Saddening to the ego; but at my age no doubt inevitable.'

Having winced at the reference to his impending death, Stanhope made a brave recovery. Like some life-pensioner with dependents, he had preservation value. The torturer who turned the rack too far lost precious secrets. So he glanced drolly enough at the shadow beyond the light, which at once became a concentration of priggishness.

'You have a responsibility.'

'Dear, dear! May I know to whom?'

A roughness, as of strangled rage, seized John White's voice.

'To posterity, which will want to learn every fact about Curtal.'

About Curtal? Good heavens! This pompous fool had the face of a masked judge. It had been noticeable outside the church today. No lines about his eyes gave them anything but searching

brightness. His contempt was what Coleridge called the concentrated vinegar of egotism. His assurance was that of a fanatic.
Disregard privacy, denounce virtue, despise the humanist as a
dishonest fool; but for the sake of The Cause demand a right to
pick his corrupt brains?

The Cause: what was it? A hysterical fury to expose only
darknesses in other men's souls. With what object? Good God,
with what constructive object?

'Pardon?'

John White was not asking pardon. He had detected the
unconscious movement of an old man's not quite steady lips, at
which somebody with bowels, seeing the movement as a sign of
exhaustion, would instantly have desisted, apologized, and withdrawn.

'I was wondering, Mr White,' said Stanhope, 'why I should
care for posterity. I never have done so.'

Bitterness was not allayed.

'You've cared only for present rewards?'

'Rewards? Those of the artist are intangible, I think.'

'At least, you never lost yourself in a crusade, never tried to
change the world?'

'I should have thought it impertinent to try and change a
world beyond my understanding.'

'The same old world; good enough for your father?'

'No; a sense of cosmic immensity. And—I'm bound to say
—modest reluctance to swell the fashionable clamour.'

'Hm.' It was scornful. To the fanatic, any moderation is
heresy. 'You think Curtal clamoured?'

'Of course he clamoured. He spoke and wrote loud. Everybody heard him, and marvelled. His voice went into every home.
Mine never did. As you hear, I speak in a whisper. What do you
suppose Curtal's ideas will mean to what you call posterity?'

Astonishment seemed to fall upon the visitor.

'Surely they'll have helped to form its intellectual climate?'

Stanhope clucked his tongue at the cant word.

'My dear Mr White, the smallest news paragraph, repeated
a dozen times, does as much.'

'I don't agree.'

'I'm unfortunate.'

Stanhope was amused at this exchange, which ended in bristling silence. He sank back in his chair, lower, lower, as he loved to do, and brought the points of his long fingers together in a gesture signifying meditation. But in reality he was enjoying the belief that he had distracted, or nettled, the brash Mr White. No longer did he sigh for deliverance. He promised himself, now that he had taken Mr White's measure, a few minutes' sport.

SIX

Thompson's Wife

THIS was not yet clear, apparently, to the visitor, whose disagreeable voice remained contemptuous. He changed his tack, however; sure indication of lessened confidence.

'Do you mind telling me your real opinion of Thompson?'

Stanhope took his time. Danger had receded. He became the leisurely connoisseur of human nature.

'Thompson? Oh, a trivial, uneducated fellow, troubled by a sense of his own inferiority. As you'd suppose, it made him grandiose. He used long words. He learned them by heart from a pocket dictionary. You could see it bulging here, over the right breast. Then he brought what he'd learned into his day's writing. "The debonair deceits of decadence" was one of his early phrases, I remember. We used to say we knew what page he'd learnt that morning. It certainly went as far as "M". "Majestic, masterly, me, miraculous, money, and myth." '

'And "malicious"?' The lowered tone acknowledged unwilling relish.

'He never mastered that word. If he'd peeped as far as "P" he'd have called it "perverse". A dull man. Slow, rhetorical, platitudinous. These were assets to a journalist.'

'Indeed? I'm a journalist myself.'

Aha! Again vulnerable! Farther down, farther down in the chair. So. That was easier.

'I don't say all journalists are dull. I, too, have been a not unsuccessful journalist. Swift was a brilliant journalist. So in our times was Shaw. Curtal himself was a fine swash-buckling journalist.'

'A good deal more than that, surely? Like yourself.'

The sneer was obvious, and negligible. Stanhope suavely replied:

'Oh, yes. But Thompson was our journalistic triumph. With a little luck, he did just what he meant to do. He impressed the half-literate, struggling to understand what their daily lives were about. They thought him "sound"—"sound" was one of Thompson's great words.'

'He'd reached "S" then?'

'See 'skipping". He must sometimes have "leafed", as the modern term is, through his dictionary.'

'But you do admit his soundness?'

'I said that was his reputation. He had no learning. In the early days of the century, when Wells and Shaw were knocking everything down, a lot of people craved to have it propped up again. Thompson did the propping for some of them. They'd ceased to believe in heavenly harps. The R.P.A., Darwin, Huxley, and destructives like Strauss and Renan, had made them all sceptics. And their natural anodynes, shag and intoxication, were missing from the new chromium-plated Utopias. Unemployment had done the rest. But they were still credulous. The modern spiteful intelligence, which I always think hysterical, hadn't been bred.'

John White shrugged off the persiflage. He said, with considering insolence:

'You disliked Thompson. Did you envy his "illiterate" following?'

Stanhope arched scanty eyebrows, without looking up. He cared nothing for Thompson, who had long been forgotten; and no question about Thompson could ruffle him.

'No, I liked Thompson. We all liked him.'

'What? You liked a man you thought stupid?'

'My dear Mr White, one always likes the stupid. They disturb nobody's self-esteem. And Thompson, under the bombast, was good-hearted. In his mean Cockney way, he was generous. He wanted to improve people, not by denouncing the present, which is always easy, but by preaching over again the commonplaces of the past. He was the Tupper of his hour. He hunted through Marcus Aurelius, Bacon, Emerson, John Foster, Arthur Helps, and so on, for aphorisms. You should have seen his copies of their books, scored and underscored—in ink, I shiver to remember—with a thousand banalities written all round the margins. "Profound!" "I respectfully question this!" "See

Plato." That sort of thing. But he was kind to his mother, his secretary, his colleagues, and, when he married, his wife——'

'His wife,' asked John White, sharply alert. 'I want to hear your opinion of his wife.'

How strange to catch some human quality at last in that cruel voice! The sound quickened attention. Why should Mr White feel vehement interest in the scowling Hester? That was a matter for delightful thought-spinning later. No surprise or curiosity must now be shown.

'Have you heard Curtal's?'

'It's yours I want.'

'I'm afraid it will be less eloquent. Give me a moment to recall the impressions of forty years ago. By the way, are you married yourself?'

The delayed answer was ungracious.

'As a matter of fact, I am.'

'Happily, I hope.'

'Quite.'

Hm! Most interesting. Too quick; too ambiguous. Probably there was imperfect sympathy, understandable with such a man. Yes, imagine him in the home!

'Good. Good. I'm glad to hear it. Nowadays, so many marriages are brittle. Well, now, Thompson: Thompson managed to join a paper for half-baked agnostics, called *The Thinking Man*. It was a moribund, pragmatical sheet, glum, very high-toned; quite unprofitable. Thompson loved it. He'd found his niche. He'd also found fortune; because in a couple of months the editor was carried off by pneumonia, and Thompson whisked straight into the editorial chair before they could appoint anybody else. Curtal told him to do that. Thompson always obeyed Curtal. And the Cheeryble Brothers, bland old bankers who ran the paper as a naughty hobby, were presented with a *fait accompli*. He'd never have done such a thing of his own accord. He was too sound a moralist.'

'You *did* dislike him!' ejaculated John White.

'What? Never, I assure you. Thompson pulled the paper together. He almost made it pay. Nonconformist sermons were preached against it. Very serious, you know; flowing on interminably, alliterative, allusive, and I must admit eloquent in

Thompson's own turgid way. His ethical conceptions didn't amount to much; but the readers liked his rolling sonorities. Also a kind of pompous common sense. As Charles the Second said about Bishop Woolley, when he converted all the Dissenters in Suffolk, "his nonsense suited their nonsense". The idea was, that if mankind was only indestructively good, the world would be a better place. Very sound, you see. We thought it might be better, but Thompsonian, and therefore dreary. He helped to form what you would call a "climate" of pre-war pacifist thinking——'

'Which you ridiculed!' interrupted the unexpectedly intent listener.

'After the event I think it wasn't the best preparation for global war. But of course we didn't anticipate global war. Poor Thompson was thunderstruck when Germany invaded Belgium. It seemed to him incredibly unethical. Then his mind split. He wanted us to keep out, to show by our unarmed moral superiority that there was a better way of living than dying——'

'What's wrong there?' demanded the harsh voice.

'You must decide. The problem's too abstruse for me. I admit there's a problem. Thompson's line was, what did the Empire matter? We ought to be small, pure, agnostic. Then the Germans would drop their arms, and embrace us. He had no other answer to monstrous and calculated evil. You thought I ridiculed him. I never did so. I was distressed by his absurdity; but I never ridiculed it. Curtal did.'

'Curtal admired him. He's told me so many times.'

'For his own reasons, when he wasn't quarrelling with them, Curtal always extolled his friends.'

'You mean he lied to me?'

'I think he probably forgot how violently he reacted at the time. He savaged Thompson right and left—most offensively. Said his love of humanity smelled like a conventicle in Wigan. Accused him of yapping while civilization burned. All that sort of thing. Part of the Curtal Technique. Thompson accepted every taunt, because it came from Curtal. That's interesting, isn't it? From your standpoint as—what is it called?—a Curtalian?'

Silence.

Stanhope, well content with the effect of his *bravura*, resumed:

'Through the whole business, though he was bitterly hurt, Thompson treated Curtal with tremendous respect. Footnotes. Leaders. "The greatest admiration for a mighty, but occasionally misguided thinker." "Look at it this way, oh Scoffer!" "John Locke, one of the most glorious intellects in our history, said . . ." But as the war went on, and the news grew worse, and his sales dropped, and he couldn't ethically get the paper for even the dropping sales, his courage sank. His gods had forsaken him. Neither Emerson nor Marcus Aurelius had any texts about a Juggernaut Germany.'

Rustling movements of irritation came from John White. Stanhope heard him mutter: 'You, secure in your ivory tower'; but that, undoubtedly, was a shot from somebody in retreat.

'Thompson had based himself on the notion of progressive virtue; the triumph of the Liberal Idea. When he was dying, I found him holding a copy of Bertrand Russell's *Sceptical Essays*, and whispering: "Sophist! Sophist!" '

'You were amused.'

'No. He was dying. We both knew it. I was visiting him in kindness, as an old, and I hope loyal, friend. Was that very discreditable? I must point out to you that Curtal refused to do as much.'

'Curtal couldn't bear sick-beds. They disturbed his bowels '

'At any rate, he refused. And yet, you know, if he'd gone, he'd have found something pathetically grand about Thompson's last awful sick-bed. Thompson was magnificent in hollowness, pathetic in consternation. No faith to sustain him.'

'What's *your* faith?' asked John White, rudely. 'Aren't you an agnostic?'

Stanhope restrained an instinctive motion of the right hand across his breast.

'Thompson was a good fellow. If he'd been educated, he'd have been an obscure country parson, quoting Thomas Aquinas from the pulpit. He was incapable of hatred. It was his wife who hated. She had mortal detestations.'

A movement came from the shadow.

'I wondered when you would remember his wife.'

How venomous it sounded! Venomous and amusing and thought-arousing.

'I hadn't forgotten that you wanted to hear of her. Now what

can I tell you? She wasn't a beauty. She had a long face, full of
darkling resentment. Black hair; black eyebrows. Inarticulate.
She disapproved of almost everything, especially Curtal, whom
she ferociously loathed. That was first of all because of his ridicule
of Thompson, whose long words she'd always taken as inspired.
His long words, his conviction of perfectibility, his expectation
of permanent income from *The Thinking Man*. When Thompson
was dying they'd all gone; and Curtal wouldn't go and see him.
She was furious—and very anxious. She didn't know what was
going to happen to her.'

'Do you know what did happen to her?'

Stanhope answered, easily enough:

'Oh, people disappear. They have relatives. They take jobs.
It was a confused time. And she had a certain pride. . . .'

Even while speaking, as was shown by the slight indistinctness
of his consonants, he had fallen into reverie about the shocks to
a whole population of that first encounter with mass killing. He
had been personally unaffected by the war's claims, being then
under powerful patronage which secured him immunity from
military service; but the general destruction had broken the
hearts, and usually the fortunes, of all those surviving Victorian
idealists who could not turn it to glib journalistic account.

It had also killed a generation rich in talent. The ardent
young poets, from Sorley to Brooke, Nichols, and Owen, had
given or risked their lives in a spirit of crusade; and of those
known to him since that meeting in Thompson's room Key, returning from ugly Army service, did so as if obsessed by a longing
for oblivion. Key was like Lazarus, in Andreyev's tale, who cast
upon his associates the eyes of one who had experienced death.
He seemed to shun even Ruddock, who had formerly been a
twin in gaiety. Sad that so charming a light wit had been extinguished by the mud and blood and terrified boredom of the
trenches.

The sequel was that, having lost his pre-war contacts, Key
sank, poor devil, from attention. He made some attempts to
catch up with the ascendant intellectuals, which were a complete
failure; and to this failure succeeded what one could only
describe as a paralsyis of the literary faculty. Key made one or
two fitful appearances in the Stanhope home.

'Look here, Graham, can't you do something for me?' he had demanded, at their last meeting.

One had been embarrassed by his air of failure.

'I can, and do, offer my most profound sympathy.'

'I was sure you'd do that. But with all your grand friends, editors, proprietors, publishers.'

'My dear fellow, you know how little notice those hard men take of outside recommendations. Either they want, or they don't want.'

'I've got kids, you know.'

'It's a distressingly difficult world, these days.'

The Lazarus eyes had been turned upon one, and away again, as if significantly, towards the little Manet on the drawing-room wall. Adelaide had bought it as an investment. Then one had seen a dejected back-view, had impulsively brought out such money as was in one's note-case, felt one's hand thrust aside. No other speech passed; no other application had been made. . . .

'That wasn't what Curtal told me,' cried John White, abruptly.

'About Key? I fancy Curtal was able to help him in some way——'

'About . . . Mrs Thompson's detestation. Curtal said she was in love with him when she married Thompson.'

Stanhope felt his old thin legs give a jerk. He remained silent, his mouth covered by one protective hand; both shocked and resistant.

'Apparently you don't believe the story.' Two steel-like eyes must be burning and piercing through the darkness, trying to read his thoughts.

What thoughts had he? Oh, God! Age put a brake on one's resilience. One's elusiveness was clogged by the stupidity of another nature. This man, perceiving confusion, would attack again, as boxers quicken their blows upon a dazed opponent. Quickly! Quickly! One must answer with aplomb!

'Believe? Curtal's stories were legion. One couldn't believe any of them. This one is Curtal at his most blatant.'

'You'd heard it before?'

'I'd heard every story that Curtal told.'

'And you think you knew Mrs Thompson?'

'As far as anybody could know her. She said nothing. She glowered. At Curtal she glowered like a thunderstorm. You saw the grimness of her original Methodism, soured by resentment, by loathing. I assume that the poor woman's dead, or Curtal wouldn't have told such a story.'

'She's dead.'

'Then she should be spared calumny.'

'Is it calumny? You're sure? I wanted to study your reaction.'

'My reaction, as you call it, is one of simple distaste.'

There was a long pause, while Stanhope, knowing that his whole body shook in agitation, tightly gripped his hands in order to conceal the shaking. He had no time to consider what John White was simultaneously feeling; and he was therefore astonished at the rough fury with which the fellow delivered a final blow.

'Curtal always said you were incapable of simple reaction. He said you'd been consumed with curiosity about their relations for thirty-five years. It was when he was trying to mimic your manner that he laughed himself into the fatal haemorrhage.'

Stanhope could hear Curtal laughing, choking, coughing with malignant glee until blood gushed from his mouth. The blood filling his eyes at the vision was Curtal's blood, warm and blinding. His heart beat with terrible rapidity. An immense shadow floated everywhere, threatening to envelop him; a voice which was unrecognizable as his own rose and faded, quavered, died; another voice, at first unintelligibly loud, and then dwindling to a murmur, ceased in God-given silence.

What was that? The sound of some movement reached his ears. Apparently Martin was within the room; but why she was there, and what she said and did, and what had happened to John White, he could not understand.

SEVEN

A New Alarm

HE WAS alone, in bed, and in complete darkness. Not even a knife-edge of light gleamed under the door, and he had forgotten where the heavily-curtained windows were. It must be very early in the morning; for no echo of street traffic was audible to him.

First sensations were those of comfort and peace. He stirred in warmth; no muscle in his body ached; he was entirely relaxed. As consciousness strengthened, an emotion of relief sweetened his dreaminess. The insufferable John White had gone. He was safe.

What happened last night? How had he managed to rid himself of the incubus? Had he fainted? Didn't Voltaire faint when tired of his company? It was a possible example! But the amusement was tremulous. He had endured an ordeal. Question had followed question for too long. In the effort to avoid questions of greater danger he had been too garrulous.

The fatal haemorrhage. He had been, he was still, horrified by the appalling sound of Curtal's laughter in his ears, and the imagining of Curtal's blood in his eyes. He knew at last the truth about Hester and Curtal. That bony creature with the smouldering fire within: there could be no doubt that she had been insanely passionate; and Curtal was not the man to thwart passion. They had been lovers. Poor Thompson!

She had tried fiercely to look into one's heart. He had surprised in her once, an expression of the cruellest scorn. He had never told anybody that. The simulated hatred of Curtal must have been burning lust. He had always suspected it. Thank God he would hear no more of the repulsive Hester.

But White would return. Dread made him suddenly cold. His teeth chattered.

·   ·   ·   ·   ·

For a time he lay still, scheming ways of escape. None satisfied him. But was it not possible that the worst was over? Yes, if White had been in Curtal's confidence for no longer than he admitted. Having declared Curtal's ridicule, and sprung his shock about Hester—what could have been his object? It was inexplicable—he could have little more in that field to ransack. But there were other fields.

'No, no; I have nothing to hide,' thought Stanhope. 'Those innuendoes are the worst.'

He meant, that he could think of nothing more which Curtal, on his deathbed, could have betrayed. Was there in fact nothing that malice could distort?

The long pageant of his life unrolled itself against the invisible ceiling. It was now dim, now radiant, now cruel and sullen, as it had been in reality. He was a very old man, whose memory, once clear, had become so fitful that it rambled here and there, as sick minds do. Sometimes a moment of triumph flashed from his middle years, a word of enthusiasm, a sunlit countryside, a phrase from a great poem; and whenever this happened he grew tranquil. But sometimes the immediate past was too insistent— the memorial service, the cold wind, the recollection of his faintness on leaving the car, and that whispered talk between Cook and Martin—and although the sheet was chill in his restlessly creeping fingers he was hot with alarm as he imagined himself once more beside the dim study lamp with the shadows of interrogation expanding in menace.

Hark! Was that a man's breathing? A cry rose in his throat. This was nightmare. He could picture the cruel face as he had first seen it outside the church.

The face was gone. He thought of the fields he had known in childhood. They spread immensely, full of closing and therefore almost invisible daisies, from the gate of his grandmother's forbidding garden, where cypress and laurel made everything dark, towards far-distant bronze hills. Beyond the hills lay infinite space. For all the beckoning promise of hills and space, he lacked courage to leave the garden, lest he should be pursued and dragged back to punishment.

This was his childhood again, a time when every timidly

adventurous impulse was checked by dread of that supervisory
woman, tall, gaunt, beaky-nosed, steely-eyed, crazily tyrannical.

She might at any moment come upon him by stealth as he
stood by the gate, demanding angrily to know what he was doing
there, reading his poor childish thoughts, and forcing him to
scheme the most laboriously evasive answers. He seldom gave the
answers he had planned, and when he did so they were usually
contradicted; but sometimes he managed to outwit her, in
moments of sweet precarious triumph. When he did this he
always feared that she would return and doubly punish him for
lying.

What an education in craft that had been! It had served
him well, afterwards, in dealing with predicaments, when careless words would have brought endless trouble; but at the time
he had felt as the hare does when face to face with a stoat. It
might again be of use in this combat with John White.

He still detested his grandmother. Her full skirts, being of
wool, or cashmere, made no sound. Her hands and wrists were
hideously grey by contrast with eternal lace cuffs. Her abrupt
movements, the result of excessive irritability, alarmed his sensitiveness as rustles in the hedge after dark always did. She
smelled of cinnamon and the vinegar which, with hard cold
palms, she rubbed nightly into his head. He thought she was
poisoning him, and deadening his brains, with the evil vinegar;
suffocating him with the odour of cinnamon.

Cinnamon, vinegar, and brandy; his three horrors!

He was a very little boy again; and very much afraid. The
sun was going down. He had been walking for hours, until his
thin little legs ached with weariness. The hills remained as far
away as ever; it was impossible that he could ever cross them
and escape. He did not hope to escape, did not want to risk the
unknown; but must go back into the dark house, where everything
was as solemn as a church crypt, and where his grandmother
would envelop him in cinnamon, stare down into his eyes, and
ferociously rebuke him for absence which he could never explain.

'Where on earth have you been, Graham?'

'I don't . . . know, Grandma. I forget.'

'Of course you don't forget. You're a ridiculous naughty
boy.'

Naughty. Naughty. He was naughty.

'Yes, Grandma.'

The old strangled helplessness was upon him.

After all, however, it was not his grandmother who caught him at the gate; but a tall fair woman of his own age, with emaciated cheeks and a nose highly aquiline and too big for her face. She smiled without warmth but with possessive familiarity. She was Adelaide, his wife, who, whether in this vision she was thirty, forty, fifty, or sixty (for she changed little with the passing of time), had directed, helped, driven him on to fortune.

He owed her a great deal. That was unquestionable. Belonging to a family of active politicians who had snaffled at least two Parliamentary Private Secretaryships in the course of a dozen years, she had all her life aimed by instinct at power. Power through and for himself. She had done a good job, a fine, efficient, unimaginative job, for which he owed her much gratitude. But he, too, had done a good job, with a thousand times Adelaide's art. It had been a handsome unecstatic partnership, admirable in every way; and it had carried him high into public notice. Not as high as Curtal, whose irrepressible gift of self-advertisement was unparalled; not, to some minds, as high as Ruddock, with his impudently satirical plays; not—as he would have wished —to great poetic fame; but in pure letters very high indeed. Oh, yes, quite to the top of the only tree that mattered, with positions and honours galore. Something to look back on with satisfaction.

Adelaide never bullied, never raised her voice, even to a stupid maid who broke a vase or stole a trumpery ring. She was unyielding in one's arms, from a constraint natural to her temperament and breeding; and if it were true, as he sometimes thought, that she would have wished to be tempestuous in love, she accepted the misfortune of self-consciousness with dignity, and did not, as some wives of her kind were more than tempted to do, accuse her husband of marital coldness. No; measuring this as she measured everything else, she redoubled her effort to be a good, even-tempered, all-arranging hostess, who never let him down.

She had flattered great men, who were all vain. She had given the necessary hints to her political relations, who acknowledged her claim to their good offices and made the applications she required. Being proud of his height, carriage, tongue, and social aptitude, she had entertained all celebrities in the arts, not as a lion-hunter, nor for escape from the socialite's fatal boredom, but with an eye to their joint success. She had supported him with approval in the flippant irony which passed in their world for good talk. Through her, he had been a guest at innumerable majestic houses; through her, he had picked the plums of editorship and professorship, and received the offer of knighthood, which at her bidding he had declined.

'More distinguished to be a commoner,' she said. 'You must aim at the Order of Merit.'

She hadn't succeeded there. Nevertheless, a good wife. A good wife. An invaluable partner. Such a relief when she died. The ten years which had passed since then had been the happiest he had ever known.

'Did Curtal tell you that?' he asked the shadow.

No answer came. The shadow was swallowed up by another, more insistent vision of Curtal with Hester Thompson, both also shadows. It was wartime, and Thompson, though not yet dying, was in hospital. Curtal and Hester were out of doors, while he, hidden behind a long curtain of brocaded silk in Adelaide's country drawing-room, strained his ears to catch what they were saying to each other.

Twilight, stars beginning to tremble within a deepening blue sky; a strong west wind that promised freedom that night from air attack by Zeppelin; the two standing very close together, whispering—and suddenly the frightful battering of a gong within two yards of his head.

Memory of the gong broke his vision. He saw only darkness.

It ceased, as he stared about the room, to be opaque, but he still could not see the dreaded figure of John White. Mystified, he cast a question into the general shadow.

'Are you there, Mr White? My sight is a little . . . There's a question I forgot to ask. You never, I think, knew my wife?'

'No.' Was the answer no more than a thought within his confused brain? 'No, I never knew her.'

'Neither did I!' said he, with silent laughter. 'I didn't tell her that, of course. It wouldn't have done.'

A change had unquestionably occurred in John White; for his response was mild.

'It never does, to tell *them*. Curtal made your wife an amusing figure.'

'That sacrilegious hound? He knew nothing about her. It suited him to pretend that everything connected with me was a huge joke. As, by your account, he did in the matter of Hester Thompson, which was a lie. There was no end to his ridicule. However, as you can imagine, I was never troubled. I knew my Curtal.'

'You loathed his ridicule. It stung your hallowed *persona*.'

'What a word that is, *persona*! I'm not really surprised that you should use it. The vocabulary of the new generation is flavoured with glib psychological terms. They mean nothing. *Persona*—imaginary or cultivated personality. The assumption is that we all slip into categories invented by charlatans and accepted by their gulls. By yourself, for example. . . .'

There was no answer. Stanhope repeated the last sentence with even greater derision, trying as he did so to penetrate the darkness. When the effort failed he switched on his little bedside lamp with an unsteady hand; but although he threw the lamp's glow to the other side of the bed it did not answer his intention. Nobody was there.

Once more he toiled upon a wearisome journey, this time through multitudinous streets thronged with silent people whose faces he half-recognized. One of them was that of his chauffeur, Cox, who stood waiting beside the car, ready to open the door, but apparently unable to see or hear him as he approached. Cox wore an artful, sinister expression which revealed overwhelming disrespect for his employer. If this were a dream, might it not be at the same time a glimpse of the truth?

What went on behind that stolid *façade*?

It was disconcerting to imagine that one's servants looked right into that *persona* which—as John White suggested—had been laboriously sustained for eighty years. Was this in fact Cox? Had not the Devil power to assume every disguise? Didn't Cox's face change, as one tried to prove one's identity, into the faces of other servants, long ago discharged, or lost as they passed to alternative employments? It wasn't Cox at all, but Murphy. No, it was Jenkins. Or was it Sanger? Man and car dissolved upon the instant; the exhausted walk through unknown streets in a darkened city was resumed. Night was upon him; he still had far to go in his search for the long-sought haven.

'I shouldn't venture down there,' said a voice. 'Don't you remember, it's the street where Gertrude lived. Where she died.'

Stanhope thought his heart stopped beating. It was some time before he could stammer a reply.

'The name isn't familiar to me,' he at last murmured, with what he prayed might appear exemplary blandness, although his voice was thick and unnatural. 'I'm afraid you must be confusing me with Curtal, who had a large acquaintance with dwellers in mean streets.'

'I'm not confusing you with Curtal,' he heard.

'I think you must be. But I see it's very obscurely lighted; so perhaps I'll accept your advice. It might be . . . dangerous.'

'It would be very dangerous,' answered the harsh voice. 'To your *persona*. Also to your public reputation.'

'I have nothing to fear in that respect. What I appear to be in public, I am.'

The laughter he heard was not White's, but Curtal's.

'So you're there all the time, Curtal,' said Stanhope.

Vehement rage possessed him. It affected his breathing. He struggled as if the hand of Death was already upon his throat.

EIGHT

Rara Avis

IT WAS a long time before the fit passed; but gradually the wild beating of his heart sank in pace and violence; and he slipped once more into reverie.

The day was just such a day as this had been. What day was it? He thought himself back in the church at Curtal's Memorial Service, and it wasn't the church at all, but the chapel of his school, to which he would have to go presently, when he had finished the long, muddy trot in vest and sweater to which he and many other small boys were condemned by a rigorous training. Having begun to develop the long legs which afterwards gave him unusual height, he was 'fancied' for the hundred yards, and whether the day was fair or stormy he would have to moil, pausing, walking, and breaking into small bursts of speed, until he had completed a trip around the lanes. One must always run as one approached the School, lest a suddenly out-leaping master who had lain in wait to spy, accused one of slacking.

Slacking was a frightful offence. It marked a boy out as disgracing the School. It was meaner than pocketing another boy's pencil, or using a Latin crib. One could earn a public rebuke; and would certainly be sneered at by other boys. 'Ugh! Slacker!' would be their grunted comment, as they passed. But these others, perhaps, were not runners; they did their penance on the football field, where they were taught to tackle low and trip and perform other highly sporting manœuvres for the good of their souls and the School.

Today his journey, made through mud and murk, was especially trying. Something had caused one of his running shoes to burst at the toe, and he could feel a soreness which would handicap him in the race. It was forbidden that he should cadge a lift in a farm cart or pony trap (there were not yet a plentitude of cars along the country roads), so that he must run gently, to avoid chafing the toe into a bloody mess. Legs ached; shoulders, when he went slowly, were so much chilled by the drenching murk that he began to shudder; and at last, in the final half-mile, as he was running up-hill, the foot slipped in greasy mud. He fell face downward, half-stunned, his teeth covered with gritty slime, and tears, which it would be disastrous to shed, burning his eyes like flames.

As he so lay, jeers from two boys who were not runners filled him with angry shame. Both boys were excused games because of cardiac or other weakness; he despised them as weaklings; but, jubilant at another's discomfiture, they laughed. The laughter grated upon his ears. Of all affronts, ridicule was the one he most feared.

At the Sports he ran well; but not well enough. Another lad, with even longer legs than his own, shouldered him aside before he could reach the tape. It was not, technically, foul running; it was the push and drive of a temperamental bully, such as he had never been able to combat. So every effort in preparation for the race was proved vain. His father would be displeased; his grandmother, from cruelty, not so displeased. She rejoiced in his humiliation. She was detestable.

He made up his mind, then, that as soon as he left school he would run no more. It was undignified. 'I loathe racing . . . jostling . . . that cad!' he said breathlessly to himself, as he trotted to find warmer clothes. He meant: 'I'm no good at it.'

The other boys of his House, maintaining a continuous roar as the runners passed, until, towards evening, their voices tired, were already like ravens. Nevertheless, they continued to bray while the seniors raced. He'd added his own mechanical cheers. He had sneaked in among his form-mates, one or two of whom, carelessly and insincerely murmuring: 'Jolly well run, Stanhope. Hard luck!' turned their backs as they followed the seniors. Insincerely, of course, because insincerity, or what Cowper, speaking of his own days at Westminster, called 'the infernal art of lying', was the lesson most easily learned, and most helpfully retained through life.

It was the ideal preparation for Politics, Business, and the Law. One of the jeering boys, Spink, had become a Judge; the other, a knock-kneed specimen whose name he had forgotten, grew rich in the City; a third and fourth, not involved in the incident, had come at least within reach of the Cabinet. None of them was interested, or useful, in Stanhope's career. He had risen in the School, to the upper-sixth form, had been a prefect, and had not, for some reason, become Head Boy. Why was that? Injustice, of course.

Was it, at bottom, injustice? A lack of appreciation of one's particular qualities? A conventional schoolmasterly preference for obedient stolidity, that made the Head underrate his capacity for leadership? It had rankled at the time; it still rankled.

All justice was partial. One knew the rules; one applied the rules; but one applied them according to secret bias. With all Law to play with, any Judge, ambitious of advancement, might aim at a Home Secretary's or a Lord Chancellor's approval by a decision according with the known wishes of Power. His motives might be understood by more scrupulous brethren; but the Law's dignity absolved him from denunciation.

Deep waters, these! One was drawing an invidious parallel. How often did critics abstain from saying or writing what would make an enemy or wreck a secret scheme! They were forced into ambiguity, or, in pursuit of some collective advantage, silence, about men whose advancement would be disagreeable to their friends. They praised those whom they would meet at dinner, or those who would reciprocate in kind. It was notoriously a part of what Curtal, in bitterness, called 'the literary racket'.

How ridiculous of Curtal, who slashed at friend and foe alike. Curtal did not understand that a gentleman, priding himself upon intellectual superiority, was bound to condemn or ignore, whatever their merits, those not of his own order.

Adelaide, incapable of irresolution, had been wonderfully prescient. One remembered a significant piece of advice:

'I shouldn't say that, Graham. You might jeopardize the Prentice Lectureship.'

The change of a phrase had been easy. One had achieved the Prentice Lectureship.

At the Varsity one had found wider scope than at school. Although, fundamentally, the rules were unchanged—one's form, one's House, the School, one's class, one's country, first, foremost, and for ever—pupilage was largely escaped. One worked, if one worked at all, not so much for knowledge as for a good degree; worked with intent to flatter the minds of examiners, cultivated adroitness of speech and the society of certain individuals—always calling them 'friends', although no affection existed—with future advantage in view. At school, especially in early days, fathers were merely parents, their rank or celebrity inadequately grasped. At the Varsity, on the other hand, one's perspectives expanded. Social position and potential aid were better estimated.

Unfortunately, Father, preoccupied with his churchwardens and parish affairs, and probably depressed at having to preach what scholarship had taught him to doubt, could give no help. He was completely undistinguished; a recluse. Geniality, wit, charm, were all lacking in his character. No boast, direct or indirect, was possible about his standing. There were no wealthy or intellectual relations. There was no money.

Therefore, like any struggling lad from the suburbs, one had to do everything for oneself. One could not invite home the spoiled son of an illustrious parent, who had unlimited credit. One had not the means to entertain at a club or fashionable restaurant. Only innate tact had saved one from a thousand solecisms; only exceptional talent had averted the humdrum life of mediocrity.

'But I shouldn't claim to have been a howling success at the Varsity.' He spoke aloud, with conscious whimsicality. 'I took a good Second; but Mark's was no intellectual college. The swells looked down on us. I was very much *rara avis*.'

Rara avis. One thus glossed failure to attract men of brilliance or overflowing virtue. Did John White, briefed by Curtal, and alert to decry, appreciate one's early handicaps?

'Listen, Mr White. You were offensive about my behaviour at Thompson's. You'd taken Curtal's yarn as true. But Curtal was a liar on the grand scale. . . .

'That day—the day of our first meeting—he wouldn't leave me. The moment I moved to go, he jumped up and came, too. Grandma's two hundred pounds had gone to his head. He was avid to seize it at once. "Strike while the iron's hot" was his phrase—meaning, I might change my mind. He didn't know me.

He couldn't realize how profoundly I'd detested her. His own detestations were never serious. We walked right along the Marylebone Road, and through Hyde Park and Kensington Gardens. Somewhere about Hammersmith Broadway, or it might have been South Kensington Station, I said I'd send Thompson the money next day. . . .

'He didn't want that. He said it had better come to himself. I said, no; Thompson was the convener. He was furious. He sneered: "You're a proper Sahib! I suppose it's having been to a Public School, where they inculcate pedantries." It was really outrageous; but I kept my temper. Also my promise. . . .

'After that rumpus—I suppose he was ashamed of it—he began to talk about the back streets of Huddersfield, and how he'd made up his mind to get away from wool and iron and coal, and make a big name in London and Literature. The most grandiose plans. Novels, plays, histories; the histories of all sorts of subjects he knew nothing about—economics, drama, religion, and what not. I asked if he'd studied them. He said: "You don't want to study them. That's clutter. They come as you write." I said, ironically: "There speaks genius." He said, as cocksure as you please: "I'll say it does."

'Anything more egregious, you couldn't imagine. Of course, he wasn't a genius. Genius is a flame; he was like a boiler—all hiss and bubble. I was aghast; rather fascinated, touched, bored. Chiefly bored. In spate, he was always a bore. Well, you don't think so; but I was his contemporary. I managed to get him away from himself, and on to the others. We agreed that Holmes and Thompson were liabilities; and saw Ruddock as valuable. I think I suggested that Ruddock might become a minor Calverley. We both liked him. He was as handsome as he was gay. Not the man he became in middle-age; swollen-eyed, jowled, coarse-lipped. That was due to glandular trouble; he was too careless to worry about it. As careless of health as he was of reputation. Very foolish. His plays were always superficial; quickly improvised, and meant to amuse for the moment. They amused—for the moment. He must have made a great deal of money. But I understand they're now, for some reason, being revived; and I'm glad his daughters—my little sweethearts, as I call them —should benefit. . . .

'Curtal used to pretend that I envied Ruddock. That was

absurd. Ruddock's levity exasperated me; I couldn't understand
why so obviously third-rate a talent should be extolled. . . .

'You said Curtal died laughing. That was characteristic. He
was speaking of me, whom he hated.'

Receiving no answer, Stanhope ceased to speak aloud. He
began, instead, to speculate upon his own incredible death, and
those who would first—as he had done of Curtal's—hear the
announcement of it over the air; those who would read the
almost certainly inaccurate obituary notices in the next day's
papers; and the very few who would regret his passing.

Rara avis! How few there had ever been. He had inspired
respect, admiration, contempt; but he had been a stranger to
that warm affection which Ruddock and Curtal roused in every
passing mongrel, and every man and woman who had word
with them. There must have been a rank smell in Curtal, to
bring dogs, open-mouthed and tail-wagging, to his side; an odour
of masculinity to intoxicate the women. But the men? That was
another matter; something incomprehensible.

In Ruddock's case the charm was all at its highest for children.
It lay in a beaming humour, a quicksilver in glance and flying
changes of expression. Children leaned upon his chair, his arm,
smiling up into his face. They trusted him. He made them laugh
by his stories, his nonsense, his apparent sympathy in their
concerns. His gift was a laughing silliness. Curtal's was jocose
brutality.

He himself had never envied these traits. He had not wished
to be pestered by dogs or children.

'I most desperately craved for them. Children. Women.'

Who had spoken? Had it been John White? Had it been
himself? But if it had been himself, he had said what was untrue.
Why should he do that?

'Are you there, Mr White? Mr White! Are you there?'

PART THREE

Dreams

NINE

Ruddock

HE ALWAYS, to himself, described Ruddock's daughters as
'my little sweethearts'. He liked to pretend that they were his
own darlings.

Both were naturally blonde, like their parents, and exceedingly graceful; as exquisitely flowing in movement as the incomparable Ellen Terry, as full of buoyant humour as their
father. More acceptably so, indeed; since Ruddock's irreverence
always left a sensitive man's *amour propre* uneasy. Nobody can
feel safe with a man who lacks seriousness.

As he grew stout and torpid, Ruddock had been apt to sit
in his chair by the kitchen fireplace, one fat hand caressing the
fat chin while he indulged in disrespect for humanity in a bass
rumble, and provoked laughter by incessant drollery. The
drollery would have been irresistible but for the thought: 'Perhaps he makes others laugh about me. He doesn't value me as
I ought to be valued.' One walked, with Ruddock, among quick-
sands.

Yes, decay had set in early. Ruddock enjoyed his life too
much. He never repined at a failure, nor exulted in a success.
An epicure, indifferent to distinction (or was that indifference
only a veneer?), he deteriorated physically and intellectually as
the years advanced. With his death, the plays he had written so
easily dropped from notice. Textbooks written in accordance with
the best contemporary taste ignored him. He was rightly dismissed
as a purveyor of commodities.

Now one heard that the plays were being revived, and compared with the best of Congreve or Sheridan or Wilde. He was
said not to have 'dated' as Wilde 'dated'. How extraordinary!
One's own estimate of him as third-rate was not affected; but the
change in critical appraisement was disconcerting. It suggested

that half of what one had written with ultra-fastidiousness might hereafter be considered archaic.

By such people, for example, as Mr John White! One knew Mr White's view of oneself. What was it of Ruddock? Caustic? Or did he already run with the pack?

The rules! The rules! Who made the rules? . . .

The two girls avoided their father's mistake of self-indulgent levity. They were as slim as the youthful Ruddock had been, and took unobtrusive care, according to the mode, to remain so. One always saw them, in dreams, as fairy creatures.

How ethereal they looked today! More like angels than human beings! The familiar furnishings of the study seemed to be visible through their lovely bodies; the fire behind them glowed as rosily as if no draperies intervened. Celestial pair!

His attachment to them dated from an afternoon when, as children of five or six years old, they appeared in the big Ruddock kitchen at Wimbledon, peeping at their father and his distinguished friend, and at last, holding hands for greater confidence, venturing into the room. Not such a room as this, naturally, with its thousands of books and its air of dignified seclusion; but a place circumscribed by a loaded and shining dresser, old-fashioned coal-heated stove and oven, plain yellow walls, and striped curtains of blue and gold. The only picture was a coloured print of horses at plough decorating some local tradesman's calendar; the only chairs two rather elegant grandfathers with high backs, and a plain rush-seated antique used by Honey Ruddock when she rested between activities. A bench on which the little girls sat for their meals was pushed under the table; a pair of miniature three-legged stools stood near Ruddock himself. One afterwards saw why this was.

Ruddock did not use a study. He worked, when he worked, on a corner of the table covered with his wife's ironing, or on a raised knee by the fire as she cooked. His feet rested upon an enormous patchwork hearthrug, or the edge of the polished steel fender. They were outlandishly slippered. Being unaccustomed to kitchens, crazy slippers, and scribblings in pencil on scraps of paper, one had felt as if precipitated into a situation embarrassingly unworthy of Literature, even of Literature produced to amuse.

'My dear fellow, I'm intruding!'

'You know Honey, don't you? She's making fresh scones for our tea.'

'But I see you're busy with your—pencil. Can you really write with . . . ?'

Ruddock's reply, as nearly as one remembered it, was: 'I'm fond of the old girl's company; and she likes to have me around. I don't suppose it would suit you and Adelaide?'

Adelaide! Good God! The thought of her presence in the room, coldly watching the movement of one's gold fountain pen, produced goose-flesh. One had drily responded: 'Adelaide and I are not as domestic as you are, my dear Ruddock!'

A fat smile—no, it was then only plump and good-humoured —greeted this indication of distaste. The smile mutely stated that Adelaide and oneself were as unimportant as Ruddock and his ridiculously nick-named wife. One could hardly dissent.

'But ideas, Ruddock; the essential brainwork, concentration. . . .'

'I catch sermons in saucepans, laughter from the arch odours of good cooking.'

'Can pots and pans ever produce great Literature?'

'Ah, that's the question. "What porridge had John Keats?" I leave great Literature to the professors!'

It was a reference to the Prentice Lectureship, then just announced; and called for no answer.

When not trifling with pencil and paper, Ruddock roamed the streets by himself, overhearing the dropped words of passersby, and absorbing incongruities which, when he repeated them, seemed the gayest of improvisations. Otherwise he remained with his family, affectionately engrossed in them, giving frivolous amusement by lazy talk which they, like other people, enjoyed as they did the nauseous horrors of Punch and Judy.

The children were Ruddock's most appreciative companions. They saw every joke, because it was suited to the state of naiveté in which they lived. Thin stuff for adult minds, busy with the abstruse; and Adelaide refused to see Ruddock plays, saying that she had left the nursery. For the same reason she never saw the Ruddock children. One or two glimpses of Honey had been enough. 'The worthy helpmeet', she called her, with some truth. But the children were enchanting.

They had not whispered in the doorway, as Cook and Martin whispered when they found him dozing. Instead, after slight hesitation, they came forward with the eagerness of new arrivals at a Christmas party which they knew they were going to enjoy. One imagined the glitter of shining balls on the decorated tree, and the radiant eyes of those who looked for the delicious things they would find when the first games and boisterous pushings were over. He had impulsively thought:

'If only I had children like these!'

No children. Adelaide so decreed. Hers was the line of rarefied intelligence. It was also the line of no-sacrifice. There she was in the portrait over the mantelpiece, like a woman of marble with her vestments tinted to heighten the face's pallor. No man could have experienced overwhelming passion for one who never murmured a sweet endearment nor betrayed delight by involuntary caress. She was an experimentalist, an observer. Oddly enough, he had always suspected her of coarseness.

And so there were no children. Until he saw Ruddock's, he had not wanted them. They would hamper career. They would introduce into his household the caprice, the greed, so evident in children to be seen and heard in the streets. Jam on their faces, inopportune sickness, whines for sweets and fruit and toys, and, as they grew older, money. Endless trouble. Endless expense. Just as well to have none.

The Ruddock girls were different.

They were so enchanting that only shame lest his adoration of them should make him ridiculous to that lazy all-comprehending mind kept him from returning constantly to the house. Like a boy who has fallen in love, he took walks which brought him near the Ruddock home, in the hope of seeing his darlings. He repressed the wish to send them presents at all times and on any pretext. When he went to tea, and they chanced to be out, his heartsickness was again that of a boy.

It attracted Adelaide's attention.

'You're extraordinarily restless, Graham. Where have you been? Where are you going? Oh, the Ruddocks' again. I can't understand what you see in that trifling man. *So* third-rate!'

'Not first-class, I agree. A certain charm!'

'Never for me.'

Caring only for the first-class herself, she had busied him with more worthy engagements. He sometimes did not see the little girls for weeks; and when they went away to a boarding-school he missed them for weary months at a time. Adelaide thought she had disposed of the third-rate Ruddock.

How old were they now?

Five-, six-, no, eight-and-twenty? It was incredible, yet surely it must be so. The elder, Emma, having married before she was of age, was almost immediately widowed through an appalling aeroplane accident. He had not attended the wedding, because Adelaide found it inconvenient to go, and declined for them both. Nor had he seen Emma in her hour of sorrow. He had written, of course, and received a brief reply; but within a month she had resumed her maiden name, put away every sign of mourning, and become as virginal as before.

'What odd people they are!' Adelaide observed, upon hearing this. 'Quite uncontrolled.' She later thought there might have been something amiss in the marriage. 'Some abnormality, I suspect,' was her comment. 'Was the husband piloting the plane himself?'

Unwillingly impressed by this hint of possible suicide, Stanhope had often speculated upon it. He did so in sleepless hours, imagining himself back in the kitchen, listening to Ruddock's ludicrous stories of Curtal, who was imitated with such glee that he seemed to become one of Ruddock's own comic characters. Levity! Levity! But one laughed uproariously, as Ruddock did; and only after a time felt discomfort.

'Ruddock, we must stop guying him. I believe you invent these tales. Curtal doesn't behave like that with me.'

He still saw Ruddock's brooding smile, and Honey Ruddock's quick glance over her shoulder from the pastryboard. She must have had some thought about himself; he could not imagine its tenour. And as he remembered this scene he added to it the two little girls, standing beside their father's chair, as close as possible to the most wonderful and amusing man in the world. Enviable, enviable Ruddock!

Characteristically, while not dressed alike today, as they had been on that first encounter, they wore clothes of similar type, which, with what he supposed to be due regard to fashion, belonged to themselves alone. They did again what they had done in the Ruddock kitchen, entering unannounced, pausing for a moment with the slightest possible hesitation, and moving forward, not towards himself, but to the fire, beside which he was not surprised to see their father sitting. Ruddock was immediately under Adelaide's portrait.

Neither girl spoke. Both smiled with great sweetness.

Anne was by one year the younger. Was she the cleverer? Had she, too, a secret deeper than that of perpetual charm? She revealed no more of carnality than Emma. Neither was ever spoken of or written about as attending the vulgar parties so dear to the gossip-writer. No word of 'romance' (as those ugly modern casual marriages or affairs are styled) appeared about them in the Press. They did not hint or proclaim attachment to any man.

Was it because they still loved their father? Were they both, under the charm, frigid? Did they hide their concerns from one whom they thought of as an inquisitive old man?

'That would wound me very much,' he sighed. But the words were uttered only to himself. 'My interest in you, which is as spotless as lawn, is insatiable. I don't expect you remember our first meeting; but I remember it as if it were before me now, as you are. . . .'

Both were talented actresses; but the talent was seldom exhibited in London. Had they their father's indifference to Fame? Did they share the lethargy which was his ultimate vice? Their shows were unlucky, they said, and got no farther than provincial try-outs; or their parts, if the plays came to town, were given to other women.

'But why? Have they rich lovers? I don't understand it. You tell me so little.'

'It's just one of those things.' Emma was usually the spokeswoman, to an accompaniment of exchanged smiles. Both were merry at his astonishment. 'You mustn't take it very seriously, Uncle Graham.'

'Is it that you don't employ a publicity agent?'

'No, we don't. Daddy never did. He liked peace. So do we.'

'But praise, fame, money; do they mean nothing? Why aren't you in films?'

'We aren't the right types for stardom.' It was a laughing duet.

'But you're so beautiful! To me, you will always be stars; radiant as a southern sky.'

He was glad they were not stars. He wanted to keep them in focus. They must not become too rich or successful. Great prosperity gave women a taste for luxury—diamonds, grand hotels, lovers, folly. It took them into a world of false values.

'To me, you will always be stars.' He meant: 'I want you to remain within my orbit.'

He wanted them to love him. He talked to them a great deal when he was alone; and if he had been fifty years younger, and free from Adelaide's persisting censorship, he would have been in love with them.

'This is a charming surprise,' he now heard himself say. 'I hope you don't mind tea in the study. I'm becoming more and more of a recluse, as you see; and this room, for me, is full of dreams. You are among my dearest dreams.'

Distinguished courtesy became, as he uttered this routine and fanciful apology, wistfulness. Moisture started to his eyes, so affecting them that the lovely pair grew wraithlike. He longed deeply for their sympathy, for some warm demonstration of feeling. He could not say 'I've been lacerated by a malicious tongue'; but he stretched out both his hands, appealing for kisses which—alas!—he had never received.

'Pride, which is my *panache*,' he thought, 'is good. But it hedges me with dignity!' He smiled with pale grandeur at the gibe, which cut deep into his heart.

Emma answered only his polite speech. She must have done so a score of times, in various phrases.

'We love this room. We always feel we're skating on the intellectual plane. Like the man who boasted that he lived near the roses.'

Skating on the intellectual plane: was the room cold? Did they think him cold? That would be a tormenting interpretation.

'I live near the roses whenever you come to see me—as you do too rarely.'

'We never had many books at home.' This was Anne, the younger, who must have guessed his wound. 'That's what Emma really meant. I don't think Daddy read much. Towards the end of his life, at least.'

'He read the same old books,' explained Emma.

'I always sent him my new ones,' whispered Stanhope, with a pang.

They seemed not to hear.

'His books were the streets. The faces of the people he saw on his strolls. He called himself a physiognomist, and made up stories about them. Some were very funny!'

'They were always untrue. They made you laugh. Your dear father saw life as a farcical comedy.'

'Isn't it?' asked Anne, very innocently. She was even more her father's daughter than Emma.

'Not a successful one, my darling. As your father's farcical comedies were successful.'

All three smiled.

He heard one of the girls—he could not be sure which—speak of Curtal.

'We saw you at the Memorial Service. We didn't like to interrupt.'

'You could never interrupt. It would have been a blessing to me.'

'We thought you looked as if you'd prefer to be alone with Mr Curtal.'

'We were close behind,' added Emma.

'Were you? I wish I'd known of it. For a few moments I *was* alone with him, until a monster . . . I've been much alone with him for the last—I don't know how many days. Or is it hours?' A dreadful vagueness seized him; he strove most earnestly to see the girls, who had become shadows.

Were they there? Had he merely imagined their coming? He listened for the sound of a voice.

It reached him as a sigh; perhaps the rustle of a collapsing cinder.

'Daddy was fond of him, too. And sorry for him.'

Stanhope answered quite briskly:

'Such a strange person to be sorry for! I knew your father's mind. I argued with him. He wouldn't admit Curtal to be the most self-sufficient egotist that ever lived. As impervious as concrete.'

Anne's voice was stronger.

'Daddy had a theory about him.'

'Daddy had theories about all sorts of things,' laughed Stanhope. 'I remember the absurd one about Curtal.'

'That he was always trying to find a twin soul—to complete himself?'

'It was invented *pour rire*, to fairify the minxes who loved him!'

'Loved? Didn't we all? Even you?'

A slight draught touched, or seemed to touch, his cheek. He saw the utterly silent Martin enter the room, pushing her rubber-tyred tea-trolley, and was reminded of slow-motion pictures of men boxing. Such pictures always made him shudder, as Martin did now. He imagined an exchange of smiles between her and the visitors; but heard no words until he himself cried out, loudly:

'Thank you, Martin. I hope there are crumpets for Miss Anne.'

Emma, to whom the trolley had been wheeled, slowly raised the lid of the hot-dish, to show that luscious butter-drenched crumpets had been brought. There were grave, smiling nods before Martin withdrew in the same extraordinarily suspensive silence. If only she had spoken! If only he had heard the noise of her skirt!

'I know that Anne always liked crumpets. So did your father.'

He could see Ruddock cutting a crumpet into four pieces, and putting one of the pieces between his teeth, the flesh about his eyes slightly bulging, his big humorous mouth closing like some elephantine maw. That must have happened thirty years ago, before the children were born; but simultaneously it was today, with Ruddock holding the plate close to his chest in a plump left hand. Ruddock's jaws moved. One saw his eyes gleaming within the swellings caused by illness, heard the familiar rumble of his deep voice.

Straining eagerly, Stanhope listened for Ruddock's words.

The tone was smothered, hardly to be caught. As he grew fat, Ruddock spoke more and more thickly, like a dog growling in its sleep. Today the sound resembled, rather, the purr of an old and contented lion.

'Yes,' rumbled Ruddock. 'I told you why I was sorry for

Curtal; but you wouldn't listen. Your habit of masterly inatten-
tiveness! The poor devil was incomplete, like a man born with one
arm. Well, now, that's true of most people. They can't understand their own restlessness, the search for novelty, the love of
crowds, the craving for marriage. In the end, finding no satisfaction in revelry, or crowds, or marriage, they wander. Some of
them cut their throats; others turn to God, which—for different
reasons—you and I never did. That's remarkable, isn't it? I
mean, about us.'

'And quite untrue,' Stanhope muttered. 'Like your other
sophistries.'

'I was always satisfied with this life—charmed with it as
entertainment. You regarded God as your intellectual inferior,
and despised Him as somebody not first-class. Curtal didn't do
that; he was never a prig, and never, like me, a lazy devil. He
tried furiously to make sense of the cosmic mess by steeping
himself in it. But he still couldn't make sense where there was no
sense. He picked up those doxies of his as an avalanche gathers
rocks and rubble. He picked us all up like that.'

'He didn't pick me up like that,' protested Stanhope.

'He didn't hope to complete himself by women, as I sometimes
pretend. He despised them. He needed a spiritual leaven. I was
no good; too acute, and too static. I'd found my own completion
in Honey and these girls. If you'd been a bit different . . . But
you're a very curious character, you know, Graham!'

Stanhope, deeply interested, muttered:

'The same might be said of you.'

Ruddock ignored the comment.

'Not so much armed at all points as defensively insensitive
to whatever might disturb your egotism. I was sorry for you only
once. It was when that little girl you were keeping killed herself.'

Stanhope jumped in his chair. Emma—Anne—must not hear
this! He was in fever.

'No, no, no! Quite untrue. Quite. I wasn't keeping her. It
didn't enter . . . She was much too proud; and I——'

But Ruddock was deaf.

'Killed herself, poor kid. I thought you'd be broken-hearted.
You weren't. The surface congealed at once. When I tried to be
kind, it was as if I had vomited in this holy-of-holies. You didn't
want sympathy. You wanted secrecy. You resented my having

come on you in Regent's Park. It was dusk; a rising moon; a lovely balmy evening; you were kissing her. Idyllic! I was delighted. So was she, the pet. But you were aghast because I'd caught the immaculate Graham Stanhope kissing his mistress!'

Stanhope pressed back in the chair, tightly interlaced fingers close against his mouth. He had no voice to speak the protest which he struggled to make.

'Poor child! She laughed. I loved her for it. She was radiant. But you could only see the humiliation to yourself, imagine me splitting to the Dragon, sniggering, making a good tale of it everywhere. I ought to have looked down my nose, coughed, and skedaddled, as you'd have done, you old prig!'

'Yes. God knows, I should have done just that.' It was a silent, an agonized admission, torn from his pride.

'But I never looked down my nose in my life. One of my vanities, I suppose. I had a thousand of them; and every one was a comfort to you. Part of your system of striking balances to prove yourself superior to other men. . . . Honey was away. I made you—forced you—forced you—to come to dinner with me. A wretched little place in Greek Street; verdigris on the cruet, wineglasses as thick as mugs; but the party was gay, the food paradisial.'

The food paradisial; the party gay. Stanhope remembered everything; what they had eaten, the thick glasses, Gertrude's sparkling eyes, her response to Ruddock's benign teasing, her joy in himself, his own agitated constraint. He even remembered hoping—yet with torture at the most momentary relinquishment of Gertrude—that if spies were present they would suppose himself, not Ruddock, the interloper.

Ruddock's rich growl continued.

'I took you aside at parting; told you she was delicious; begged you to chuck everything and bolt with her. Ha-ha! Good God! I might as well have suggested *hara-kiri*.'

'For me—think of my position—all I'd worked for—gained—it would have been *hara-kiri*.'

'Frightened of the Dragon; the Dragon's posh relations. They'd have made it hot for you. Oh, yes, I know what people of that sort can do. I've had some experience of it. But the girl was worth any rumpus. She'd have made a man of you. You know? The Elixir of Life! By Jove, I did like her. I saw she was devoted to you. Wonderful! When I read the little report of her death, with its reference to "George Stanhope, a friend of the deceased" —was that a little deceit of yours, or a lucky misreporting?—I hurried to see you—in this room. "My dear old chap—" You brushed me aside. "Keep your nose out of this," you said; "I'm sick to death of fuss." That's what you said; do you remember? It was enough. I gave you up for good.'

Swept anew by the emotion of that hour, Stanhope incoherently protested.

'I was paralysed . . . Adelaide . . . You didn't know. Hadn't the subtlety to read me or understand me. Too long by the kitchen fire, grinning, talking nonsense, snoozing. . . .'

'You'd let her down, my boy. And you knew it.'

Stanhope no longer saw Ruddock. He cast tear-dimmed eyes upon the girls, who had not once stirred. He held an unsteady hand to receive the expected cup of tea; but for some reason, although he saw Emma's hand extended, he had no sense of physical contact with the saucer.

'This is quite extraordinary,' he said. 'I must have fallen asleep for a moment, and dreamed that your father was here. Am I dreaming, also, that you are here? Didn't Jackie telephone asking you to come? Did I only imagine I'd . . . ?"

They smiled as sweetly, as silently, as they had done at the first meeting, long ago. He saw his hand trembling as it reached in vain for the now invisible cup. The picture vanished.

TEN

Early Days

As THE minutes passed, his sense of shock diminished. Thank God, this had been no more than one of his dreams, uneasier than most because Ruddock's lifelong kindness had seemed, like so much else in his life, to have been sham. By some mental distortion he had attributed John White's spitefulness to one who was never spiteful. Ruddock had not been there, by the fire. He had not spoken; had never betrayed the secret they shared.

But the dream most painfully revealed the turmoil into which he had been thrown by Curtal's death and White's inquisition. He was very tired. His hands still trembled. When he would have risen in relief, to stamp about the room, his legs also trembled, so that he fell back into the chair, where he sat watching the sportive flames which had recently so deceived him.

His mind travelled, for solace, to more golden aspects of the past.

What vistas had opened in that first glory of young manhood at the beginning of the century, when he and the others were rich in confidence and what they believed to be a plenitude of new ideas! The babble of voices—Thompson's pompous, Holmes's tonelessly insistent, Curtal's rasping—had been an offence to one's ears; but the life, the superb life, in those youngsters had been intoxicating. He and Curtal, in particular, leaving together, walking together, meeting again and again in the following weeks, had discussed the cosmos for hours on end, rivalry forgotten in the excitement of speculation.

What they said was jejune enough, in retrospect. At the time it held the glow and heat of conviction. Curtal, it was true, was uneducated. His reading was small—almost ridiculous in its narrowness, its dependence on little manuals and a score or two of the robuster classics; but he had seized a few ideas, picked others up as he went along, and borne down opposition with ruthless vigour.

'You and I will never agree,' he declared. 'But you'll learn.'

That was a true saying. It was equally true of himself. And they had never agreed.

Curtal was what was known as a reformer. He had been a reformer since childhood, when a stupid schoolmaster boxed his ears for demonstrating the master's ignorance of a local by-law.

'Get this mess tidied up,' was his cry. 'Send the bosses and the drones to some place like Siberia or the Sahara. What we want in England, in the World, isn't the vote-catching swindle they call Democracy; but a real classless society, where everybody's used to the limits of his powers. No gentry, no plutocrats, no Government—old William Godwin had the right idea there, at any rate—about the best men giving their best for the lot. We'll get a millenium within a century!'

'Give me my dreams,' had been his own unspoken prayer. 'Of reputation, great and beautiful possessions, a life spent in the refinement of aesthetic values, away from all this noisy irrelevance, where men squabble and boast and tyrannize, as this fellow will do all his life!' But to Curtal he had said: 'Godwin's notions have been obsolete for a century. You've never read anybody else. If you blare like this, you'll earn cheers from the sweaty multitude; but there won't be any millenium. Only the rise of thousands of mediocrities grabbing at power. Chaos! The worst form of anarchy. We need, not the wreckage of society, but an intellectual *élite*, high above the jostle, making almost divine laws, revered by the obedient mob, the orderly hewers of wood——'

'Obedient mob be damned!' bawled Curtal. 'The shout's for liberty!'

'I know. "The Rights of Man." You really must read Burke and Coleridge. . . .'

'Ah, Coleridge! A bloody poet! Wasn't he the English Opium Eater?'

'My dear ignorant Curtal!'

Yes, yes, yes; 'my dear ignorant Curtal.' Stentorianly ignorant all his life; and now dead. The old debates returned to Stanhope in flood. They were deeply moving as proofs of former ardour.

'Wonderful! Wonderful! I had great insight; Curtal blasting energy. I was John Donne, to his surly, burly Ben Jonson; Coleridge to his Cobbett. The eternal antitheses. Who now questions Coleridge's greatness? Who compares Jonson to Donne? Who thinks of Cobbett as a political sage? It will be the same with Curtal; while I shall be remembered as the apostle of light!'

So his boasted indifference to posterity had been a lie? He lay back, quietly chuckling.

Delusions of greatness led to impotence. He must try to set these juvenile egotisms in their true perspective; think himself back into another world, to which they were appropriate; hold fast, in spite of repugnance, to the vicarage, the greengrocer's shop, the walks with Curtal through Hyde Park and Kew Gardens, the visits with him to teashop cellars with their mortuary odour and marble-topped tables, the argumentative rides on open-top horse-drawn green, white and yellow omnibuses. . . .

London was darker then. It was full of dark entrances and littered streets, immense policemen, white-faced cadgers, gas-lit windows, and, it now seemed to him, the smell of beer. He loathed it. Ruddock didn't. Thompson had never known anything else. Curtal, striding along in his cocky way, talked to the cadgers, patted their arms, perhaps gave them pennies, looked boldly in at the windows, ventured into the dark entrances, and bawled in a loud voice in spite of every effort to hush him.

It had perhaps been embarrassment that caused one to lead him from the streets into open spaces, where his outbursts were less likely to be overheard.

War in South Africa having ended at last in the defeat and public exaltation of Boer generals, and a new Liberal Government 'of all the talents' having attained power, the way seemed to be open to vast expansion of the spirit. Tories were smashed. They would never again vulgarize politics. Imperialism, inflated balloon of national vainglory, was dead. Kipling, apostle of Imperialism, was buried in its ruins. With him had gone all the admiration for wallahs, pukka sahibs, and their wives, who took out in power what they lost in complexion and longevity.

This, at least, was Curtal's account.

'All gone,' he declared, to the religious assents of Thompson, the glum nods of Holmes, and the mischievous 'hear-hears' of

Key and Ruddock, who had no social ideals but thought of life as a jest. Encouraged by these proofs of attention, Curtal would add: 'You can forget Kipling as you forget Shakespeare's bluster about "this precious England, set in the seven seas"!'

'Silver,' corrected Holmes.

'Amend it to "Great Britain, its Colonies and Dependencies",' advised Ruddock, with his radiant grin.

'England did the bad work. The others helped to swallow the profits. My God, when I think of Kipling and Warren Hastings, my gorge rises. As it does when I think of Cecil Rhodes and stout Cortez!'

'Bravo! Bravo!' cried Key. 'We'll soon finish the Empire!'

One had not joined the chorus, knowing that Curtal's ignorance of history was grotesque. It was always grotesque. It had helped him to set everybody by the ears with vehement balderdash. One had thought of Kipling: 'I'm not so sure that he's dead. Vulgar, yes; with a brainless military belief in national supremacy. One mustn't defend him, of course. That would mark one as an outsider. But fashions change. This one may do so. I commit myself to nothing.'

Committing oneself to nothing, one had smiled, remaining aloof from the rest, who were in full cry.

The vogue, then, was for a domestic revolution; not the kind of thing Curtal wanted, which was merely a super-mess, but the Nonconformist brand of good works. There were to be no more slums, no more rambling unemployed, starving and receiving charity, no more displays of arrogant national bunting. The Empire must be handed back to all aborigines, with gifts and apologies. Not Heaven, but Utopia, was the prevailing carrot. 'We are all Socialists now.'

Such ideas were insufferably vulgar. They disturbed the vision of spiritual grace. Art, finely polished and expressive of inward calm, ought to be the inspiration, and its apotheosis the ultimate aim. Not Hobbes, but Descartes; not this fellow Wells, after whom Curtal was in full cry, but the thwarted neo-Platonic mystics. The artist should live within, apart from his fellows, in monastic seclusion. But for as long as this turmoil lasted he should—here was a great paradox—prosper in the material world by preaching idealism.

One had illustrated this theory in a long metaphysical poem, *Hesperus*. Some folly, in which pride and what John White would call condescension were mingled, led one to show the manuscript to Curtal.

The raucous outburst following this *naïveté* had been unpardonable. It still rankled, although one's tear-starting heat was gone.

Curtal flung down the exquisite manuscript.

'If you want my opinion—as I suppose you do—it's bloody awful!' God-like authority spoke. 'Tennyson, William Morris, and your own damned nonsense. Why, it's almost as bad as Thompson's muck. You don't believe a word of it!'

'Certainly I do. I've put my soul into it. Everything I do believe.'

'Good God! Is that all you believe? I've been mistaken in you.'

'I wonder why you say that?'

'Because I believe in telling the truth. When the rest of us are trying to keep in touch with reality——'

'With superficial reality—the stop-press news, the passing show of events. My interest is in the permanent things, beauty, poetry, the intangible. To you, poetry means nothing.'

There should have been an explosion. There was not. Curtal had one of those odd turns of mood which a lifetime had left unfathomed.

'I shan't answer that. What you call superficiality is the world we live in. Your "permanent things" are prehistoric illusions. There's no room for them. We've got to get on with the job. My God, Stanhope; take the wool out of your ears and your eyes and your brain. I know you want to stuff your bed with it. But I tell you, as man to man, it's no good. I *know*.'

Yes, one had quivered.

'You know. Meaning, you've swallowed the new bigotry. Science is your Pope.'

It was Curtal who persisted.

'You're not a poet, you know. You're a thief among the tombs. A bloody ghoul!'

Thief! Ghoul! When one had laboured night after night, recasting, re-phrasing, determined to use, as Coleridge said, 'the best words in the best order'. And that brute, who crammed a hundred *clichés* into every page he wrote, presumed . . . For those words, Curtal should rot in hell!

Nevertheless, the poem was forgotten. One had taken it from the shelves a few nights ago, read ten pages with admiration, lost interest, and replaced the book in melancholy. Not a poet. Not a poet. Handmade paper and vellum binding mocked an old egotism.

The broadsheet they started was an assault upon fame. It attracted attention, and it was thought 'fun' by smart folk. Curtal's attacks on smugness, Ruddock's lazy derision, and one's own acute, sometimes destructive, ironies at the expense of established reputations, all made a show in its pages. Key was comparatively a failure, Thompson much too grandiose, Holmes a dead weight; but Curtal and oneself were alive, full of quality. Both knew it. Curtal, strutting, expounding, bullying, knew it best of all. A horrible exhibition. . . .

The result of 'success' was a debt to the printer, settled under threats and after a row which Curtal enjoyed like the gamecock he was. The broadsheet came to an end. Curtal, in spite of every appeal to dignity, insisted on writing a boastful farewell to the perceptive few. It was entitled 'Colours to the Mast!' It arraigned the intelligence of a nation, and made the collaborators appear a bunch of conceited apes.

The truth was that, as always, there were the indifferent many and the small and cultivated minority. Among the more aesthetic of these, the mode was for everything French. It was so with oneself. The French were civilized; one was civilized; one was sick to death of the ineradicable Englishness of Curtal and, as one privately called them, the Greengrocers.

With stealth, therefore, one planned an excursion into *belles lettres*. No word was spoken to the band. All was done in secret. One would astonish everybody by appearing within cloth covers. 'My book . . .'

Luck turned up in a pale, heavy-lidded neurotic named Marvell, who, having a little money, fancied himself as a precious *avant-garde* publisher of tiny booklets of verse. Only verse, he said; the best, the stuff that others were afraid, or too blind, to publish. But with marvellous finesse one convinced him that verse needed highly distinguished prose support. What better than a biography of Stendhal? Already Francophil, with a taste for absinthe,

Marvell was caught. The man to write it? That, of course, was more difficult. . . . It would have to be . . . have to be . . .

It had to be oneself.

The book was up there on the shelves, bound uniformly with a set of Stendhal's own works in pale blue half-calf. One couldn't distinguish it, in this light, from *de l'Amour*, *La Chartreuse de Parme*, *Promenades*, and the rest; one liked to believe it snared their aura of immortality. At the time it had brought tear-summoning cruelties. The Greengrocers were not impressed. Old men, reviewing briefly in learned journals, called it 'trivial'. Insufferable youngsters, writing, full of envy, with great brightness, accused the author of knowing no French and missing every nuance of the master's original mind. Devils! Devils! He hated them still!

Nevertheless, in spite of a few blunders which one now brushed aside, the results of this book were momentous. A few admirers gave one kind words; two or three strangers wrote letters; and one such letter, addressed in a splashing, dashing hand, surpassed the others in importance. It was from Henrietta Pigott.

Difficult, now, to understand Henrietta's reputation. Her life as artistic patron had been short in all respects, especially one's own; but at the time she represented the acme of smartness. This, indeed, had been one's reason for sending her a copy of the book.

'I loved it!' splashed Henrietta. 'Do come and see me!'

It was triumph. At one bound, one was in the great world, on one's own unique merits. As young Eugène de Rastignac, surveying the streets of Paris, exclaimed: 'Henceforth there is war between you and me,' so young Graham Stanhope discarded the Greengrocers, and swore that everything was at an end between them.

ELEVEN

Henrietta

AT REMEMBRANCE of his exultation, which now seemed, although justified by more than fifty years of success, so *naif*, Stanhope allowed his chin to drop to his breast. The room's warmth was exceedingly pleasant, the more so because, out of doors, a noisy cold wind threatened snow.

He was young again, entering the world from which he had previously been excluded. He had just received Henrietta's letter. It was several weeks since he had seen Curtal and the others. And he was in an ecstasy of hope.

In those days motor omnibuses had been recently introduced, and were subject to ridiculous strandings by the kerbside. One wore top-hat and tails for afternoon calls in Mayfair. Hansom cabs were going out; the Pigotts travelled in a thrilling-belled electric brougham. Moustaches were newly unfashionable; the starched collars which had propped many an ambitious chin and produced many a nervous ailment were narrowing. West End streets were quiet as the countryside, unlittered, free from oil-stains. Silence, cleanliness, and dignity without; luxury within. And one was privileged, for the first time, and in delight, to be within.

In the *monde*, one's height and good looks and debonair manners—so different from the rough and ready carriage of the Greengrocers—had naturally been assets. It was then not correct for young *arrivistes* to be rude; one had always abhorred, and never practised, offensiveness. If one's stomach was filled, one's name pronounced with *empressement*, and one's range of acquaintance, at the cost only of clothes, cab-fares, and politeness, increased every week, the least one could do was to comport oneself with grace. Never had tailors' bills risen so high, nor been so difficult to meet. But one was *there*!

Some discomfort attended the re-awakened memory of Henrietta. There had been so much promise in the early days; and, in the end, so deep a sense of humiliation.

She was in her late thirties at the time, *petite*, almost blonde, daringly indelicate in slow drawling speech, quite unshockable and without mercy. Her husband, a barrister with one undistinguished foot in the House of Commons, was extraordinarily stupid; but he had inherited wealth, he enjoyed a safe Tory seat, and he could afford to run a big house in Mayfair and an even bigger house in Sussex. Since neither he nor Henrietta understood the art of self-amusement, they entertained a great deal, patronized the Opera, bought pictures and *objets d'art*, and employed a superlative cook. Henry supplied the money; Cook worked the social magic; Henrietta exploited both.

She exploited everybody, not for any permanent advantage, but for her own amusement. She was a natural parasite.

Thinking this, Stanhope's mood changed from one of comparative complacency to one of resentful unease. He neither saw Henrietta nor imagined her voice; his mind was occupied merely in self-exculpation.

'I was as cool as she. But as a man I dislike what I remember of her.'

That was true and untrue. He had known for fifty years, without confessing the fact to any other person, that the shallow and selfish creature had used him deliberately. She saw herself as a clever, gracious lady, stooping to raise the promising unknown to distinction, and at the same time adorning her parties with the latest novelty. Whenever a new amusement or decorative aspirant caught her whim, the old one was discarded. His own amusingness had lasted for six months.

At his first visit he found her in a roomful of buzzing strangers. Being apparently engrossed in conversation with an oldish bearded foreigner, she glanced at himself with—he afterwards remembered—competent quickness, noted his good looks and the cut of his hair and clothes, made two or three unintelligible introductions, and turned away.

Calculated! Calculated! But he had been unnerved. Seeking relief, he had fallen into the company of another young man, also a novice, and also unnerved by similar treatment; but as neither was aware of the other's identity there had been some inquisitive sparring between them. The young man was Prince, the satirical novelist, dead and buried long since. Three or four novels, and total exhaustion of the vein, left Prince to that lowest infirmity of ignoble mind, the spiteful reviewing of his betters. Their encounter, years later, was marked by calm on the one hand, animosity on the other. Poor worthless Prince!

At this first meeting, with only ambition in common, they soon parted. A thin young woman with a long neck and unconcealable ears revealed that she was a conceited pianist. On learning that he had never heard of her she flounced away. It didn't matter; lacking *réclame*, she quickly vanished from Henrietta's parties. He remembered her as no more than embodied huff.

These were the two identified persons among a chattering crowd. Henrietta continued to talk to her Professor, ignoring all others; and within twenty minutes, deafened, and oppressed by disappointment, Stanhope was on his way home. The splashing, dashing note had been delusive. A fashionable hostess had invited nonentities to an *omnium gatherum*.

'Never again!' he exclaimed, striding along. 'The insolent cheek of it!'

He imagined Curtal, if Curtal ever heard of the fiasco, bellowing with glee.

Youthful arrogance. Folly. But the rapid departure had not escaped those cruelly observant eyes. A week later Henrietta wrote again, in the same splashy hand, complaining that an old bore, by monopolizing her, had prevented the talk she had longed for, and begging him to come to tea one day in the following week. 'I promise there won't be anybody else here!'

At first he had angrily protested 'No!' Pride was then uppermost. But the stink of burned cooking from downstairs, the smallness of his study, and of course the unassuaged longing for the *monde*, produced a different mood. He remembered Henrietta's drawing-room, without the crowd, with his first appreciation of its luxury.

He had seen there, against a lucent green wallpaper, paintings by Manet, Renoir, Sickert, and Orpen, bought, it transpired, on the advice of a Jew named Finkelstein, who had afterwards become a familiar acquaintance. Finkelstein, dazzlingly clever, mysterious, and full of taste, shot himself within two years for no ascertainable reason; but before dying he had revealed in semi-casual talk a hundred details of Henrietta, whom he valued at much less that the smallest picture in her possession. No tears were shed for him. He did not inspire love. Nevertheless the pictures of which he had advised the purchase increased in value (as she did not), and when disposed of at Henrietta's death they fetched something like sixty thousand pounds in the sale-room. Had Finkelstein, in a limbo of his own choosing, laughed?

How opulent all who visited the house felt at sight of those vivid and lovely pictures! They were a bouquet to hungry aspirants. So, in another field, was an ebony grand piano; so were the unopened rare books and the carpets from China, which were soft enough to absorb the tramp of regiments, and so delicate in colour that they could be breathlessly admired for endless time.

Luxury! It inspired one to believe that one had attained to Aladdin's wealth; as the bowls of flowers, brought newly every day from the gardens and greenhouses of the Pigott mansion in Sussex, made one dream of Paradise. Luxury! He had re-read that cordially-apologetic note—now seen to have been so insincere—and it had conquered him. She must have known that it would do so.

The second visit was quite unlike the first. The room was in a blaze of sunlight. Only one other guest was present, Trumble, the miscellaneous scholar, who had means enough to roam the earth at whim, and was equally amusing on the Man in the Iron Mask, excavations in Egypt, Bonnie Prince Charlie, medieval English poetry, and Alpine climbing. He talked, laughed, showed a mouthful of giant teeth, winked often in good humour, and cast cheerfulness upon the party.

'I remember,' thought Stanhope, today. 'Well, I was pretty good, myself.'

That curious vacuum which so often follows private vainglory occurred. He realized that, being over-anxious to hold his own, he had exposed to both Trumble and Henrietta the superficiality of his experience. Trumble hadn't minded; he was free from all conceit, liked youngsters, and looked upon his own affairs as unimportant. That showed greatness. But Henrietta, avid of other people's absurdity, must have enjoyed exquisitely malicious amusement. She was the perfect female cad.

Not cool enough to understand this, he had thought her superb. She played Trumble with facile address, adding to shrewd familiarity with his oddities the kittenish archness of an affectionate disciple. Smiling glances at himself at the same time ridiculed the old man, and said, in effect: 'Quite a comic creature! You and I can see him as he is, cranky and entertaining. And we have other comprehensions, too; the comprehensions of youth. We'll explore them presently.'

When Trumble, who was leaving that night for New York— 'back in a fortnight; after cracking a few jokes about Columbus at Columbia'—jumped up in haste, Henrietta detained Stanhope with a hand upon his sleeve.

'Goodbye, darling Trummy. Give my love to America. Don't risk a single quip about George the Third or the Tea Party!' And, when the door had closed upon Trumble's last tremendous wink at his fellow visitor: 'Funny old man! He's terribly pleased to have an audience. Now tell me all about yourself, Mr Stanhope; and how you came to write that enchanting book. Everybody I tell about it is excited—Mr Trumble not least!'

He was pumped, weighed, smiled upon, and watched by her demure pale blue eyes, which, he afterwards perceived, were unsoftened by lines of pain or affection, but expressed the malicious hardness of her nature. His ingenuous expositions were punctuated by indulgent promptings. 'Yes? . . . Yes?' She didn't really listen; yet she heard. And at the end of quarter of an hour, having yielded his quota of amusement, he was dismissed.

Yes, dismissed. He could imagine her boredom. But at the time he was unaware of it.

'She's wonderful!' he had thought excitedly, persuaded that he saw her with the most subtle penetration. This was not a woman to elude; but one of rare taste and intelligence, who drew one's best and highest from its treasure-house. 'She's as quick as fire! She gains time by that drawl; it enables her to re-focus all that's been said and all she's known beforehand. It also heightens the effect of all she says. She must know that. But her true quality is sympathy. And I was a success. No doubt of that. Oh, yes, a great success, with Trumble, as well as herself. She was pleased with everything that happened. I was very good. . . . Curtal wouldn't have been. The room would have been too much for him. He'd have been *gauche*. He'd have contradicted Trumble. My God! Wouldn't he have made a fool of himself!'

The thought had been extraordinarily pleasant.

The suburban vicarage to which he returned that day made him shudder. It was a shocking reminder that luxury was almost as far away as ever. The house was full of shabby furniture, faded carpets, terrible engravings in frames of polished light wood, and, in the gloomy parlour, complete calf-bound sets of Scott and Thackeray which nobody had opened for twenty years. They were in great mahogany cases, behind glass, together with formidable, equally morose, volumes of *The Leisure Hour* and *The Quiver*. An epitome of glumness!

A cook-housekeeper, Miss Champion, dominated the kitchen. She was aridly devout, and her meals were penitential. She left them unsalted and unsweetened, on the pretext that feeders should do their garnishing to taste. Her nose had a red tip, and her mouth was as grim as a mantrap. One ridiculed her with ironic suavity, and she ignored the irony as she ignored the front-door bell.

The Old Man, Father, untidy, short-sighted, with nervousness betraying itself in a *tic* and an excitable Adam's apple, struggled all the week with his choristers and wardens, and on Sundays with a stolid congregation of censorious unbelievers. He was a six foot skeleton; and out-of-doors he looked like a mute on stilts. Weak sight made his mournful grey eyes evasive. Having propped a book or ecclesiastical journal before him against an old empty photograph frame, he ate all the unflavoured food without caring what it was; and when it had given him indigestion he withdrew in silence to a mouldering den which scowled with unreadable books.

After his death, some that were unscowling turned up behind those literary chokepears. Dozens of them, from Casanova's *Memoirs* to *Cora Pearl*. How shocking the discovery was! But in the light of further knowledge how pathetic! Not the foulness of hypocrisy, but the hunger of an emotion-starved man, probably a hedonist, had lain behind that gaunt silence. The silence had never been broken; no understanding ever existed between them.

Stanhope's own little study, a back room overlooking the dingy garden, represented his protest against the universal dust-laden gloom. Very Beardsley-esque, with original black-and-white drawings by Herbert Cole, Ospovat, and Sime, intermixed with a few by unidentified artists of a similar order. Indian rugs, which in those days were cheap, one or two Chinese jars or plates, hand-wrought brass fireirons, and a crowd of books published by Smithers, the Unicorn Press, or from the Bodley Head spoke of the owner's aesthetic taste; and in the midst of all was a secondhand kneehole desk at which, with plenty of ruled paper and an array of fancy pens, the poet and critic laboured to polish work destined to—'Oblivion,' said a voice.

Stanhope jumped. For a moment he fancied that John White had intruded even here. It was not so. Nobody was within sight. The sound must have been made by a suddenly-accelerating taxi in the distance.

Memory carried him again to Henrietta's luxurious homes.

He had not been as cool as she. When invitations came again and again, sometimes to the house in Mayfair, sometimes to the Sussex mansion; when she introduced him to men and women of note, singled him out as her companion in walks through the woods and over the Downs, and made him her escort to the theatre, his vanity was intoxicated.

It led him to suppose her fascinated by his mind and person; so fascinated that she desired him as a lover. The unemotional manner must be meant for the world; for himself, when they were alone, it held tantalizing intimacy, distance, encouragement. How could he have failed to respond to the encouragement?

'I was as cool as she!' he now cried, desperately. Then, in an undertone: 'No, I wasn't. I made a fool of myself.'

This was the first time he had ever granted as much. His words caused pride to suffer more deeply than it had done in the hour of surprise and resentment.

She had dropped him overnight. He must have presumed a little; shown in his manner too confident an expectation of favours to come. Folly! Yes; but no man, in such a situation, presumed without reason. Her encouragement had certainly been deliberate; probably it was given to supply a pretext for dismissal. Who could tell? The nature was shallow; the adroitness that of astonishing sophistication.

Thereafter, meeting her at a show of paintings by a newer protégé, he had received no more than a cold bow. When he made the mistake of approaching her as familiarly as he would have done, without rebuke, a week earlier, he was ignored. No more invitations came. The doors of house and mansion alike were closed.

It was, for him, though as it proved not for her, the end of their acquaintance. At his still greater success, three or four years later, she wrote again. By that time he was well in with Lady Chard, had married Adelaide, and was on the high road to fortune. He had not answered the letter.

TWELVE

The Dream Ends

CURTAL, thank God, had known nothing of the Henrietta episode. One went no more to the greengrocer's shop. Certain Cambridge intellectuals were rising to influence; and although not originally of their number one had had the wit to applaud their highly-exclusive taste. It accorded with one's own. Curtal then seemed a very common little man indeed, far from the possibility of inclusion among the first-class few.

Nobody could have foreseen his leap to fame. He went up like a rocket, high, noisy, and argumentative about every topic of the hour. No periodical was free from his shouts. Though the fastidious stopped their ears and tittered at his rowdiness, he made the wider ranges of mankind cheer him as their prophet. At first one smiled at the din; but when the first of his damned evangelistic books of castigation and prophesy appeared it seemed only right to send him a note of congratulation.

The note went unacknowledged, in accordance with the man's natural ill-breeding. One shrugged, turned to other interests, tittered as the others did at Jack-the-Giant-Killer among the Bishops, and busied oneself with French Academicians. Meanwhile Curtal crowed like Chanticleer.

'Extraordinarily ignorant,' said the Few. 'Hurray!' bawled the Many. 'A mighty thinker!' wrote Thompson. 'He can't *think*,' said the Few; 'a sort of Dickens.' To compare a man with Dickens was, rightly, to condemn him as an outsider. Curtal was the great outsider.

The trouble was that Curtal would not stay outside. He angered conventional people; he disgusted the aesthetes; but in his own eyes he was pure light. Furthermore Curtal, in his egotism, chose to regard the hiatus in their close acquaintance as desertion on one's own part.

96

The word 'desertion' was ridiculous.
Ridiculous. Stanhope shivered.

The fool had shown pique. One night at Lady Chard's, when that admirably loyal and authentic patron of the arts gave a small dinner-party, they met again. Lucy Chard, having invited Stanhope to come early, gave him a drink and cigarette, and made him sit near her by the fire. Having done this, she mentioned that she was expecting Rossiter, who owned the *Sunday Courier*.

'Delightful man,' she mourned—for her velvet tones always suggested the loss of a favourite spaniel. 'He tells me he's looking for new talent. I naturally thought of you, dear Graham.'

'Always superlatively kind,' he replied, with a quick rise of the heart.

'I like to see my boys established. So I've promised that he shall meet the three most brilliant young men in town.'

'Are there so many? This is a sad disappointment!'

'One of them has jaundice.'

'Ah, you told him I was coming!'

'The other . . . I wonder if you've ever met Tom Curtal? My pet! He's quite the most vivid talker——'

Curtal! Oh, God! Stanhope remembered how instantly, and how far, his spirits plunged at the name. It was as though somebody had said: 'By the way, you're to be drowned tomorrow!'

'My most intimate friend,' he had managed to reply. 'I won't say we shared the same perambulator; but short of that——'

Curtal had interrupted the claim—whatever it was going to be—by stumping into the room, quite at ease, with nothing of the gaping errand-boy in his manner, but quiet assurance, even dignity. The transformation was extraordinary. Watching him, Stanhope had felt a chill which was increased by the fact that Curtal's greeting was the curtest of nods. No hand was advanced to meet his own. This, disagreeable in itself, became calamitous because Lucy Chard must be contrasting it with a just-proclaimed intimacy.

To his relief, Rossiter had arrived immediately afterwards; a dull-looking man with porridge-coloured face and a sweep of black hair over grim eyes, whose habit was to leave all talking to the other person. That, as he knew, induced nervous self-distrust.

His vanity, Stanhope later discovered, was colossal. He saw everything in terms of money and 'pull', and prided himself too much upon judgment of character ever to accept recommendations, even from great ladies.

He said to Stanhope, much later:

'Old Lucy's swans are mostly geese. I saw Curtal couldn't be told anything.'

'Too independent, you mean?'

'Too conceited. I run my own papers. That's why I let him go to Trusty, where he keeps the whole place in a dither. *Prima donna* stuff. Shouts. Walks out.'

'I notice he sometimes doesn't appear.'

'They can't print it. He'll ruin himself, and everybody else. He'll end in the gutter.'

Curtal hadn't ended in the gutter. He'd ended in a crowded Memorial Service and yard-long obituaries. But Rossiter's reading of character gave Stanhope the preference. Stanhope, it appeared, could be 'told'. Was that a compliment, or the reverse? It meant that through high-paid work, publicity, and nerve-ridden subservience, the balance between Curtal and himself was, for a time, adjusted.

From that moment of hostile greeting and express public rivalry he had been haunted by terror. If Curtal survived him, he believed the man's stored venom would be released in a posthumous lampoon so virulent that reputation woven year after year by strand upon strand of gossamer grace and tact and adroit seizure of opportunity would at once be destroyed.

This was why, at news of Curtal's death, his first conscious reflection had been:

'There'll be no lampoon. I'm safe!'

Safe! Safe! A singing of joy had followed. The wind was less keen; the sun broke through the November murk; he felt an accession of love for mankind. But, besides a threat, a prop had been withdrawn. He was alone, unsupported by that powerful mind. Nobody, it was true, any longer knew a single thing that he wished to keep secret; but nobody remained to whom he could turn for utter comprehension of the age that both had lived through.

It was a loneliness beyond imagination by the young.

Was that the explanation of Curtal's blabbings to John White? Why make White the confidant? Who was White? And

if Curtal had told him, as was clear, the truth about Hester
Thompson, what else could he not have told? Good God, where
had he stopped?

This cold sweat was appalling. It made one's hands, one's
lips, one's empty jaw tremble.

Just so had his teeth chattered under his grandmother's fury,
and in school, when he had been forced to lie about cribbing or—
that was one of his worst hours—some too accurate answers to
certain exam-questions. The accuracy had been a damnable
folly. He couldn't possibly admit that he had seen the answers
overnight; so a lie, oh, a lie with the clearest of clear eyes, was the
only course to follow. He had persisted. His lie had been received
with disbelief. There was a great stink. But nobody had seen him;
a lot had been said about his proved integrity; the paper had
been re-set and by miracle answered tolerably well. He had
escaped. But the reaction had been ghastly.

Two other occasions flashed upon him from the darkest
of thunder-clouds. First, that misunderstanding of Henrietta's
wishes, her look of disdain, her brutal dismissal; and second, the
discovery of his darling Gertrude, dead. How terrified he had
been! Wave after wave of terror came now from the darkness.

'It's all right. It's all right. They called it misadventure.
That's what it was; misadventure. Nobody but Ruddock ever saw
us together. He didn't tell Curtal. He couldn't have told Curtal.
Curtal knew nothing about it, I say!'

Didn't he know anything about it? Curtal, who accumulated
within his horrible memory every indiscretion and confession
into which his contemporaries slipped?

The picture of Gertrude lying on the bed, cold, pallid,
staring, had brought a scream to his lips. She didn't accuse him;
she had never accused him; her stoicism had been immaculate. It
had been far beyond what fine ladies would have supposed
possible in a girl without expensive breeding. Her dignity, her
sweetness, both of which came from the heart, shamed him still.
His horror at finding her dead was as vivid as it had been in the
moment of first shock.

Not so vivid; overlaid by a thousand self-comfortings, later
interests, amusements, achievements. He had believed it could
not be borne; he now knew that it had been borne through the

many devices of will and circumstance. The knowledge was a relief; it was also an unforgotten reproach.

He walked with her again. He remembered the first naive expressions which had won his interest, and the gaiety with which she had turned to him—the childlike gaiety, in which he never once discerned the flaw of consciousness—when they met, or their hands touched, or their steps were discovered to be in unison. His responses, to begin with, had been ironic; they had moved quickly to irresistible infatuation.

The infatuation had betrayed him to Adelaide, his wife; and Adelaide had acted at once, with the frigid insistence of her class and type. The relation came to an end. That was the only happiness he had ever known.

Had he slept? Darkness was yet about him; and, although he could not distinguish the hour, he had been roused by the chiming of his bedroom clock. So he had been here all the time! He was warm again; free from nightmare. Blessed sanity had returned.

But what a dream it had been! He had been led by wanton voices from the air and from within to accuse himself almost of corruption. That was really preposterous. Those voices must never more rouse fear in his heart. He would be calm and unafraid.

How had the dream begun? First in the accusations roused by Curtal's death, which a clergyman's ignorant eulogy quickened into animus. From age and illness, he had been unfitted to bear the stress of considerable emotion. The young man, John White, by assailing him outside the church, and calling so soon with assertive impudence, had heightened strain to the point of fever. Fever was gone.

Was that the clock ticking? It was very loud, like the tapping of a death-watch beetle in old timbers. He listened. The streets were quiet; for an hour, two hours, only an odd car or cab would pass the house, probably altogether unheard by himself. Then the deep roar of life would begin again. He must hasten to sleep before that roar oppressed him. After sleep, he would without qualm see the grey daylight of November. He would recline while Martin drew the curtains and set beside the bed a tray bearing his morning tea. When ready for his bath, he would ring the bell. Routine would function as usual.

That would be better. He would be a man again.

PART FOUR

Hope

THIRTEEN

A Glimpse of Sunshine

BY MORNING, every cloud had been blown from the heavens. As Martin drew the bedroom window curtains, Stanhope's eyes were dazzled by glittering sunshine, and charmed by a square of blue. The wind had fallen; but it was strong enough to rattle the panes in passing. This was winter.

He sat up in bed, sipping hot tea, contemplating Martin's bony shoulders and stiffly corsetted waist as she knelt before the grate. They were female; but not feminine; angular in the style of ascetic art, not agreeable to his vision in the manner of Ingres. A scraping sound, involved in the removal of last night's ash, was followed by the crackle of firewood, a puff of smoke towards the ceiling, and, very soon afterwards, through the transfer of Martin's intervening body, the sight of flaming coals.

'A very nice cup, Martin,' purred Stanhope, with gracious courtesy. 'It's done me good, I think.'

'How's your cold, sir?' demanded Martin. She could never match his courtesy; and she was flushed and breathless from work at the fire. Her cheeks, usually white, showed round patches of brick red; her grey hair, not yet properly combed and brushed, reminded him of an old sponge. The thought crossed his mind that it would be ironic if, after the whispered conversation he had overheard between Martin and Cook, he should outlive them both. They would be disappointed if this happened. He did not wish it to happen.

'I have no cold,' said Stanhope. He sneezed.

A very peculiar expression primmed Martin's lips and gave critical hardness to her eyes.

'It doesn't sound like it,' she replied.

'At least, we won't dwell on the possibility, Martin. That sneeze was probably its farewell.'

'You caught a proper chill yesterday, sir; going to that Service. You ought to have stayed in the warm. It's all about it in the paper this morning. There's a picture of you outside the church. Cook showed me.'

'I can hardly wait to see myself!' exclaimed Stanhope, in gaiety.

'That young man who came last night, I think you're talking to. And tired you out. He looks a dwarf, beside you.'

Ah! John White! It did one good to hear him belittled.

'To tell you the truth, Martin, he is a complete dwarf.'

'But then you're so tall, sir. Make anybody look like a midget.'

Damn it, she was humouring him! Women of Martin's class talked like this to very young children, encouraging what was called the superiority complex, and unfitting them for the world of reality.

'A regular sky-scraper, in fact!'

His tiny joke dropped between them like a ball thrown by a child's strengthless arm. Martin gave him a pinched, hard-eyed smile; but did not respond.

'Cook says, what would you like for your breakfast this morning, sir?'

Cook, of course, knew perfectly well what she proposed to allow him. There was something unhealthy in these professions of solicitude. The wretched women were sure he was going to die. Chill; bed; doctor; pneumonia; peritonitis; all over. A six-finger exercise in prophecy; with the will, and a small legacy apiece, to follow.

Ghouls! He would disconcert them yet, as, indeed, he had done—when was it? Yesterday? It must have been yesterday, because the photograph was in this morning's paper. 'Oo, look! It's him! Yes, and when he got home he was almost gone!' . . .

He would have liked to demand kidneys and bacon. That would be bravado. Kidneys and bacon would ruin his bodily comfort for the day. But they expected a supplication for no more than dry toast, marmalade, and weak coffee. Or the skilly they called porridge. Or a slice of thin bread and butter with a scrape of Gentleman's Relish. 'What's he want, then?' 'Leaves it to you, Cook. No appetite this morning.' He saw the exchange of meaningful looks. 'How much longer do you think?' Bah! He would have none of their rubbish. He would insist upon being treated as what he was, a man of health and vigour.

'Tell Cook that for breakfast I should like above all things two large slices of toast, some of her delicious *paté*, and some stewed fruit—no, tinned apricots, if she has them. I need food with flavour. And she's not to forget that these people are coming to lunch; so that it must be a particularly nice lunch. Steamed fish, I think; saddle of mutton, done to a turn. With red-currant jelly; and the Pouilly; and the thirty-seven Corton; and, of course, afterwards, Armagnac. A feast for men and women who can still enjoy food. My mouth's watering already!'

'Very good, sir.'

Martin withdrew. He followed her, in spirit, to the kitchen. He saw Cook's jaw drop, and her hands perch themselves at what was once her waist, as Martin said: 'He's potty this morning. Raving about food. Give him his usual dry toast, Cook; or we shall have him howling later for bismuth!'

What horrible women!

Servants were an anachronism. He was lucky to have these two in the house, together with Cox. He did not know what he would do without them. Hence the need for continuous finesse in hiding his comprehension of their mean little minds. What was the phrase in *Julius Caesar*?

> He doth bestride the narrow world
> Like a Colossus, *and we petty men*
> *Walk under his huge legs* . . .

Oh, yes, of course this was a prelude to the tag about underlings. Cox, Martin, and Cook, although underlings, had all the contempt belonging to ignorance. They, assuming him to be senile, did not always trouble to hide their crude thoughts. They didn't guess how easily he read minds.

Somewhere in the house, all were occupied. Jackie, as he called her to himself, meaning his secretary, Miss Boothroyd, would not arrive until nine oclock. She lived somewhere in Battersea; a secret life. She was quite young; she might, for all he knew, be engaged, married, divorced. He did not believe in any of those possibilities. She was pellucid, intelligent beyond the comprehensions of Cook and Martin.

A dark girl, who reminded him of Gertrude in her quickness and—it was much more important—her beautiful gentleness, she spoke clearly, listened, and always understood what he meant. Good girl. He had never once detected her in a falsehood or an equivocation. . . .

Why, here she was; so he must have fallen asleep again, in spite of the sunshine. But the sunshine had passed to other windows.

'Good morning, Mr Stanhope. I've brought your letters, in case you'd like them.'

Brisk, crisp, with perfect assurance. Also, in her suit, which was of the colour of a summer sky at dusk, as lovely as those spring flowers, scillas, primroses, exquisite daffodils, which he most valued. Good God, how he longed to see the English countryside, in spring, if only once again! The longing, coming so suddenly, made strength fly from his bones.

'But I'm getting up, Miss Boothroyd. Did Martin give you a wrong impression?'

'All Martin said was that you hadn't rung for your bath.

'Well, that's true. I've had some conversation with her this morning. She wants to bully me into invalidism.'

He liked Jackie's quick reply.

'She does it from kindness, Mr Stanhope.'

'Hm.' It was news to him that Martin was kind. 'All the same, she bullies.'

'I'm sure you wouldn't let anybody bully you.'

'I'm sensitive to atmosphere. To suggestion. And there are many ways of bullying, from termagancy to the owlishness of pressure groups. Martin and Cook are an owlish pressure group. They mutely intimidate by holding bed and black draughts over my head. They're not listening, are they?'

'They couldn't hear us, even if they were at the keyhole, which they're not. I hope you won't imagine things about them, Mr Stanhope.'

'I imagine all sorts of things, when I'm alone. Conversations, pictures. Not always pleasant ones. It may be because I'm getting a little deaf.'

'Your hearing's perfect. Like your eyesight. Both wonderful!'

How amusingly firm and at the same time childish she looked! Her hair and eyebrows were both of a rich chestnut colour, which was unusual. The eyes were blue. When she smiled, as she did now, one saw how charming her mouth and teeth were; and her carriage delighted the eye. Extraordinary poise. She must know all about these signs of an agreeable nature; but she never exploited them. A good day school; too poor and individual for the University; secretarial training; recommended to him by Lottie Trench; and his efficient aide now for a year or more. On the whole he felt more affection for Miss Boothroyd than for anybody alive, except the Ruddock girls. This was why, to himself, he called her 'Jackie', and often 'dear Jackie'. But he was careful always to address her as 'Miss Boothroyd', to demonstrate the respect he felt. The profound respect.

'I also have quite a number of my own teeth. One might describe me as a living proof of the survival of the fittest. Did Martin tell you I sneezed this morning?'

'Not a word. Did you?'

'I think it was dust. When she lights the fire, you know. The smoke puffs out.'

'I expect there was a lot of wind in the chimney. It's very windy; rather cold.'

'I can tell you walked here. It's given you a colour. I used to walk a lot, myself, at one time. But I liked to have a companion.'

He looked closely, half-hoping to have disconcerted her by suggesting that she, too, had had a companion; and, as always, was left to embroider curiosity with invention.

'You're not like William Hazlitt, then,' remarked Jackie. 'He says, "I love to go alone." '

'A surly brute,' sighed Stanhope. 'All writers are surly brutes.'

'You're the only writer I know. I can't believe that.'

This pleased him tremendously. He felt his lips trembling. How grateful he was for kindness! It was the one thing his dreams denied him. That the words should come, spontaneously, from one he trusted was particularly affecting; for Jackie saw him too close, every day, to misinterpret his real nature. He wanted to believe this. It was most important.

What was his real nature? No, no, no; he mustn't fall again into the pit of introspection! He returned Jackie's smile.

When she was gone, he repeated the precious speech more than once, lying with correspondence, which he had not read, scattered over the eiderdown like a snowfall, and enjoying an interlude of sweet content. At last he rang for his bath. Yesterday's and last night's terrors were forgotten.

FOURTEEN

The Party

AT LUNCH-TIME he was still in a mood of unruffled benevolence; and as his visitors were punctual they found him at his best.

Sybil Moir, the eldest of them, mousy-white-haired, talkative, avid of gossip, and an acquaintance of many years (to himself he denied her the name of friend, although he used the term without compunction in addressing her), remarked as much. She rustled into the room like an ancient privileged spaniel which has long scratched at the door. Her electric blue dress, shot with reflections like a thousand daggers, made him close his eyes; her kiss upon his thin cheek, resembling a blow from a well-aimed tennis ball, made him stagger. 'Fortitude! Fortitude!' he prayed. Sybil had no time to observe stagger or flinching eyes.

'How well you look, Graham!' she gabbled. 'I was afraid I should find you under the weather. No sherry, Martin; I'll have Dubonnet. I saw you were at the Memorial Service. I didn't go, myself. So cold; and I always thought him a common little man. But I should have gone, if I hadn't been afraid of the cold. I stayed indoors, and read a filthy novel; always my delight. Isn't it splendid there are so many of them nowadays! Quite an imposing list of people. I suppose they all love to see their names in print. That's a vanity I'm spared. But you were photographed, too. Such good advertisement. Hullo, Lionel! Did *you* go?'

She turned to address a young man who had followed her into the room.

'No, I didn't. I was in the country. In any case, I shouldn't have been photographed.'

'You might have been. "Graham Stanhope with handsome friend." '

Lionel Pride, Stanhope's protégé, who was being groomed to write the biography, ignored Sybil's jeer. It was noticeable that he used the elaborate modern enunciation which proclaims the most fastidious taste in the world; a fact which Stanhope, who thought all ostentation vulgar, deplored. Nevertheless, Stanhope was impressed by Lionel's mastery of technical terms in music, ballet, and abstract painting, which in his own youth had been no part of aesthetic good form. The flaxen and smooth-cheeked boy looked, at thirty, quite five years younger than his age. If his gold chain-wristlet unpleasantly suggested effeminacy, one must not draw the obvious inference.

'I was in the country': evidently Lionel had considered it not worth while to honour a corpse. He was attentive to the living Stanhope. That, whether oblique or gross, was a compliment. Yes, one could deal with him in spite of the bracelet. *Were* there any women? Was he, like so many modern young men, a gynaecophobe?

'Did you come up this morning? You must have left the countryside in darkness.'

'To lunch with you, Graham, I'd travel through an Arctic night.'

'Who wouldn't?' clamoured Sybil. Very slightly too florid? Dear vulgar Sybil!

The third guest, Mrs Pinchin, was unknown to the others, who marked the fact by disregarding her. She was here to make the party a foursome, and as a worker in one of Stanhope's 'fields', the poet Cowper. Apparently she had a new theory about Cowper's insanity, hermaphroditism, and inertia; and while the theme now bored him almost beyond endurance Stanhope felt he must be courteous to an admirer. He was, further, not altogether lacking in the desire of the star for the moth.

Curtal meant nothing to Mrs Pinchin. Since he had never written about Cowper, he was for the present no more than a speck upon her literary horizon. She remained mute, accepting sherry as she would accept cold tea, and was probably unaware of any difference in the flavours.

'Did you go, Mrs Pinchin?' demanded Sybil, after some lip-twitching over the Dubonnet. Her relish for the sweet warming drink was ludicrous.

'She'll want port after luncheon,' thought Stanhope. 'She'll flush that loathsome beetroot red. Her hair, abominably in need of dyeing, gets very thin. Very bad, at sixty!'

'I? Oh, no.' Mrs Pinchin looked vague. Pale, short-haired, short-sighted, and shyly explosive, she was a left-handed bookworm with vestiges of the schoolgirl. 'He's outside my range. You see, he was sane.'

Sybil's deafness betrayed itself.

'Insane? I always suspected it. Paranoia, I suppose——'

'Manic-depressive,' suggested Lionel, laughing. He had not mis-heard the remark.

'Do tell me how you know!' pleaded Sybil, quite enthralled.

Stanhope laughed silently. He loved confusions.

'Sane, dear Sybil. No man more so.'

'But she said——'

'A slight misunderstanding. Mrs Pinchin meant that she concentrated on insane poets.'

'Poets? Oh, I see. But aren't they all insane? I mean, either real or pretending? That's what I dislike about the modern poets. All writing rubbish, and artfully watching to see what you make of it. We used to call it "showing-off". But it's now the accepted fraud. Don't you agree, Lionel?'

'Your flashes of insight are always irresistible, Sybil! I shouldn't dream of disagreeing.'

Sybil, being stupid, was encouraged to persist.

'Bogus stuff about being "dedicated" and "committed": such baffling and pretentious vocabularies. Ransacking the Thesaurus, I call it!'

'All part of the literary mystique.' Lionel showed brilliant teeth. 'Giving the sub-conscious its head!'

She turned upon him.

'Well, that's another——'

Martin, understanding Stanhope's nod, refilled Sybil's glass.

'And what do you think, Mrs Pinchin, of this *affectation* of insanity in the modern poets?' he asked, with great blandness. 'This hunt for the peculiar word and thought?'

As he expected, mockery puzzled the bluestocking, who blinked, slightly moving her shoulders as if she were back in the fourth form, wriggling before a sarcastic mistress.

'I don't know. I read nothing later than eighteen hundred. That's my limit.'

There were two cries of dismay.

'Incredible self-discipline!' exclaimed Lionel, in admiration. 'Not even Southey and Walter Scott?'

Mrs Pinchin showed mild resentment.

'I find the eighteenth century engrossing.'

'Mrs Pinchin is a literary expert,' remarked Stanhope to Sybil. 'One subject.'

Sybil gabbled:

'Oh, I know it's the latest thing. How many semi-colons and dream images. I should have thought it was very boring to spend every day in the same spot. Like a tethered goat!'

While Mrs Pinchin flushed at being called a goat, Stanhope answered for her.

'Not, I assure you, to the dedicated scholar.'

'Oh, well, I know it would bore me. I like variety. How long have you been an expert, Mrs Pinchin?'

'On my present work,' answered Mrs Pinchin, dreamily, 'three-and-a-half years. I've been doing research on Cowper's family. There's no doubt there was a venereal taint——'

'Good heavens!' Sybil's scoff changed to eager interest. 'Venereal! And I suppose the doctors in those days——'

Her eyes raked Mrs Pinchin's dedicated face. Stanhope could see that she wanted to find it that of a madwoman. She next swept Mrs Pinchin's dress, which was plain but not conventual. Being then unable to eyebrow another woman, she drained her second Dubonnet. She herself scampered through any book in half-an-hour, without noticing the self-betrayals or the semi-colons, keeping abreast of what was smart, and, as was proper, forgetting what she had read within a week.

'The doctors had very little knowledge. They saw everything in terms of flux and imposthume, bolus and clyster. People died like flies.'

'Dear me! I knew they died, of course; small-pox, scrofula, and that sort of thing. But you've gone into it all. I can't tell you how much I admire erudition,' cried Sybil, scrambling for safety.

'You think it next door to martyrdom?' suggested Stanhope.

'You always scorn my mind, Graham. I assure you it's a very good mind. I've been told so.'

'It resembles the gorgeous Himalayas; peak upon peak,' he gaily answered. 'I could explore it for ever. Ah, here's Martin, to say that luncheon is ready. Let us explore that, too. I hope you're all as hungry for food as you are for knowledge.'

He never talked sincerely at meals, regarding his heterogeneous guests as so many infants from the kindergarten. So he now benignly smiled upon the seated company, intent only upon diversion. Sybil's lips twitched as she eyed the decanter; she was already flushed. Mrs Pinchin was clumsy in helping herself to vegetables; and under her horrified gaze a brussels sprout rolled across the table like a large green marble. Faint pink stained her cheeks. Lionel, smiling satirically at the absurdities of both women, sought his host's eye in amusement and dutiful admiration.

Just so, in youth, Stanhope himself would have behaved. His junior was therefore beyond condemnation for doing the same thing in style; and, in sympathy, he imagined Mrs Pinchin ten years hence, when her book on Cowper, if it was ever published, had been remaindered. By then, probably, she would be persecuting another ancient lunatic, such as poor Kit Smart, girding her loins to attack the entirely baffling peak of William Blake. Her appearance would be that of a desiccated white rabbit whose sprouts were gobbled directly from the dish, or even from the saucepan, as she dedicatedly struggled with the Prophetic Books. Poor distasteful creature!

Turning, still in fancy, to Sybil, he saw her, garrulous to the last, cramming her greedy mouth once too often, and being cut off in the middle of an undigested sentence. This was a truly horrifying picture. He dismissed it in haste, contemplating Lionel. Lionel, who by then would have discarded the adolescent wristlet, and developed very distinguished grey hair, would be a second-rate Graham Stanhope, super-elegant, and, unlike his original, a mere *pococurante*.

Little beings. Little beings. Necessary at times, as now, for the relief of boredom, but gladly dismissed after the meal. Other pigmies would replace them here or in the society of dilettanti and bluestockings. He alone, kind and observant, would remain.

Doing what?

He awoke from reverie, to find Sybil engaged in malicious gossip.

'I don't know what his wife thinks of it,' said she. 'The affair's quite notorious; and she can't not know about it. Yet she goes on with her tatting, or whatever it is she does, while he gallivants all over Europe with this other woman, a Lesbian who's having monstrous affairs under his very nose.'

'What does he say to her Lesbianism?' inquired Lionel, with that indulgent smile which might mask either contempt or anxiety lest she should blurt out his own secrets. Sybil, with her insensate love of scandal, was capable of any enormity.

She briskly rejoined:

'My dear, what *can* he say? Of course he knows she's a Lesbian; but she's also heterosexual. Not to say promiscuous. That's what makes the imbroglio so fascinatingly indecent.'

They spoke, apparently, of people well known in their world, whose names Stanhope had not caught. And, as they spoke, it occurred to him that such scandals were the same that he had enjoyed about other flitting figures half-a-century ago, when he first entered the *monde*. He must have heard a hundred such tales at Lucy Chard's and elsewhere, sometimes about writers and artists, sometimes about the *ton*. How stale they were; how tiresomely recurrent!

What did Mrs Pinchin think of all this?

She seemed half-asleep, turning in her mind the gossip of two hundred years earlier, when Samuel Johnson battled with his wife's drunkenness and cast Hestor Piozzi to the sanctimonious wolves, and the Miss Berrys flirted with Horace Walpole, and Horace Walpole dodged Chatterton and ignored requests to help Cowper. Mrs Pinchin was not unlike the others; while they destroyed the reputations of the living, she dwelt with the long-dead. There was a mass of filthy scandal under the Georges.

Not one of them spared a word for Curtal, whose misdeeds were of yesterday, and who was as dead today as Swift or Wilkes, Castlereagh, Parnell, Dilke, or Wilde. So the private lives of famous men were ransacked in every age, to amuse the parasites; and their greatness was ignored because it was without spice.

Thank God, no calumny hung like miasma about himself.

Sybil's tongue had flown to a new subject.

'Well, he's a very clever man; you must admit that, Lionel. Poisonous; but clever.'

'Emetic rather than poisonous,' declared Lionel, with contempt. The indulgent smile was now fixed. His eyes glittered. 'Such a good husband, I hear. I shouldn't have called him clever. Industrous, ubiquitous . . .'

'Ah, you're jealous of him, Lionel!'

'Why should I be?'

'Well, for one thing, his mere ubiquitousness. His energy's tremendous.'

'I don't deny him that vulgar trait.'

'Industry,' laughed Stanhope. 'That's the eighth deadly sin. One might as well call call a man "worthy" as "industrious". It suggests such undedicated mediocrity. May one ask the name of this tedious paragon? I was thinking of poor Cowper, industriously translating Homer.'

'Oh, he's not tedious,' protested Sybil. 'You should see him on Television. Like a hawk; a panther. His victims loathe him.'

'I still haven't heard the name,' Stanhope insisted. 'I can't wait to know it. Not that I ever watch Television, myself.' He refrained from saying that he believed that there was a TV set in the kitchen; Martin, at his elbow, might be offended. He heard her listening with heavy-breathed interest.

Mrs Pinchin was the one to answer. She turned with an expression which he would have thought impossible to her. It was heightened for combat, and revealed extraordinary life within the vague placidity. Here was something far deeper than her absorption in the lunacies and veneries of another century.

'John White,' she said urgently. 'My husband's friend. And, of course, mine. It's very strange, when one knows him well, to hear him condemned.'

There was a startled, almost an angry, silence.

'What name did you say?' demanded Stanhope, who had heard only a mumble.

'How interesting!' gabbled Sybil. 'How interesting!'

Lionel's smile persisted. His eyelids had dropped, giving the smile venom.

'John White,' repeated Mrs Pinchin. 'My husband's close friend.'

The name so unexpectedly pronounced sent a violent shock through Stanhope's body. He had forgotten John White in the past three hours.

FIFTEEN

Discomfort Returns

W HEN further reaction was possible, it took the form of vehement dislike of Mrs Pinchin. Her enthusiasm became intolerable. She was a person of obtrusive and revolting opinions, a pedant, a bore. But in the midst of exasperation he felt pleasure at Lionel's discomfiture, which significantly revealed character.

Both annoyance and betrayal were quickly past. Lionel had such self-command that he drank wine as if dismissing a triviality. Mrs Pinchin's flush did not deepen. Her little mouth merely tightened in obstinacy. Sybil alone, rushing in as usual, kept the topic alive and dangerous.

'Oh, do tell me! Do tell me! I never met anybody who knew the creature. He's got such burning eyes; like a moth's under the magnifying glass. They make me think of the wolf in *Red Riding Hood*!'

Stanhope's poise returned. His heartbeat was normal.

'Oh, Sybil!' he sighed. 'Your fancy likens the whole race to insects and vertebrates!' He said this, although his recollection of White's air and voice and pounce confirmed each of her surprisingly apt comparisons. Out of the mouths of fools and prattlers! Striving for detachment, he added: 'Mrs Pinchin, I'm afraid you've brought out the hornets. Do you think you could tell us something about Mr . . . White's origins? I'm sorry to say the name's unfamiliar to me.'

'Graham eschews the bliss of ignorance!' laughed Lionel, derisively. 'He wants to know the worst!'

'Or the best, Lionel. I never agreed in thinking bliss a cheap commodity!'

'I don't know what his origins were,' pondered Mrs Pinchin. 'I never thought to ask.'

'Was that from fear of a snub?' Stanhope, in asking this, was influenced by memory of White's insulting brusqueness. It still made him shiver.

'No, no, Mr Stanhope; not fear, I'm sure. Respect, I think. Or just the feeling that it doesn't matter. You see, Tom, my husband, knew him before we were married. They both worked for *The Reformer*——'

'Ultra-Left,' interjected Lionel, correctly presuming that Stanhope had not heard of the paper. 'Reformers reforming the reformed.'

'What a process that is!'

'It's very outspoken. Critical.'

'Not to say censorious!' cried Lionel.

Mrs Pinchin blinked. She continued:

'Mr White's wife had a terrible accident . . .'

'Was it attempted suicide?' demanded Sybil. 'Somebody told me . . .'

'Oh, no. They were going out to dinner. Her dress caught fire. Mr White managed to put it out; but they were both burned. She'll always be badly disfigured. Before the accident, she was beautiful. Neither of them has ever been the same since; it was such a shock.'

Stanhope murmured his distress.

'Most interesting,' commented Lionel, without distress. Far from being horrified by the story, which he must have heard before, he seemed to exult in it. 'Does he now feel aversion for his once-beautiful wife?'

'He's passionately devoted to her.'

'Ah!' cried Sybil. 'He probably hates her. All husbands hate their wives. Don't you agree, Lionel?'

Lionel's cool amusement was checked.

'I'm not married, Sybil.'

'But then you hate all women, don't you?'

That sounded like an accusation. Nevertheless, Lionel suavely answered:

'Not more than a dozen; all of them particularly obnoxious. Hating is such a bore.'

'Oh, I look on it as fun. It is, to me. But then I'm too good-natured to really hate anybody. Mr White seems to hate all the people he argues with on TV. He knows so much more about everything than they do. Does he suffer a lot from crossness, Mrs Pinchin?'

Mrs Pinchin pressed her lips together more firmly, and looked like a child whose toys have been confiscated to teach her unselfishness. Stanhope, with fine grace, rendered first aid.

'Mrs Pinchin admires the man, Sybil. Lionel doesn't. You've suggested a reason for that, which we don't accept. You, I gather, know him only as a TV personality; always an over-dramatic rôle. I wonder anybody survives it. As for me, I'm still longing to know where he came from. London? The North? Wales? What sort of school did he attend, for example? Lionel, do you know his school?'

'One of the minor public schools, I believe. Not mine.'

'Oh, this school snobbery!' shouted Sybil. 'It runs through the whole country. Squabbling about the eleven-plus. All the common boys muffling their necks and going without overcoats, to copy the undergraduates. You'd think one couldn't hear their accents! Come to that, Mr White's is none too good.'

'But then you judge everybody by Lionel!' mocked Stanhope.

'And yourself! You must have had your accent from your clerical father. I'm sure he spoke beautifully, as you do. Quite a model!'

'Perhaps Mr White has his from *his* father?'

'Who was his father? We don't know. Is his father alive, Mrs Pinchin?'

Mrs Pinchin looked confused.

'I couldn't say,' she admitted. 'He doesn't speak of him; and I never asked.'

'How strange! Perhaps he was illegitimate? You don't know: I suppose you're naturally incurious.'

'Not about Cowper, you remember,' said Stanhope, smiling at Mrs Pinchin in apology for his other guests' rudeness.

Sybil rushed in again.

'Oh, yes, mad poets. We never finished about them, did we?'

'Mrs Pinchin's been busy on one for three-and-a-half years,' interjected Lionel, sarcastically. 'You can't expect to cover them all in five minutes, Sybil. Especially as you never listen.'

'Oh, I do listen. But I think like lightning.'

'We know that,' laughed Stanhope. 'Like Juggernaut, you leave a trail of maimed subjects behind you.'

Finding herself unpopular with the whole table, Sybil looked offended, and finished her wine. She was at her best only in attack.

The talk strayed to less dangerous subjects; and Stanhope's itch to discover more about John White was baulked. Several things, however, quickened his thoughts. He had learned that under Lionel's polish lay the bitter resentments of wounded vanity, that John White appeared in some sort of panel on Television, that his wife had disfigured herself through careless-ness in front of some sort of fire, and that in spite of the ensuing disfigurement White remained loyal to her. Most creditable to him. But why the fanatical interest in Curtal? Why, unless he was naturally vindictive, the fiendish harshness to oneself? He must question Mrs Pinchin in private.

On the pretext, therefore, that she had come as a specialist to consult another specialist, Stanhope detained her when the others left.

'Come into the study,' he said. 'We can be more at ease there.' And when she had exclaimed at the splendour of his library, and looked closely, with short-sighted eyes, at the portrait of a superbly arrogant Adelaide, he made her sit down, offered cigarettes and, in vain, further drink. 'I was interested in what you were saying about John White. I'm sorry that Mrs Moir was so noisy, and Mr Pride so unhelpful. They're both a little assertive. The truth is, I know nothing of Mr White. I assumed him to be a journalist, and now I find that he appears—as we heard. Did the accident happen to his wife recently?'

The object of these mild inquiries was to give Mrs Pinchin confidence, and, while proving himself gentle, to maintain the aloofness proper to his age and distinguished position. He was alert for any sign that she thought him inquisitive.

Evidently she had no suspicion. She was a simple woman, respectfully married to a man of sharper wits than herself, and, as Sybil had announced, naturally incurious about what went on around her. What a relief this simplicity was from Sybil's and Lionel's aggressive cynicism! Yes; but Lionel, surely, had been smarting from a sense of personal injury? . . .

'It happened about two years ago,' answered Mrs Pinchin. 'There's never been the smallest change in his affection.

Naturally it's been an ordeal for her; but I think she's satisfied
that John's still as fond of her as ever.'

'Any children?'

'One little boy, who at first wouldn't have anything to do
with Elizabeth. He's better now; but that was an added trial.
John has been very good with him.'

'All sweetness and light?'

'Oh, yes, always. Tom, my husband, thinks the world of
him.'

'What about his supposed malignity?'

'That's only a story. You know how people invent things
about those they see on Television. Of course, John feels
strongly.'

'I gathered that,' said Stanhope, in his dryest tone. 'How—
if it's not disagreeable to you—do you account for Mr Pride's
adverse opinion? It's evident that they're acquainted—estranged
—allergic, as it's called.'

Mrs Pinchin peeped quickly, drew breath, answered with
earnest candour.

'I didn't say anything about it at the table; but it's true that
John was rather severe on Mr Pride in an article. He pointed out
that Mr Pride . . . Oh, but perhaps, as Mr Pride is a friend of
yours, I ought to say that?'

'No writer objects to hearing about the discomfiture of
another writer . . .' A small breeze of memory caught Stanhope's
attention. 'Oh, wait a minute. Did he, by any chance, say that
Mr Pride hadn't read what he claimed to have read? Something
. . . something . . . I've forgotten. If it was clearly so, how naughty
of Mr Pride!'

'It was. I heard John talking about it to Tom.'

'Ha-ha! And of course you, who double- and treble-check
every reference, saw the naughtiness. I think you behaved very
tactfully in saying nothing about it.'

'Well, I naturally didn't want . . . I was interested in seeing
Mr Pride. He was exactly what I'd expected.'

Stanhope laughed inaudibly. He asked:

'From John's and Tom's conversation?'

The eyes turned upon him were no longer vague. Lines about
them which had previously been lost in the general smoothness
glowed with unexpected intelligence.

'I'd read Mr Pride's book myself. So I knew what they were talking about.'

Another shock assailed Stanhope. This woman was bafflingly more than a simpleton and humble acolyte. He, too, had been charged in his day with airy inaccuracy. Could she by any chance be comparing Lionel with himself on the subject of Cowper? That, although he continued to smile in the safety of age, was disconcerting.

Mrs Pinchin began her rigmarole about Cowper's ancestors. It was laboriously ridiculous. She'd found nothing that mattered. She was as much puzzled by the fits of insanity as everybody else had been; but, having picked up some medical jargon, she maintained opinions which Stanhope knew to be false. His impulse was to say:

'My good girl, this is elaborate bunkum. Cowper was a dodger. He didn't want to grow up. Peter Pan in a bag-wig. He was afraid of marriage, and jilted the girl who wanted to marry him. Then he tried, or said he tried, suicide—to escape. That was bungled; he still had life to endure. How about insanity as a substitute for suicide? That was better. It found him a mental nurse; and, when insanity grew tiresome, he snuggled himself into the Unwins' home, with Mary Unwin as a substitute Mama. . . .

'Got that? He had another bout when Lady Hester, or whatever her name was, grew too arch; and at last, when Mary Unwin, in turn, wanted to marry him, he played the trick a third time. That was all. He didn't want a job, or a wife. He wanted the placid enjoyment of cosseting. If he could have crept back into the womb, he'd have been happy. The religiosity was nothing but what Mr John White calls a "guilt complex"— something I don't understand. As for the stuff you've invented about venereal disease, it's as preposterous as the yarn about hermaphroditism. I wish you'd go. Go! Go!'

He said nothing. He looked grave, courteous, sympathetic.

'All you tell me,' he replied, when she had done, 'is most interesting, most suggestive. I shouldn't like, at this moment, to express a decided opinion——'

'No, of course, Mr Stanhope. If you thought I was on the right lines——'

'Oh, I've no doubt of that. The case hangs together, you see.'

'But, Mr Stanhope, I don't want to bother you, and I know your book was an assessment of Cowper as a poet——'

'Quite. Quite.'

'But you took an entirely different line. You said his madness came from excess of sensibility——'

'Did I? Yes, of course I did. At that time our . . . general knowledge of heredity, psychology, pathology, and so on, hadn't crystallized . . . crystallized . . . A-a-ah. A great deal of work has been done since then on Cowper, in France, in the United States. I like to feel that what I wrote has been, in a small way, useful; but I should be the last . . . I should like, if I may, to study the evidence at leisure.'

'Could I leave the manuscript with you? Would you awfully mind?'

'By all means. Send it—oh, you have it there; how delightful! —leave it with me.'

He was checked by a colossal yawn which, thank God, she took for an old man's uncontrollable sign of physical weariness. She edged forward in her chair; he laughed a little in self-excuse, and rose. She, too, was forced to rise. He took her papers; and with the art which he had always commanded in dealing with suppliants he—as it were—bore down upon her, so that, being a small woman, she was overwhelmed by his height. Within two minutes he was alone, quite exhausted.

SIXTEEN

Dr Meredith

'I TELL him just as much as I think fit,' was what Stanhope always said to himself about Meredith, his regular doctor. 'Not a word more.'

He said it again today, as the plump little man took a low chair alongside, and breathed heavily. There would be the usual pretendedly-casual pulse-taking. Then the stethoscope would be brought into play without comment; after which he would re-button his shirt and waistcoat, and feel pleasure at Meredith's routine inquiries about bowels, bladder, digestion, and sleep. 'Yes . . . yes . . . yes . . . yes.' The whole thing was a farce.

Furthermore, Meredith was a simpleton who understood nothing about states of mind. He put on a learned air, like an animal in a fairy story, said nothing, grunted 'hmphm', sat for five minutes while Stanhope related a few anecdotes of dead writers, politicians, or painters, and at last slowly rose, having satisfied himself that the patient would last another week, until his next visit. 'G'bye.' 'G'bye.' So much for Meredith.

The doctor was not above five feet six inches in height. He had a round pink face, the eyes of a gobbler, an indiarubber mouth like Edward Gibbon's, and a hoarse voice that suggested a good meal, lately taken, of braised steak with onions and tomatoes, followed by apple tart and cream. Also some not quite vintage burgundy. As to a glass of port, Stanhope had doubts. There was certainly never any odour of brandy.

Meredith resembled an expanded baby, who had swollen, rather than grown, since days when a nursemaid pushed him to Kensington Gardens in a perambulator, and sat with other nursemaids, discussing babies and the Royal Family. Master Roly-Poly had become Doctor Roly-Poly, having placidly and by miracle acquired medical degree and hospital experience without comprehension. Women probably found him an immense comfort. They, too, told him as little as they thought fit. An absolutely decent fellow, not conventional, not haphazard, but a good-humoured sybarite. No match for a man of surpassing irony.

Well, very few men could pass that test. Or had ever passed it.

This afternoon, curiously enough, Meredith varied the routine. Having pushed Stanhope's wrist back into his own keeping, he sighed, and produced a leather band to which he imparted a magic and disagreeable pressure. This was painful. Relaxing the pressure, Meredith sighed again, and was thoughtful. A thermometer came next. One felt it hard and for an instant cold under one's tongue; and listened to a watch ticking in Meredith's pocket; one looked at Meredith's protrusive eyes, which were averted: and noticed that his mind had passed into coma. The thermometer was withdrawn, and silently consulted.

'Sleeping all right?' Meredith asked, returning to life.

'A little over-tired,' admitted Stanhope, indulgently. 'Oh, yes, I sleep all right. Result of a good digestion and good conscience.'

'Hmphm.' Meredith retreated into non-committal geniality. 'Good digestion and good conscience, eh? Only murderers have good consciences. They eat good meals before they're executed; and savour them. Were you out yesterday?'

Conscience? Murderers? Stanhope did not follow the questions. He said:

'I had to go out. What, d'you think I caught cold?'

'Did you?'

'I sneezed twice this morning.'

'Nothing in that. Clears the sinuses. All the same, you might stay in bed for a bit.'

'Oh, nonsense, Meredith. I can't stay in bed. I'm an active man.'

'I know. Be a little less active for a day or two. I'll send round something to make you sleep easily.'

'Good heavens! I should have more bad dreams.'

'More? Does that mean you've been having them?'

'I'm always having them. An old man's life is made up of dreams. A return to juvenescence.'

'What sort of dreams do you have?'

This was astonishing. To hear the fellow talking about dreams was to see him in the rôle, not of Freud, but of Medicine Man.

'Are you setting up as a psychiatrist?'

'Half the g.p.'s job is psychiatry.'

Stanhope was seized with hauteur.

'You need an elaborate system to read a mind like mine. I've touched life at many points; and read some of the profoundest and subtlest minds of the last four hundred years, from Descartes to Bertrand Russell. Read some of them intimately, at close quarters; others, such as Pascal and Hegel, in the printed word. You'll have to do all my reading, and a lot besides, to understand my thoughts. I'm an exceptional man, you know, Meredith.'

'You're exceptional, all right. Otherwise these dreams wouldn't be interesting.'

'If they are dreams; and not realities.'

'Oh.' Meredith looked at the fire. One would have thought he expected something to come out of the chimney. 'What, people talking to you?'

Stanhope took fright. They mustn't have any more of this.

'No, no, no. I've had three bores to lunch today; tiresome enough.'

A long pause followed. Meredith said, at last:

'D'you think you'll dream about *them*?'

'Ph!' Stanhope flicked his fingers. 'I've already forgotten them.'

'They didn't excite you, then?'

'They left me comatose. As you see me now.'

Meredith eased forward in his chair, preparatory to rising.

'All the same, I'll send you the sedative, and tell Martin to put you to bed with a couple of hot bottles. You want to nurse that cold.'

'I have no cold. We agreed on it.'

'A little temperature.'

In his annoyance, Stanhope could not prevent himself from crying, rashly:

'Not to speak of the dreams, eh? Or do you call them hallucinations?'

The plump face was masked.

'I call them nothing. You're running a trifle above normal, that's all. G'bye.'

Meredith heaved himself up, offering a hand soft and cool as a full-blown rose, after which, unconsciously trembling, Stanhope watched him go.

The trembling lasted for as long as the sense of having betrayed something which should have been kept hidden. He ought not to have shown his annoyance. What on earth had made him use the word 'hallucinations'? It had deeply agitated him. With Meredith's 'people talking to you?' it suggested mental weakening. That was what Meredith implied, wasn't it?

Rubbish! There was no mental weakening.

Admittedly some uncertainty had arisen as to the physical presence of this man White, and the Ruddock girls. Ruddock himself couldn't have been there. That was 'hallucination'. As to the girls, the question could be settled at once by a reference to Martin. But what would happen in Martin's mind if she were asked whether certain persons had, or had not, visited him? She'd run at once to Meredith. 'You're quite right, Doctor. He's wandering. . . .' Hallucination. Hallucination. Meredith would bring along another doctor. 'About these hallucinations of yours, old chap. Just a second opinion, you know . . .' Second opinion; some long-faced charlatan claiming to be a specialist in the *psyche*. They'd question him; go farther, farther. . . .

This was terrifying! The imagining of it robbed him of breath. It brought a veil down over his eyes, over his thoughts, until, although fully conscious, he seemed to be paralysed. Evening would come, and peopled darkness. John White would again appear at his chair-side or bed-side, primed with new diabolical questions and incalculable information about the past. What had they said of White? 'He hates everybody he argues with on TV.' 'He only hates his wife.' 'Vindictive' . . .

Vindictive; hadn't that word been his own? Was everything that had been said his own?

He struggled to his feet, and shambled, stiff-kneed, to the fireplace, where the marble mantelpiece was cold to his fingers. It would be welcomingly cold against his burning forehead. Downstairs, Meredith was probably whispering to Martin, Martin whispering back. 'Don't let him see you're watching.

Behave naturally.' 'Yes, sir, I see, sir. I'll be very careful.' Then
Martin would whisper to Cook; Cook to Cox; Cox to other
chauffeurs. Whispers would surround him. Hark! He could
already hear them!

There was no sound but the clock's ticking and the thumping
of his heart. This was all a most stupid fever, against which he
must be on guard lest it be detected. Martin would give that
sharp glance when she brought the tea, look over her shoulder
when she made up the fire, and when she said 'I've put the hot-
water bottles in the bed, sir,' and 'Here's the pills the doctor
sent, sir. Shall I help you take them?' The most vehement caution
would be needed to defeat her bestial inquisitiveness.

SEVENTEEN

The Two Women

WHAT had Meredith meant by saying that murderers had easy consciences? He was no murderer.

He must be calm. The word had been used in reply to his own defiantly jocular claim to easy sleep. No intention lay behind it. None. He must not allow himself to read into a chance word something that wasn't meant. Only at this moment of heightened sensitiveness did it arouse tragic memory and suggest menace.

Nobody had ever accused him of anything so ludicrous as murder. His reputation was spotless. He had kept it so through the years. But, looking down on the flaming coals, he saw faces among them, one, in particular, of a bearded man whose name he had long forgotten. The beard had been black, streaked with grey, and the eyes sunken deep in their sockets. Dull eyes, he recalled, of no quality; their owner revealing none of the shrewdness which he must have possessed. Other memories were of·a shabby frock-coat, a wing collar, a black tie, ugly hands holding a black fountain pen.

The setting was a dingy room whose dead grey walls, dusty electric light globes, and wintry gloom froze his blood. Two or three unhelmeted policemen, two or three other men in dark clothes, and a couple of sorrowful women who wore mourning, completed the picture. Both women were unknown to him; apparently they were neighbours. They had previously been tearful; but their tears were gone. The only extreme agitation was his own, a compound of grief and fathomless anxiety.

At a later date he had accounted for the Coroner's considerateness. When no longer an official, the man was a reader. He understood more of his witness's pain than he allowed to be seen; and if he understood the fear, also, he did nothing to exploit it. At the time his mercy was something to thank God for.

'Did she ever say anything to you that suggested an intention to take her life?'

'Never.'

'Did you know she had the tablets?'

'No.' That was untrue; he had known.

'Had you quarrelled?'

'Never.'

'Mr Stanhope, I must ask you this: were you her lover?'

'I was not.'

'You're sure? She was not a virgin.'

'I think there had been'—oh, God, the closing of his throat, the sweat under his arms; but a violent effort to appear candid! —'an unhappy love-affair. She told me that.'

'You were simply——'

'Simply a friend. An affectionate friend. I tried to help her. She was a very clever, intelligent girl. I encouraged her to read. I lent her . . . Yes, sir; simply a friend.' Something in the Coroner's expression had warned him against too elaborate a protestation.

'Tell me why you went that day, how you discovered the body.'

'I was taking some books she'd asked for. I had no answer to my ring, my repeated knocking. It seemed strange. She was expecting me. Or so I thought. So I went downstairs to the landlord, who had a key to the flat. He hadn't seen her; and came back with me. We went in.'

'You found her on the bed?'

'Yes, she was lying in bed. I thought she was asleep. When I couldn't rouse her, I telephoned for a doctor. The landlord telephoned.'

'She was then dead?'

'The doctor said so.'

'Yes, he has said so today. You can think of no reason why she should take her life?'

'No reason at all. I can't believe she meant to do such a thing.'

'She was expecting you? A normal, friendly visit?'

'A normal, friendly visit.'

'You took the books away again?'

'I . . . took the books away again.'

'Thank you, Mr Stanhope.'

'Thank you, Mr Stanhope.' 'Thank you, Mr Stanhope.' He could hear the man's quiet voice, hear it echoing from those ugly green walls and sounding like a declaration of mercy. The relief was so overwhelming that blood had burned his cheeks. Tears came to his eyes. He took his seat again, at first dreading the suspicious examination of those in the room, and only afterwards finding that every stare was for the Coroner. Questions and answers had been too quiet to arouse hostile curiosity. He was but one of those who waited, as if apathetically, for the proceedings to end.

'Death by misadventure; no reason to suggest . . .'

There had been nothing sensational in the newspapers. Two or three lines only, referring to him as 'a friend of the deceased'. He had not been identified by the hack reporters, who knew nothing of his work or his world. Within twenty-four hours the extremity of his dread was over.

Only two people besides himself knew of the association. One was Ruddock, who met them together one evening, at dusk, at a time when Adelaide was staying with relations in Provence. Ruddock, that quiet laughing man, understood everything at a glance, caught their shoulders with the rich impudence of old friendship, would not allow them to pass, delighted Gertrude by his jovial nonsense, and begged them to dine. She had looked 'Yes, please! Please!'

'Do give me this pleasure. I'm all alone. My evening out!'

What else could he have done? He had known it to be unwise. He was jealous of Ruddock's quick triumph. He was struck by Gertrude's inability to dissemble or think of their love as in any way furtive. On that golden night nothing could be refused.

They had taxied to Soho, Ruddock, already portly, sitting on one of the little flap seats opposite, with his back to the driver; and they had spent an evening of delightful merriment. Gertrude was like a proud bride, sparkling and adorable. There was spontaneous liking on both sides. He alone felt the sense, not of sin, but of fear, as he thought of Adelaide. Wasn't that natural? By any calculation, he was the transgressor, and would be so regarded by all her friends. The fear came in waves, as memory now did, sometimes stealthy, sometimes minatorily loud.

'I've escaped for tonight, for these exquisite weeks. But—always—always—I shall have to go back!'

The ejaculation had proved bitterly true. That had been the climax to their happiness. He saw it now as the hour before despair.

Ruddock called on the evening of the inquest, without saying how he knew of it, offering unbearable sympathy. Just a word, and, for the first and only time, a caressing arm about one's shoulders. The arm had been shaken off, the sympathy repelled, from pride, from agony. No sympathy was ever again offered, in any circumstances. This was the cause of the dream in which Ruddock accused him after thirty years of silence. He had always dreaded that accusation. It was brought by outraged conscience; the good conscience of which he had lyingly boasted to Meredith.

The other person who knew, as was inevitable, was Adelaide. She must already have suspected, and pried in clothes, in desk, in books. 'Why is he so happy? So unlike himself? There's a woman!' And so there was. One small note, left by chance in a book which Gertrude had returned, was all she found; but it was enough. The damned callous brute!

Stanhope took several vehement steps away from the fire. Adelaide had come into this very room, here, where he stood, holding the note in her hand. She had shown no indignation. She had only, after the manner of her heartless kind, delivered an ultimatum.

'Either you stop this ridiculous affair now, at once, or I leave you.'

He had been unable to defy her. To have done so would have meant, at that time, and in the circumstances of their social life, a sudden ruinous ebb tide. There was no quarrel between himself and Gertrude: he had spoken the truth. There was a parting. He quietly explained what had happened, and what he was compelled to do. Gertrude listened. That was all. His career, his good name, was at stake. His debt to Adelaide could not be repudiated. He was a man of honour. It had all been whispered and heard in silence. She had run to him at the last, perhaps hoping that he would act romantically—he could not tell. She was very pale. There had been no quarrel; no reproach; a superb and touching dignity.

It was not true that she had expected him that day. He hadn't been able to work or think or endure the bleak loneliness of his study; and had gone—why? The books were a pretext. He did not know what he had intended or expected. As he told the coroner, he had taken the books away again. He had also, with instinctive precaution, recovered while waiting for the doctor three other books which bore inscriptions to Gertrude in his writing. Nobody but himself had seen them. His few letters were missing, evidently destroyed. She had left nothing, except the books, to suggest that they had been friends, or more than friends.

More than friends. When once he knew that she was dead, he had not looked at her again.

'I couldn't have risked any scandal,' insisted Stanhope, thirty years after the event.

The whole structure of his life would have collapsed. Adelaide had the money, the social power which supplied prestige. Under her classic frigidity she was as vengeful as Catherine de Medici, and would have invented a hundred stories to his discredit. A hundred! A thousand! Such women as she were endlessly ingenious in slander of a husband. But she would also, without scruple, have destroyed the carefully woven pattern of flattery, graciousness, and disparagement by which the superior literary critic attains power. How well she had known the strength of her position, the vulnerability of his!

'The delicate poise,' he muttered. 'The assembly of intangibles. I couldn't risk it. I couldn't risk it. Well, if you call it murder, wasn't she the murderess?'

The one fatal slip. A simple letter of half-a-dozen lines, left in a book on his desk. It was evidence. Previously, whatever suspicion she might have formed, she could never have proved anything; but those indiscreetly loving lines were all she needed.

How discreet, otherwise, they had been! How discreet! He hadn't had the heart to warn Gertrude too openly against any sort of written word; it could have made her suspect him of being a common intriguer. She was impulsive, lacking in disguise. And, when the discovery was made, he hadn't had quite the command of himself to bluster, lie, or counter-attack. Another man would have done so. Curtal, in the same predicament, would have carried the matter with a high hand. Such behaviour was impossible to a gentleman.

So there had been no arraignment of Adelaide's frigidity. No defiance. All, on his part, had been apparently honey-smooth. Otherwise, of course, within, where for once, after that first turn of a girl's laughing face had seemed to burst his heart, suppression had failed.

Well, then, it had been goodbye to Gertrude. Her pupils enlarging, until they swallowed the irides; her lips pressed together, pale and swollen in the deeper pallor of her cheeks. No word uttered. What thoughts had passed in her mind?

'Do, for God's sake, say that you understand my position!' he had cried, very desperately.

'What is there to say? You're leaving me.'

'But you appreciate that I'm in an impossible situation.'

A nod. A half-smile. What had that smile hidden?

He had to admit that, afterwards, Adelaide had behaved well. She had not referred to the matter again. When the inquest was over, and she had returned from the country to find him sitting at his desk, staring at blank paper, she had lightly touched his shoulder with her white hand—Gertrude's hands had been as beautiful, but of a less exquisite whiteness—and gone away at once. Only at dinner that night did she say, with every appearance of unaltered kindness:

'I think I have some good news for you, Graham. Peake was staying with the Hunts. We had several talks. I found he was thinking of Percy Jay for that job on the *Mercury*. He angled to find out what I thought of Percy. I said "very good, very sensible", and so on; but left it to be inferred that he wouldn't have been *my* choice. I didn't, of course, mention you as an alternative; although I knew you'd been interested in that particular job. After all, it's a thousand a year, with enormous prestige, which I know is what you care about most.'

A slight pause occurred, as if she underlined the importance of reputation. He had not answered; and she had resumed:

'The matter didn't crop up again until last night, when Peake suddenly asked what you were doing. I rather expanded. Your idealism, and so on. He liked that. He's a pathetic little man, really; wants one to believe, in spite of every sign to the

contrary, in his high ideals. So I expressed admiration for them.
I said how much *you* admired him. I think he saw you in a new
light, which was what I intended. It all happened quite naturally.
He asked if I thought you would like to work for him. I said I
felt sure you would. I said nothing about Percy. Nor did Peake . . .

'He gave me a lift to town this morning—a wonderful new
Rolls. We spoke of the Hunts, and country life, Beethoven—he's
got as far as the Kreutzer Sonata—and some new woman pianist
whom he admires. . . . He evidently wants to be thought cultured;
and he likes to give the appearance of depth. Great insight into
character, you know. His last words as we parted were: "I shall
be writing to Graham." "Graham" you see. I look on it as a won
battle.'

Recalling the long speech, which had been remembered
exactly as to emphasis, if not in the actual words, Stanhope
paused. He had not been misled. She had meant 'as another won
battle.' She was rewarding him for good conduct over Gertrude;
reminding him, in effect, that she thought only of his good, and
that in the past she had used her beauty and family connections
to his advantage.

He had been properly grateful at the time. The job had been
offered to him. He had accepted, and used it for the next seven
years to express his own, as well as Peake's, high ideals.

There must nevertheless have been strange doings in
Adelaide's mind. She had perhaps indicated, in silence: 'That
gairl could only kill herself for you; I advance your career.' Had
she also wanted to escape the charge, which might have been
brought, that she was a murderess?

Not Adelaide! She was too consciously a great lady to
entertain such a preposterous notion.

EIGHTEEN

Jackie

WHAT was that? The only perceptible movement was a changed light in the glass covering Adelaide's portrait over the fireplace. The continued presence of this portrait was an act of piety, the symbol of lasting acknowledgment to his grand benefactress. He saw with relief that the reflection was that of Jackie Boothroyd.

Had she heard his accusing cry? He sharply drew breath.

'Oh, Miss Boothroyd; did I say what I shouldn't say?'

Her smile, always frank, was a reassurance. But of course the frank smile need deepen very little to become brazen. Eavesdroppers developed monumental craft.

'No, Mr Stanhope. You said nothing at all.'

'I was discreet, was I?'

'Always discreet.'

Admirable! She had calm. He really believed that she liked and respected him. She must be the only person in the household who did so; the only disinterested employee he had. But wouldn't she find his inquiry odd? She'd say to herself: 'Oho! What was he thinking, then, that he should be afraid I'd overheard it? *I must find out.*'

He finessed.

'My thoughts were innocent. But I asked, because I'm apt to indulge the old man's habit of talking to myself. The old woman's habit, too. Do you know it? A nurse I had as a child used to say very coarse things about my grandmother. I didn't know then that they were coarse; but I found out later. Most uncomplimentary. She, being deaf, couldn't hear herself. Her face was as benevolent as vast quantities of soap and water could make it; but she wasn't in the least benevolent. She was like a Dickens grotesque. It makes one wonder whether Dickens's grotesques were as crude as fine ladies and gentlemen suppose.'

134

Jackie, impulsively cheerful, smiled again.

'I shouldn't have thought there could be anything more grotesque than real people, Mr Stanhope?'

'You say that suggestively. You're not, by any chance, referring to me?'

She shook her head, adding amusedly:

'My father sometimes talks to himself. He's by no means old.'

Stanhope mused. He said, at last:

'I hadn't realized that you lived with your father. Isn't that strange? My ignorance, I mean. I wish you'd tell me something about him. I should be interested. For example, what does he do for a living?'

'He's a solicitor's clerk.'

This was almost more surprising, for some reason, than artist or bank manager.

'How unexpected! Does he know any Law?'

'He never tells us how much or how little he knows. He's a silent man.'

'Like me; discreet. Well, of course, as a solicitor he needs to be. It would be unlucky if he thought aloud among his firm's clients.'

'He only does it when he's sitting by the fire, at night, and has forgotten we're there.'

Yes, yes. By the fire, at night, supposing himself to be alone. It might happen to anybody. To oneself, for example, sitting here, dreaming. But did this exemplary father people the room with the accusing ghosts of former friends? What a mockery the word 'friends' could prove! They spoke with tongues too harsh for love. Be silent, 'friends'!

'What does he say, when he talks to himself?'

Miss Boothroyd showed embarrassment, not by shrugging, not by colouring, but by the almost breathless haste of her answer.

'Oh, I don't know. That he's disgusted with the Government, or the local Council, or something he's read in his paper. Strikes exasperate him. He thinks they upset other people, innocent people. Or he calls himself a stupid, unimportant man. That's when he feels he's been clumsy, or inconsiderate. He wouldn't wish us to hear him, in case it did something more to hurt our feelings.'

'Your feelings? This is very subtle. He knows he's important
to you?'

'He's essential to us.'

'Is anybody that? I suppose when one has a family. I have no
family; no relations at all. In some ways it's a convenience; but
I see . . . If one has no family, and no friends—no longer any
friends—there's a temptation to . . . Your father sounds en-
dearingly modest.'

'He is.'

There were tears, Stanhope believed, in her eyes. He said,
hardly aloud:

'Like his daughter.'

She answered only with a glance, which he thought proved
character, as well as composure. Modest. Modest. How many
modest people had he ever known? Ruddock; the Ruddock girls;
Gertrude. For an instant he believed that Jackie was Gertrude
herself.

'I didn't disturb you before; but a Mr Venables, of the B.B.C.,
telephoned to say that they're preparing a memorial programme
to Mr Curtal. Mr Venables would very much like to come and
see you about it. He suggests bringing a tape-recorder.'

Blast! Stanhope, having been lost in tenderness, was swept
by fury.

He sought always to suggest that he and anger were strangers.
Others must believe him to be impassive, far above the earthy
irritations of commoner men. Yet nobody, not even Jackie, could
have missed the abrupt uncrossing of his extended legs. They
straightened, and were drawn back again, in a single convulsive
movement. Lamentable! The heart had quickened its beat.

Curtal, in a like situation, would have exploded. He'd have
shouted: 'Tell the B.B.C. to get to bloody hell out of this! I'll
have nothing to do with their body-snatching!' You'd have seen
his little eyes blacken. A cornered bull was no more savage. But
Curtal had no dignity. He raged and ranged like a Hyde Park
spouter. It was different with oneself.

What then? The truth about Curtal, cad, liar, lecher, for-
ever on the make, was impossible on a radio programme. But so,
for a man of principle, were the unctuous platitudes of most
memorial programmes.

'Hm. Hm. As you know, I detest the radio. Such vulgar self-display. They tell me John White . . .' No, he hadn't said that; it was a first unuttered improvization. His official answer was: 'That's very charming of Mr Venables. Most flattering. You told him I should be delighted to pay tribute to my old friend?'

'I told him I would ring him back after tea.'

'Ah, yes; after tea. A breathing space. How considerate of you. I'll have a quiet tea, and plan what we should say.'

Miss Boothroyd looked up in surprise.

'Oh, but, Mr Stanhope, have you forgotten the Ruddocks? They're coming to tea.'

Stanhope felt overwhelming confusion. Was she there? Could this be, already, the return of hideous dream?

He stared at the fire, shaken by the beat of his heart. Momentary darkness made him fear that he would swoon. Through the darkness came his own voice, in a sigh.

'I'd forgotten.'

Thank God, the voice and person of Jackie were real. If he stretched out his hand he would be able to touch her.

'Would you like me to put them off? You're too tired? I'm sure they'd understand.'

He was himself again, by an effort of the tough, undefeated will.

'On no account put them off. It was just that it had slipped my mind. I was under considerable strain yesterday. Did I ask you to do it yesterday?'

'Yesterday morning, before you went to the Service. You wanted to talk to them about Mr Curtal.'

'I wanted?'

'They were better, you said, than Mr Curtal's own children, who were only children of the brain.'

Children of the brain! Why, the fellow had probably left a hundred bastards!

'Did I say that? The pretty fancy of a poetaster, Miss Boothroyd! Did you know I was that? Mr Curtal said so. Had you any other reason for supposing he'd left no fleshly children?'

A faint colour deepened Jackie's cheeks.

'Only that the papers didn't mention them.'

'Ha-ha! That was conclusive, of course!'

'Most people have to depend on the Press,' she said, a little drily, 'for news of what happens in the world.'

'Journalism is a noble profession,' Stanhope declared, in his silkiest tone. 'And journalists are omniscient. Therefore, either Curtal left no children, or his mistresses, like your father, keep their mouths shut. It's unusual; perhaps possible.'

Jackie had listened attentively.

'The papers, if I may mention them again without being laughed at, said Mr Curtal was "notoriously attractive to women". What sort of women, Mr Stanhope?'

'Bad men,' murmured Stanhope, 'attract every sort of women.'

'Was he a bad man?'

'Very bad. You'd have liked him very much. When he entered a room, every woman in it became a wanton. Or she detested him. It's the same emotion in reverse.' Stanhope roused himself after this only half-conscious and half-serious answer. 'Why, Miss Boothroyd, I'm talking scandal, which, as you know, I never do. Like all men, including myself, Mr Curtal was a mixture of good and evil, with evil predominating.'

'I don't think there can be such a mixture in you, Mr Stanhope.'

'What! All evil?'

He saw her colour quickly; and new warmth flowed in his veins. He was overjoyed at her admiration. In sophisticated society, no admiration is genuine. His own had never been so.

Had he ever whole-heartedly admired anybody in the world?

'So you thought the Ruddock girls would comfort me, Miss Boothroyd. As the next best thing to Curtal's children—if he ever had any!' The thought flashed across his mind: 'or my own, whom I never had!' 'I wonder if they'd be gratified. They loved their father with all their hearts. They really only tolerate me, you know, because I was his friend.'

She did not expostulate; if she had done so he would have detected the lie. She said, very quietly, as if she had been his wife, or a daughter:

'That's not true, Mr Stanhope. They're devoted to you; they love coming here; and they do you good. You oughtn't to be ungrateful.'

'They always do me good? Not always.' He remembered that
the exception had occurred in a dream, and corrected himself.
His tongue slipped into the use of her Christian name. 'Yes, yes,
always. You do well to remind me, Jackie.'

'Mr Venables is hoping to get them both for his programme.'

'Oh?' It was sharp. 'He's asked them, has he?'

Her smile marked the jealousy of his question.

'No, he said he hoped to get them. I think he wanted to be
sure that they'd be acceptable to you. His idea is to build the
programme round you.'

Stanhope laughed, and slid down in his chair. He wished
Jackie would stay with him, talking thus, for ever.

'Why, that sounds like premature immortality, Miss
Boothroyd! Something I never counted on. But what an immeasurable talk you must have had with Mr Venables!'

She was exquisitely calm under his teasing.

'He speaks rather fast. It was quite short, really. He's very
enthusiastic.'

'About Curtal?'

'No, about you.'

'Ah, he's what's called a "fan". Most unusual!' Stanhope
thought: 'I'm so old, that I treat as slang—as Henry James did—
words that have been legitimized!'

'Decidedly a fan.'

'Oh, dear, dear! That makes it very hard to refuse, doesn't it!'

'I hope you won't refuse, Mr Stanhope.'

'Hm. Hm. Of course, I should like to refuse. An old man's
hemmed about with parasites. Did he say anything about
somebody called John White? A Television personality, they told
me today at luncheon.'

'Nothing, Mr Stanhope. Did you want him in the broadcast?'

'He is the last person in the world whom I should want in the
broadcast, Miss Boothroyd.'

She smiled, preparing to leave him. Stanhope took her hand,
which was warm and firm, and at once released it. She passed
from the room, while he, drained of strength, closed his eyes.
Jackie was incapable of imagining such black thoughts as pressed
once more upon his brain, stupefying it.

NINETEEN

Mr. Venables

MR VENABLES was there when the Ruddock girls arrived.

He looked like a blond, happy schoolboy, and was so small and beautifully proportioned that he must have been his mother's pride and, finally, perplexity. One pictured her as asking: 'Why doesn't he grow bigger? Did I pray for him to remain my baby for ever?' His speech, which was staccato, with many an unfinished sentence, indicated fear lest his most elusive meanings should seem laboured; and to Stanhope, accustomed to addressing strangers with majestic aloofness, this butterfly performance was as disconcerting as jazz. It put strain upon his attention. Nevertheless, he immediately liked the boy, and thought all must do so.

Egotism suggested that Venables's flight from the specific was due to expectation that an old man would be 'difficult'; and that suave demands for re-phrasing would be followed by artful cuts in the recording-tape.

'I won't have that,' thought Stanhope. 'I have a right to be "difficult". My reputation's involved. Who the devil are these people—I don't mean Mr Venables, but the unseen hidalgos of Broadcasting House—to decide what it's proper for *me* to say?'

The anticipation of being constrained, in old age, and in relation to Curtal, by a hidden, dominating power, recalled those vile years of tyrannical supervision by his grandmother. He had then succumbed, a little boy without resource; now he would not succumb.

'Either I say my own piece as I want it said, or I decline altogether.'

He offered Venables a parchment hand, smiled with proper abstracted dignity, and made a movement to pull forward a second armchair. The movement was gracefully forestalled. They sat facing each other, Venables leaning forward with the gaiety of one whose adroitness was never at fault.

'This is very kind, sir. Far kinder than I had any right. . . .'

'I did him injustice,' thought Stanhope. 'He won't press me.'

Aloud, he explained, easily:

'Nelson Ruddock's daughters happened to be coming to tea with me today. I thought it would help you, perhaps, to meet them, as it were, unofficially. Their father knew Curtal as intimately as anybody except myself; and they may have interesting childish memories.'

'Thank you, sir. Your secretary was good enough . . .'

'They have beautiful voices,' added Stanhope, full of love for his darlings, 'which must be valuable in broadcasting.' He could not doubt that in this quiet room his own voice held a wistful music; but that was only a part of his thought.

'Quite beautiful,' agreed Venables. 'Both delicate artists. Like their father. I'm sure you loved him.'

Was that true? Apart from one doubt, it could be granted. Yes, yes; quickly!

'Everybody, including his daughters, loved him. He never said a harsh thing. He was lazy, good-humoured——'

'And a wit?'

'Do you know, it never struck me that he was a wit. He made one laugh; but one forgot why. I've read that of Sydney Smith. What I remember is more the radiance of goodness.' How easy this was proving! Every answer came pat. But Mr Venables supplied the answers. He was purposely dangling as bait a lighter subject than Curtal. 'Yes, the radiance of goodness.'

'Wonderful phrase! The plays confirm it. People laugh; they've been made happy. I wonder if a Ruddock programme, with you . . .'

Stanhope, faced with radio memorials in which he would be perpetual chorus to the dead, took fright.

'No, no: don't speak of such a thing! My broadcasting gifts are negligible.'

Venables smiled, tactfully setting aside the alarm, or—less charitably—testiness.

'I'm distracting you, sir. The worst of a discursive mind. I'll stick to Curtal. We feel it's particularly desirable that you should be the . . . Sixty years of close friendship, no rivalry, no break of any kind. . . . I imagine you were the stabilizing . . . Writers aren't in general . . . We must beware, though, of overtaxing your strength, your patience. . . .'

Stanhope, given a lead by that cunning 'you were the stabilizing', was conscious of a roughness in his own voice.

'Curtal made demands on both. Unremitting demands.'

'He was a demanding character; I understand, and admire your patience. We certainly mustn't . . . You must tell me if I . . .'

Persistent creature! Beneath every compliment lay determination. The process of streamlining had begun!

It would continue in this way—little darts aside to pleasanter topics such as the Ruddock girls, withdrawals of unwelcome suggestions, gentle pressures, smiling silences—until resistance broke down. What was that story one had heard of an unfortunate broadcaster, so much badgered by a chit producer that he ran to the lavatory to hide burning tears? Venables wouldn't badger as crudely as that. Nor would one weep. But the streamlining? The streamlining! Every piece of manipulation would be ascribed to fear of causing weariness!

'*I'm afraid I'm tiring you, sir. . . . Could we have that again? I wonder whether you'd mind if we omitted . . . It's not strictly relevant to the picture, d'you think?*'

'*What is the picture, Mr Venables?*'

Or: '*Your reactions are most interesting; but our listeners . . . Could we have a little more about . . . for example, Curtal's extraordinary loyalty to his friends?*'

Ha-ha! The legend again! One would gravely retort:

'*What loyalty are you referring to, Mr Venables? I'm afraid I can't subscribe to a studio portrait.*'

At this dry protest, the fat would be in the fire! The Venables charm would fade; its place would be taken by exasperation.

'*Well, really, Mr Stanhope! This is a Memorial Programme!*'

The glance a stare; royal displeasure; oneself brought sharply to heel by the representative of a monopoly spoiled by the furious siege of would-be stars, and all-too-confident of its power. A consolidated swelled head!

Nothing of this had passed, or would pass. One was still facing an agreeable young man who brimmed with eager kindness. One was being treated with respect as a very distinguished man indeed. Well?

'Yes. I must have known Curtal, in poverty, in affluence, for nearly sixty years. It doesn't seem like that. One doesn't measure time while a friend is living. Everything's in the present; a flow and interflow of feeling. "I shall see him tomorrow—or next week; we must hammer this out. Perhaps I can clear up this point; or he can convince me." Do you see? When he dies, it's hard to give a mortuary cast, an historical sequence, to one's recollections. In fact Curtal's been too much with me—almost literally so—in the last few days, not as a dead man, but as an energetic, exacting, rather noisy personality. Noisy, insistent, well-nigh raucous. He seems to have been—not so much sitting, as jumping about, in that very chair. . . .'

Venables did not exclaim, as John White might to one's discomfiture have done: 'Isn't that just unctuous guff? The sort of thing we expect from Pecksniff!' He cried, almost laughing in satisfaction:

'Exactly what we . . . Your friend as he *is*. The man who's—one may say—just gone out of the room. . . .'

The boy's gaiety was such that Stanhope clapped his hands together.

'Oh dear, Mr Venables! One's at one's worst! Who is ever merciful to a recently departed guest?'

So they were both laughing, as easy as two youngsters *en rapport*. Venables cried quickly:

'Would it be so with Curtal?'

'As the dust settled, yes.'

'Sixty years of rubble? I don't believe you do, in fact, back-bite!'

Flashing memory of a thousand resentments lighted Stanhope's mind.

'You don't? Well, then, I don't. I never did.'

'Sometimes tempted?'

'Oh, one learns to accept one's friends. Otherwise, what becomes of friendship?'

'His, for you, was ardent, wasn't it?'

As if every affront from that bitter tongue didn't come forth

from its hiding-place whenever one thought of him! As if Curtal
hadn't been so candidly rude every time they met!

'Yes, I think it must have been. Not always happily expressed,
of course. But yes, I'm proud to feel that it was.'

What a lie! What a lie! With John White's store of malicious
anecdote only partially revealed; with all the angers of half-a-
century controlled and driven within by forcible control of
hysteria; with all one's tears of passionate sensitiveness and hate
and misery hidden. . . . Was it a lie? Was it?

How much half-truth had Venables absorbed? He was so
naturally charming that every perception could lurk in con-
cealment within the boyish gaiety. But he must have been alert
all the time, for he said:

'I see we shall have to allow you a good deal of . . .'

'Rope? To hang myself?'

'Say "latitude". I don't want you to feel . . . strings. . . . You
know?'

'Even if my memories aren't all handsome, Mr Venables?'

'From my point of view, the racier the . . .'

'Ah, "racy"!' Stanhope's amusement was damped. 'I must
admit I shrink from "raciness".'

Yes, the first shadow had touched Venables's face with
gravity.

'We want the man himself. A portrait for posterity. It could
be heightened—lightened—by little . . . hm . . . spiritual warts?
They add. . . . You know?'

Ah! Ah! 'heightened—lightened'. The ingenuity of these
people was diabolical. One would be led on. '*How far did you
trust Curtal? Did you feel you could be absolutely candid with him,
brother to brother?*' '*Certainly not.*' '*Because he was irascible? It's his
reputation, you know.*' '*Good heavens, yes. He was like a wild beast.
Snarled, shouted, went berserk. But I can't say that in public.*' '*It would
be very amusing.*' '*No.*' '*Well, then, when he had that row with the Bishop
of Wellingborough; do you think he had the worst of it?*' '*Of course he did;
but that lands us at once in Theology.*' '*True; we should have to be a bit
careful. About his domestic life; was he happy, d'you think?*' . . .

And so on. Racier and racier; more and more vulgar; more
and more pally and familiar and indiscreet. A few leg-pulls—
weren't they called?—when the interlocutor allowed himself

some arch offensiveness to give a travesty of oneself to the grinning multitude. At last, the crowning indignity; one would be addressed as 'Graham'!

It was at this moment of imagined horror that the Ruddock girls arrived. He had never been more thankful to see them.

TWENTY

Relief

THESE were not the silent figures of his dream, who tip-toed into the room with eyes only for their phantasmal father. They were impulsive, tender young women, radiant even upon an ugly November day, when the sun was gone, the clouds threatened a bitter rain. Their coming brought him, hands outstretched, to his feet. The hands he grasped were as firm as velvet-covered steel.

'What life you give me!' he ardently exclaimed; and, turning to Venables: 'These ladies are Nelson Ruddock's daughters. You already know them for themselves; what you don't know, and what I shouldn't dare to say if you weren't here, is that they've been my sweethearts for twenty years.'

Thank God, Martin had brought chairs enough for them all. Only a moment passed before they were seated and at ease.

'Mr Stanhope doesn't tell you that he's spoiled us for those twenty years,' Emma explained to Venables. 'He's most accomplished at spoiling.'

'He chooses the unspoilable,' laughed Venables.

'You are right,' whispered Stanhope. 'They are unspoilable.'

'We have a sensible mother,' said Emma. 'Father was less sensible.'

'It was Father who was Mr Stanhope's friend,' added Anne. 'But he pretended he came to see us, bringing rich gifts. Usually edible gifts.'

'Did I do that? What shocking bribery! I wonder your sensible mother—whom I respected and feared—didn't show me the door.'

'She might have shown you the door if the edibles had been rich; but they weren't. It was the non-edibles that took our breath away. We still have them. And as for being afraid of Mother, nobody was ever that.'

146

'Oh, dear; the ordeal of that all-comprehending glance!' protested Stanhope. 'You can't imagine its effect.'

'I think Mr Curtal *was* a little nervous of her,' suggested Emma.

'Only when he first arrived. He said he wasn't sure that she'd want a bear in the kitchen.'

'Yes, always the kitchen,' Stanhope murmured. 'Did he call himself a bear?'

'It was because, when we were very little, he always crawled about the floor, roaring.'

'That was his natural voice!' The news that Curtal had played bears with the children when they were very young, presumably before his own sight of them, was not agreeable. 'I'm afraid I never crawled about the floor. You were then too old for such games; and I should have felt it ignominious. But Curtal had no dignity.'

'He was a very good bear,' remarked Anne, reflectively. 'But of course he knocked his head against the table a good deal; and had to be comforted with cakes. We put them on his nose to catch.'

'Surely he never caught them?'

'Always. Though he was awkward in other ways, he was a superb catch.'

'The relaxations of the famous!' said Stanhope, aside, to Venables. As he pictured Curtal, in triumph, making little girls laugh, and afterwards laughing to Ruddock, perhaps with a child on his knee, high spirits were lowered. There could be no doubt that they had laughed at himself.

'I think we shall have to have Mr Curtal as a kitchen bear,' meditated Venables, seeing everything in relation to his programme. 'It will be a new aspect.'

When Martin appeared with her tea-trolley, giving a dry old-fashioned almost-human smile at the girls, Stanhope approached his lips to her ear.

'You remembered the crumpets, Martin? You know Miss Anne . . .'

'Yes, sir; they're on the tray.'

'Of course. Thank you. I see the dish. I almost smell the crumpets!'

Here, again, was no dream. He heard the rustle of Martin's dress, saw colour in her white cheeks, and the movement of her sharp eyes. She was taking stock of Venables. It was because of this that Stanhope, addressing Venables, explained the crumpets.

'Part of the ritual. Nelson Ruddock loved crumpets. We always, in winter, salute his memory with them. I hope you'll do the same.'

'I shall feel myself privileged.'

How the boy sparkled! Three young men had been in the house within nineteen hours; he was so much more attractive than either of the others that no comparison with them was possible. One's hard terms about youth vanished upon this single contact. But there had also once been three striplings of a former generation—Curtal, Ruddock, and oneself. Did they conform to any standard? Wasn't the difference as striking? *Plus ça change.* . . .

One hadn't liked Lionel today. Could one bear to contemplate his prototype, the Graham Stanhope of yesterday? No! Prig, *arriviste*,—and worse. Kitchen Bear Curtal's criticisms of that man had certainly been valid, unpleasant as it was to admit the fact. What of the others? Venables, in his gaiety, recalled Ruddock. The girls must have instinctively felt that; for they treated him at once as a brother. And Curtal? Did he make John White more comprehensible?

Accepting a crumpet, from which he took one bite of ceremonial courtesy, Stanhope sipped his tea, speculating upon the recurrence of type, liking Venables as he had liked Ruddock, no more than half-attending to the conversation. He took, at present, no part in it, being content with his thoughts and his eavesdropping, and charmed by the skill with which Venables drew from the loving Emma and Anne details of their father's life.

'He read his plays aloud to Mother as he wrote them, scene by scene. They laughed together. He called her the perfect critic —less erudite than Uncle Graham; but with a finer sense of *nuance*.'

This was said with a laughing glance of kindness at Honey's inferior, who heard the very tone of Ruddock, rich and lazy, in the teasing reference.

'Did he change the scenes if she found fault?' asked Venables.

Anna hesitated. 'Did he, Emma?'

'I don't think she ever did find fault.'

'The best critics never do. I should so much like to meet her.'

'You must do so, then—for your programme. She'd love it. Father called her "Honey"; a name she still deserves. It was from the colour of her hair; but her nature, too.'

'True. True. But she didn't like me,' thought Stanhope. He heard Venables say:

'Do you call her "Honey"?'

'No, it was Father's name.' What a complete answer! Emma turned again to Stanhope. 'We were to give you her love, Uncle Graham; and demand that you should come very soon— tomorrow, or Friday—and eat cakes with her.'

He was at once alert; like a boy invited to try his hand at the darts-board.

'Oh, dear me, how I shall enjoy that! Please tell her. . . . I feel like *demanding* to be allowed to come back with you today! But that wouldn't do. I must have the appropriate appetite. As I'm sure Tom Curtal always had—catching cakes from his ubiquitous nose. . . . I won't be outdone, in consumption at least, by Tom!'

There was a stumbling urgency in the way he spoke. His excitement was so great that they must have heard the cup slightly rattling in its saucer. Hearing the sound himself, he confusedly set cup, saucer, and plate upon the floor beside him, not without further clatter.

As he raised his eyes again, he caught the passage of a quick glance between the girls and Venables. It was not conspiratorial. It held only concern. But the common anxiety aroused by an old man's trembling hand reminded him that, however considerate of him, they shared a youthful freemasonry from which he was excluded.

He longed to cry: 'I see. I understand. But do remember that I, too, was once young!'

No such protest was uttered. He smiled. They smiled again, apparently accepting him without question as a comrade.

It could not be so. Nevertheless, the next word came with resolute gaiety from himself.

'I wish you would tell Mr Venables a great deal more about

your dear father, and about Mr Curtal. I shan't interrupt. It
will be relaxation for me.'

Venables expressed delight.

'Thank you, sir. Thank you. As we have . . .'

It was Anne who spoke, without hesitation.

'Well, then, we think you ought to know that Father was
devoted to both Mr Stanhope and Mr Curtal. . . . No, he made
no difference between them; they were his friends. They knew his
admiration; he never flattered; he was ironic. In fact, he teased
them both alike. I think that was why they were so fond of him.
It was his way of showing affection; there was no cruelty at all.
. . . Mr Curtal argued with him like little boys playing cricket—
you know how they do: "Out! Out" "I wasn't!" "Yes, you were!
Out! Out!" He was all the little boys at once. Father called him,
after some music-hall comedian, "the one-man uproar". He
came storming in, telling us, the moment he was inside the door,
about his latest frightful wrongs and sufferings . . .'

'What were they?' whispered Stanhope, to himself. 'Compared
with mine?'

'. . . how he'd been given a savage review here, and another
there, and been slandered by some scoundrel who owed him a
grudge, or who was carrying on a literary vendetta. Vowing
revenge on everybody. Father would listen, and smile, and
sympathize—never suggesting for a moment that Mr Curtal's
habit of cudgelling everybody else was probably responsible.
Then he'd talk nonsense; and in the end Mr Curtal, after bluster-
ing a lot more, and accusing Father of being on the side of the
devils, would tell about his triumphs and his latest ideas, which
Father would pretend to find preposterous and unanswerable. At
last he'd go away, quite happy, splitting his sides.'

'And?' asked Venables. He must have moved his head a
little, to indicate that something should be said of their host.

'Oh, Mr Stanhope was altogether different. He never stormed.
And he didn't go away splitting his sides, either. He would look
at us, and look at Father, as if he was pained at so much levity—
as he called it; but Father teased him, too, and told stories of
Mr Curtal that made him laugh. I don't think he ever wanted to
go. . . .'

'I never wanted to go.' It was an unheard whisper.

'Sometimes he didn't laugh; and Mother would say to

Father: "He's not well, or happy. You ought to have been kinder." But he always came again, very soon, to show that he bore no ill-will.'

'I bore no ill-will, my darlings. I was often unhappy. Your mother was right.'

'She was always right. She still is. Mr Curtal used to apologize for being so noisy. He said he couldn't help it; he'd been brought up rough; he'd behave better next time. He never did. He said: "I expect you worry about the neighbours." She didn't at all. The neighbours thought we were mad, anyway; and if they knew the noisy person was Mr Curtal, they crowded their windows to see him go away.'

'Your father was very quiet, I suppose?'

'When he read a scene where the characters insulted each other, he might raise his voice, but normally he was like somebody talking to himself. He pretended he was notoriously hen-pecked.'

'He had a great big voice, when he wanted it,' explained Emma. 'A cabman was once bullying Mother, thinking she was a mouse with two frightened little mouselings. Father came up unexpectedly, saw the situation at a glance, and spoke. All he said was "Off!" but the cabman was struck dumb. He went scarlet, and flew away as if he'd seen the Devil.'

'A glimpse of Hell! Your father didn't swear?'

'No. It was the stentorian shout, and the fling of the arm. We were terribly impressed. He didn't seem to find swearing necessary. Mr Curtal did. He needed big swollen-faced oaths, to relieve his feelings. Father once said it was to make up for his smallness, like a little dog barking at all the big ones it met; and Mr Curtal retorted: "Do you think you're a big dog, Nelson? Why, I could snap you up like a lump of sugar!" But that wasn't true. Except on paper, Mr Curtal was rather timid.'

Stanhope, listening eagerly, but with constrained amusement, was caught by this last preposterous assertion. He could not check a movement of surprise, and a single question.

'Do you seriously say he was timid?'

'Oh, yes.' Anne turned very quickly. 'He was terrified of you. He said: "When Graham gets Polar, I feel like a bluebottle on a flypaper." '

'Buzzing, I suppose!' exclaimed Venables, as if the scene were before him.

Stanhope said: 'This is one of the most extraordinary things I ever heard. Do you know, I never in my life saw any sign of fear.'

'He didn't mean you to, Uncle Graham,' interrupted Emma. And Anne added: 'He said he'd spent his whole life defending a little ego from the Great White Wolf.'

'Wolf?' Stanhope was still further astounded. 'Are you suggesting that *I* was the bully?'

'That was what Mr Curtal claimed.'

'Good heavens! Why, the fellow was a natural bruiser!'

All, including Venables, burst into laughter at the breathless protest. It was the merriest sound ever heard in this decorous house. The room became, for an instant, Honey Ruddock's kitchen.

Their laughter saved Stanhope, who was convulsively involved in it. And yet, at heart, he was far from amused. The story of Curtal's fear—a lie—could only have been one of Ruddock's ludicrous inventions.

There had been thousands of them, created for the entertainment of those two children, and hoarded as part of their living memory of a dead man. Ruddock made birds, cats, horses, and pigs answer his polite questions; and without moving from his chair peopled the kitchen with a multitude of grotesques. He could not meet a stray cur without he must pretend that it had panted an anecdote; and as all dogs, cats, horses, and pigs appeared to recognize him as an old friend the lies were given verisimilitude. Now came this yarn about a kitchen bear. Childish creature!

The charge against oneself, so paradoxical, and so entirely false, was established in the girls' minds. They no doubt repeated it in good faith; but the effect on Venables would be disastrous.

'No, no, no; your father's fantasies outstripped nature. I can't let this one go uncontradicted.'

As he added to his protest, he was wondering whether a half-truth lay within the lie. Was it not possible that Ruddock had concocted some such story, not with the aim of attacking Graham Stanhope, but as the result of some deep thrust into Curtal's egotism? Full of levity as he was, Ruddock had an acute eye for character; and he had meant to suggest, perhaps, that the hypersensitive Curtal, in order to forestall the corrosive action of a finer brain, a subtler temperament, had developed the tactic of striking first, with noisy vehemence. . . .

'No, Uncle Graham. That won't do. We heard him say it, himself,' insisted Anne.

'A number of times,' her sister added.

'In that case, you must give me time to reinterpret the experience of a lifetime,' said a voice, which, although it was so small and dry, must have been his own.

'Will it affect our programme?' asked Venables, very gaily, as if he saw only comedy in the situation.

'Whatever the truth,' continued the same voice, 'if you present Curtal as coward and blusterer, you destroy the programme.'

Emma was the less impulsive of the two girls. It was she who made the correction.

'He was neither a coward nor a blusterer. He exaggerated, for the sake of effect, like a soap-box orator. When he said he was afraid of you, he meant that he respected you. He was afraid of Father in the same way, as somebody who couldn't be deceived by rhetoric. And he was full of real admiration of your qualities. We thought Mr Venables should know how simple and lovable he seemed to two children who saw him with no knowledge of the public figure.'

'Good judges,' agreed Venables, looking sage.

'Mr Stanhope will tell you how he appeared to another man. But when Mr Stanhope wasn't there, Mr Curtal always called him, quite faithfully, "our dear brother, Graham".'

' "Great White Wolf",' whispered Stanhope, moved, as he had thought it impossible to be moved, by this assertion of respect.

'That was in play; when he and Father were talking nonsense.'

'Did they ever do anything else, about me?' But the words were unspoken.

'They were often serious. They exchanged ideas. They talked confidentially. We listened. That was how we came to understand how deeply three such men could love each other.'

Stanhope had no answer. Lost in emotion, he bowed his head.

TWENTY-ONE

Postil

ONE more influential shock was to be delivered during their visit. Venables, having agreed to come again next day with his tape-recorder, had taken leave; the girls remained. As always, Stanhope kept them with him as long as possible, thriving on their animation; but he shunned further discussion of Curtal. It was less agitating to ask questions about work and play.

'Your mother, I know, is busy with good deeds; that's her nature. And it's yours, too. But they tell me your father's plays are being revived everywhere. Are you to act in them?'

No, they were not to do so.

'We shall put the royalties in the bank!' declared Anne; 'and have to do a lot of book-keeping.'

'We didn't want to be accused of self-advertisement,' explained Emma.

'Besides, we quarrelled about which should play lead.'

'No, we didn't. We simply know that we don't carry the guns for starring in the West End. But Jack Hutchings has written a play for us.'

'Ah, a play; a play of your own!' Stanhope was eager with applause. 'What exciting news!'

'Jack specializes,' said Anne, 'in writing plays for the overlooked.'

'It's about two jealous sisters . . .'

'Good heavens!' cried Stanhope, with an old man's raised hands. 'You'll be seriously mis-cast!'

The girls exchanged laughter.

'You've just accused us of being sentimental about Uncle Tom,' retorted Anne. 'This is where you're sentimental about us.'

'Tk-tk! How perverse! My view of you is entirely realistic.'

'We're not paragons, you know,' said Emma, smiling. 'We're human, all too human, as somebody said. Was it Tolstoy?'

'Nearly right, darling,' exclaimed the lively Anne. 'It was Nietzsche.'

'At any rate, he came from abroad. A Dutchman, whose name I forget, wrote a book called *The English: are they Human?* We're English; and we're devils!'

'Oh, dear me!' Stanhope was fretful. 'At my age, I ought not to be teased any more.'

'Uncle Graham! You're always treated with tremendous respect!'

'Reverence, in fact! That can't be good for you.'

He gave a mournful groan.

'I should like to tell you—but I shan't—about the severity of young men who want to visit me. I don't mean Mr Venables, who, nevertheless, is bringing his instruments tomorrow, including, I feel sure, a rack. Tell me of this slanderous play.'

'Two sisters—we told you that. Anne is the kittenish one; on the verge of becoming a cat. I, on the other hand, having passed the rubicon, am a dipsomaniac. It's a very modern play, you understand; everybody in it is vile.'

'But why do you attempt such parts? You're sure to fail in them; and nothing is so damning to actresses as failure.'

'Jack thinks otherwise. He says we shall be splendid.'

'Evidently he's not in love with you, as he should be.'

'No; he's what you once called a xenophobe.'

'I couldn't have borne to use such a monstrous word. What does it mean?'

'Your memory isn't as good as ours, Uncle Graham. We've proved that this afternoon. It's conditioned by the prevailing wind.'

'Which, for me, is always from the north-east,' sighed Graham. ' "Into my heart an air that kills." Well, of course, that's not true, either. It's like your father's tale of Tom Curtal; a vast exaggeration, with a little grain of verity in it to tease the mind. You're infecting me with your nonsense. I have a long and varied memory. Sometimes the pattern is dim; sometimes a coruscation of light so dazzling that it strains the eyes.'

He covered his eyes illustratively with one long white hand.

'Oh, that reminds me,' exclaimed Emma. 'Do you remember somebody called Raikes? I don't know whether "Mrs" or "Miss". Her Christian name is Sadie, or Sally.'

A violent qualm caused Stanhope to press the arms of his chair. Feeling for Sally was dead; but the mention of her stirred him like the sight of a ghost.

'I dredge the name . . . from a remote . . . past,' he replied, with painful effort. 'Yes, Sally Raikes. She was a very pretty, "kittenish" young woman. Never, I believe, a cat—in any sense.'

'Well, she grew up, at any rate,' objected Anne. 'And she's now old.'

'It seems incredible. One thinks of lost friends as they once were.'

'She was at the Memorial Service. She spoke to us,' said Emma.

Stanhope, with more than half his lifetime to travel, made the slow journey back to a stuffy room into which he had just admitted the sweeping wind of early morning. He shivered, as he had done then. Curtal, with a night's black bristle upon his cheeks and chin, sprawled asleep in a big leather-covered arm-chair. His own sensations were those of sick misery.

'How strange,' he pondered, smelling the odour of brandy, leaning upon Cox's arm, reliving those bitter hours of his youth. 'Why should she speak to you?'

'She thought she had seen us on Television. And she'd heard one of us whisper: "Uncle Graham." She said: "Excuse me; but is Mr Stanhope your uncle?" We said: "Not really; but he was a friend of our father's." She said: "I used to know him. I expect he's forgotten me. What was your father's name?" When we told her, she cried a little, and said she'd known him, too. Then she said: "I suppose you never heard him mention the name of Sally Raikes?" We tried to pretend that we had. I don't think she believed us; we aren't good enough actresses, when taken unawares. She then asked if we had known Mr Curtal, and cried some more, so that we began to cry, as well, feeling very sad. It was through talking to her, and crying, that we had no chance of speaking to you.'

Stanhope breathlessly waited for more. It did not come.

'And was that all?'

'Nearly all. She said she lived in the North of England—

Durham, I think it was—and had been there for many years; but she felt she must come down for the service. Mr Curtal had been such a close friend. So good to her. She said he'd helped her; but not in what way. She was obviously very much upset by the Service. She held our hands as if she couldn't bear to let us go, and said she remembered Father very well; smiled and cried very touchingly. We begged her to come home with us, to see Mother; but she refused. She'd never met Mother. She kept on thanking us; and then she vanished. We lost sight of her all at once.'

She had vanished, as before. He no longer wished her, as he had done that night, to suffer.

'No message to me?' he asked.

'None.'

'I expected none. How did she look?'

'Very small. And white-haired, with very bright blue eyes.'

'Yes, they were always like sapphires.'

He could not imagine Sally as white-haired. She must have seen him in the church, and deliberately not made her presence known, deliberately sent no messages. Her abstention was one more fact to be woven into his thoughts of an episode, important at the time, which Curtal could not have communicated to the Inquisitor.

They were gone, he was alone, and the room was silent. He felt exceedingly solitary as he recaptured echoes of those laughing voices, and longed in vain to hear the voices once more, once more and always.

So Sally had lived all these years far from London, concealed not only from Curtal and himself, but quite as effectively from the egregious Holmes. 'She cried a little.' It was significant that she had given her name to the girls as Sally Raikes. Equally significant that she had sent no message to himself.

It meant that Curtal had been the man. She must have communicated with him, perhaps seen him again, perhaps told him why she married Holmes. Had she said "I couldn't bear to marry a superior"? She wouldn't have said that; vanity would have checked her. But Curtal had been good to her! How astounding! That implied monetary help; well, Curtal had plenty of money. He was free with it. She had refrained from mentioning her other friend, who had been given no opportunity to show kindness or unkindness. Curtal was the 'close friend' of devoted memory. She had taken a long journey in cruel weather to show her gratitude to him.

What a corollary to the story those girls told of an innocent and affectionate uncle! Dismiss the story as one must, it remained extraordinary. It could probably be accounted for by the facts that Curtal was a great liar and the girls members of a family in which love was paramount. It was a happy gathering of simple folk around one good man.

'Yes, Ruddock was a good man. Not a weak man, as, at heart, I was always a weak man!'

The ejaculation caused him to jump. He brushed its meaning aside in impatience. One said such things in momentary folly, without in the least meaning them. Nevertheless, Ruddock had been a good man, strict in his own conduct, uncensorious regarding others. That was virtue.

One said 'strict in his own conduct': had he ever boasted of purity? Didn't he eat and drink with the relish of self-indulgence? 'Strict' meant morally strict; he didn't cheat, and he didn't womanize. Not that he had much interest in women, apart from Honey and the girls. One had learned only from an inadvertence of Curtal's that he was in the habit of referring disrespectfully to Adelaide as 'the Dragon' . . .

Curtal simple and affectionate: Good God, how could any estimate be farther astray: as well use the terms of Frederick the Great or Napoleon! What about his women? A too-facile affectionateness, the Ruddocks would say. Easily roused, importunate, very 'successful'; and, when the affairs became notorious, self-exculpatory. It had always been the women who pursued, he said; but that was because in crude youth he'd been impressed by Shaw's impudent *Man and Superman*, which he hadn't understood. Also, because his marriage had been a disgusting mess.

Marriage to the amorous Cora! Good God, what a name, and what a woman! The lust in her made one shrink as from a jungle pool. She, at least, had pursued. She had taken Curtal to be a stallion. But with all his carnality Curtal was a man of intellect. He'd driven her frantic. Where a more sensitive man would have been intimidated by the insatiable demands of a nymphomaniac, he shrugged, walked away, left her screaming. In the end, her screams had become those of madness.

Simple, affectionate Curtal! When she was certified, he celebrated the event by telephoning to demand one's company at dinner that night. Yes, he'd insisted. 'You've got to come, Graham. It's absolutely essential. I won't take "no".' In this way he had forced one to go, in curiosity, in—it was true—active alarm for his welfare. Yes, the active alarm which one could not resist, or, now, deny.

They had met at a familiar restaurant in Soho; Curtal white, nervy, quarrelsome, so that one expected a row for some imagined offence. No offence was mentioned. For once, the fellow was without the power to harangue. He licked his dry lips, kept his head down, shrugged, said nothing. Only over dinner, when the *apéritif* had been swallowed, and they had chosen food from the menu—Curtal's choice was some Neapolitan mess—he had called for champagne.

'To celebrate!' he'd said, showing the mottled teeth in a grin of excitement. 'I tell you what it is, Graham. I'm quit of Cora. She's put away. Raving. Homicidal. Trying to knife me; to knife herself and everybody else. You're the first person I've told. We're going to get drunk together—once more!'

What hatred there had been in the tone! What horror—shamingly confused with the loathsome satisfaction of a child that sees another child punished—one had felt!

Curtal had seen, and with diabolical insight understood, the conflict.

'You look disgusted, my boy. Disgusted and elated. By God, you're a Sadist!'

His little eyes had shone like spots of concentrated evil.

Jackie Boothroyd interrupted the vision, with letters for approval. Stanhope was instantly soothed by her nearness; she had that power. Except for Sally Raikes, all those whom he had loved had wielded it—Ruddock, the Ruddock girls, Gertrude, now Jackie. It came from within, a deep tranquillity of soul.

'Do any need signing? If so, please sign them for me, Miss Boothroyd. My hand's unsteady. What are they?'

'They're mostly requests from students who are writing theses, Mr Stanhope. For doctorates.'

'They want to suck my brains, do they?'

'They ask for your help, Mr Stanhope. I've said, as usual, that if they'll put specific questions you'll try to answer them!'

'What a game it is, Miss Boothroyd! A survival of the patronage cult. I don't want to see what you've said. I'm sure it's courteous. I'm very tired this evening.'

'You've had a busy, exciting day, Mr Stanhope. Were you pleased with Mr Venables?'

'Your friend?'

'His voice on the telephone was very attractive. I didn't see him, of course.'

'No peeping over the bannisters, like the well-bred Miss Bennets when Bingley called? That was from the window, I remember.'

'I was busy with your correspondence, Mr Stanhope.'

'I can never disconcert you, Miss Boothroyd. You know I try to do so, don't you?'

'I've sometimes thought you did.'

She was adorable. Too charming to waste her time in writing letters for a crotchety old man. He waved the letters away, smiling, thanked her, regretfully watched until she disappeared, and called out: 'Good night! Good night!' as the door closed. She must have been kept, by his thoughtlessness, beyond her usual time for going home, and must now wish to hurry. She would walk past the post office, drop his letters into the box, and continue onward, to the father who sometimes, thinking himself alone, spoke harshly of the Government, the local Council, or his own futility. How delightful to follow her, to see that modest eccentric, and take a seat at the family table!

So dreaming, he stretched his legs and contemplated the fire. The only light in the room came from his table-lamp, and in the restful darkness he felt happy, revived, hopeful. 'I've been a success today. They've all believed in me. I've been gracious, almost noble.'

There was no echo; no derision; no harsh grunt from the absent and forgotten John White.

TWENTY-TWO

Adelaide

THE kaleidoscope turned once more as he drowsed, so that its fragments sank into a new pattern. Perhaps the illusion arose because he heard the clock chime half-past six, and associated the hour with some auspicious past event. It was his fancy that every occasion had its point in time, which in after years rang a bell for memory.

Now he dwelt upon social triumphs; his public speeches; nights when he was guest of honour at a banquet, and hovering strangers beamed upon him, proud to receive the notice of a famous man. Obsequiousness was too strong a term for their heightened *bonhomie;* it was an instinctive flattery offered to success. No doubt they, as promoters of the occasion, purred at the sale of many tickets. They would have smiled less sweetly if he had been unknown, or a cause of loss.

'I liked it,' he thought. 'I believed myself to be entitled to it. That's over. Finished. . . . Venables, today, wanted to please. He wouldn't have behaved so to a nonentity. I still accepted the flattery; not because I needed it as balm, but because I was gratified. Probably he doesn't admire me at all. But then we were both evasive. The nearest I came to candour, which would have involved saying: "Cut out the flim-flam", was when I imagined Curtal's characteristically offensive reaction. Curtal had no manners. He didn't care whose feelings he hurt. By God, how he hurt mine! . . .'

The pattern shifted slightly. Long ago, in dining at great tables, he himself had been guilty of the social hypocrisy he despised. He had listened with flattering courtesy to titled bores or garrulous politicians, forbearing all retort, and allowing them to patronize him to their hearts' content. No doubt he had smiled as ingratiatingly, bowed as low, as the worst flunkey of them all.

The greatest nobles, he had read, were those most humble to the sovereign, from belief that in exalting his singularity they boosted their own hierarchic importance. Such an object had not been in his mind. He had taken pride in great company, even after learning that the great would boast to their wives of having met himself. 'Who else was there, besides the P.M.?' 'Oh, So-and So, Such-and-Such . . . Stanhope was there—Graham Stanhope. Very agreeable.'

This snobbery ran through all classes, and all men. At eighty, and alone, one knew oneself to be naked. Before then, the conjurer's performance with knives or bottles was nothing to the gas-filled balloon of the social order. Once it collapsed, Cabinet ministers and their ladies, dukes, princes, company directors, editors, bosses, and artists alike were liable, in the modern world, to become bankrupt fugitives. The President of one day was 'under house arrest' the next; and was then no more heard of. No Roman emperor, opening his veins or slaughtered by his guards, was more suddenly deprived of power and life.

How uneasy the world had become; and, in that unease, how precariously hung one's own carefully-achieved distinction.

Far better to recall splendid hours without ambition, when rambles in London with Curtal or Ruddock filled the eyes with colour and the mind with excitement, or sedate journeys through Europe with Adelaide nourished his understanding of culture. On those sedate journeys his importance had been diminished by Adelaide's greater importance; but enough had been left to him for complacency, and when alone he had walked abroad—from some defensive impulse—in statuesque loneliness, thinking: 'I am here. Nobody, nobody can rob me of this Selkirkian grandeur.' The grandeur consisted in looking, solitary, upon historic scenes, touching precious relics of the past, imagining himself warrior, statesman, or poet in the presence of demigods whom he had revered from boyhood. None to share, to spoil, his dream. Only of late years had he appreciated the meaning of that word 'nobody'. It was his comprehensive synonym for 'Adelaide and her insufferable set'.

There were dinners at the homes of Adelaide's 'set', where

confidential communications were made in undertones by great men about other great men, giving him the illusion of being yet another star in the galaxy, possessed of secrets, wielding immeasurable power. No doubt the politicians and newspaper-proprietors had thought to manipulate him to their own use; perhaps they had done so. Yes, they had done so.

That absurd delusion of greatness! The flattery had gratified his ego, and made him pompous. His carriage had developed the hauteur of authority, his chin had risen higher, his courtesy had become more condescending.

'Quite the drum-major!' said Curtal, meeting him at a ceremony.

His denials had been sensitively quick, and his anger swallowed with difficulty.

Curtal had understood. Curtal always understood. He strutted a little here and there, with superciliously closed eyes, to show what he objected to; and his stocky figure made the parody irresistibly grotesque. Then he resumed his interminable bullying manner, shaking a disapproving head. Within a minute he was boasting of his feats, how this fellow had called him the greatest man of his generation, and a little Jew boy had touched his coat in reverence, and a rich exploiter had offered him ten thousand pounds to write a history of religion, or music, or some equally impossible subject.

'But I shan't do it,' was the grandiose conclusion.

'For the good reason that you couldn't.'

'Oh, yes, I could. Two or three hacks for the donkey-work. Parasites abound. Then I should weigh in with six months' polishing. Give it the authentic Curtal touch.'

'Curtal, the English Dumas?'

'Ph! Far better than Dumas. He was an old hack, himself. I could do with the ten thousand.'

'So could we all.'

'What, you? With a rich wife?'

'Pocket money! Pocket money!'

'You wouldn't know how to spend it. No big ideas. That's what keeps you nibbling at other men's brains. . . . But I'm bursting with big ideas!'

'Like the frog in the fable!'

'Ah, of course! He was what you reminded me of, just now!'

Asinine pair!

But one had been deflated once again by this memory of Curtal; and must now recall purer enjoyments. Dawns of gold and blue and ochre glowing across the Mediterranean, sunsets that made the whole Atlantic flame, starry skies and mountainy glory that left the spirit prostrate, green meadows and hedgerows, blossoming fruit trees, golden cascades of weeping willow in the English spring; and, above all, misty autumn evenings in London, when spreading murk veiled the street-lamps and created a dream world. Wonderful, wonderful city; where men and women, outwardly bovine strangers, cherished a secret splendour of heart!

'Don't be too blasted poetic!' said a voice from the past.

He shrank, with a twinge of the old indignation. Curtal, having no poetic feeling, could not bear the display of it in another. He would as readily have mocked Shakespeare and Shelley to their faces, challenging Shakespeare to justify his Lancastrian twist to history—'Why, you're just sucking up to the old girl, kicking the Yorkists because they're out of the game!'—and condemning Shelley's flight from the sublime doctrine of Godwin into the cobweb sophistries of Plato.

'They're all damned cooks!' he would bawl. 'Mystics, metaphysicians, history-*chefs*, and the rest of them. Like Stevenson with his bits of purple, and—among ourselves—that silly ass Blenkinsop with his pretty-pretty whimsies. They daren't face reality! They won't, and can't, think!'

Think! Did the man call his exuberance 'thought'? What delusion would he next embrace? Why did one endure the coarse stupidity of a mind pointing confidently to a mechanized future that banished art and subtlety? Such a future would be unendurable. Curtal himself would find it so, when he was ignored by his very converts!

Crude parody flew to his tongue whenever one quoted the divinities. The habit arose from what 'the *cliché* boys' (Curtal's name) called the inferiority complex, formed by dingy back streets in a manufacturing town, uncouth speech, coarse language, and an instinctive knowledge that finer-tempered men had delights which he could never share. And yet one was always on edge in case his taunts should come too near one's heart.

'Don't be too blasted poetic' changed easily to 'Bloody prig!'

After the meeting at Lucy Chard's, when they had no conversation, they continued estranged. Curtal could not forgive what he called treachery, which in fact was a better man's refusal to grovel before his imagined genius; and he made his immense load of work an excuse for protracted sullenness. The truth was, he suspected Rossiter's preference for oneself to be the result of intrigue.

This had been revealed years later, when the association with Rossiter (like all associations with Rossiter) was over. They were speaking, after a meal at the Club, of old times.

'That was dirty work, you know,' Curtal had grunted, chewing his sour pipe. 'Anything to do me down.'

'What? Why do you suppose everybody's trying to do you down? The invitation to me came from the blue.'

'Like the attentive lackey's tip! "Oh, look what Father Christmas has brought!" But what had you and your pals been whispering up the chimney? I know it's your way to pretend you're the Chosen Person.'

'I don't pretend I'm a Chosen Person. I call myself lucky. I call you lucky. I never accuse you of intrigue; why always suspect me of it?'

'I know you.'

'How little you do know me! It's a dwarf's knowledge!'

There had been a disagreeable grin from the mottled teeth holding that disgusting pipe; a glance of mockery from the little eyes.

'It didn't matter. I got a better job.'

One had smiled, despite a fluttered spirit, thinking: 'Which you lost, dear boy, by your egotistical presumption!'

The thought was not spoken, from fear of provoking an outburst; but Curtal, seeing the smile, guessing the thought, and already conning another grievance, first scowled, then laughed, then thrust an open hand roughly against one's chest.

'You tricky devil!'

Stanhope could not remember whether Lucy Chard had brought about the reconciliation. It was most likely Ruddock's

work. Ruddock, who did not cultivate enmity, would not tolerate
it in others. But Lucy was a managing woman, who, if she had
been less *grande dame*, would have been a mere busybody. Keen
sight, and confidence in her ability to handle men, were accom-
panied by unstudied charm. She had no husband or children to
push, her husband having died of dysentery in the Boer War, and
her children having never been born. Her protégés were her
children, she said; thus pathetically revealing the ardour with
which she would have fought for children of her flesh. Lucky
protégés, to be spared ruthless slaughter in a nearer cause!

The contrast between Lucy's comfortable home and
Henrietta's show-place was very marked. Henrietta offered one
a bath of luxury based upon money and the ambition of patronage; Lucy, with no new pictures and opulent furnishing,
relied upon lineage, high quality in her guests, and agreeable
intimacy. Her judgment might be little more exact than Henrietta's
—great hostesses have the instinct of gamblers rather than the
fastidiousness of purists;—but it was more intelligent, and it was
disinterested.

'I make careers,' was her quiet boast.

She made matches, too. Should one be grateful for that?
Adelaide had been first met at Lucy's; and this conjunction, unquestionably, had been planned. How far Adelaide was privy to
the design, only she and Lucy could have told. Neither at any
time did so.

He had gone to dinner on a normal invitation, expecting to
be well amused and made much of by his hostess. On arrival,
thinking himself the first-comer, he had stepped forward to
greet Lucy with a fine air of ease, familiar with the palely lighted
room and the assurance that she would be sitting, as usual, close
to the fire. Only when he had made half the journey did he see
that she was not alone.

Her companion was a tall, cool, beautifully elegant young
woman with a doll's unmovable blue eyes and a pair of dazzlingly
white shoulders, who sat upright without touching the back of
her chair. The young woman's nose was high-bridged; she wore
no jewellery—or at least none that sparkled;—she had intimidating reserve; but when she acknowledged Lucy's introduction
she smiled in a way to suggest that greater cordiality would
follow better acquaintance. This was his first and strongest

impression of a character afterwards much considered. Never, he now knew, entirely explored.

Old Trumble, the scholar, shortly afterwards completed the party; and Trumble was as lively as he had been on their encounter at Henrietta's. He was a big man, fleshy but agile, with a constant grin that vouched for unlimited good-humour. His entry to any room had the remarkable effect of creating optimism in all present. He lifted their burdens, without accumulating any weight upon his own broad shoulders; and in fact was a selfish man who ensured his personal comfort by risking no intimacy closer than that of the dinner-table.

Stanhope had not realized this at the time. He knew only that Trumble was the same in all companies, and that he radiated cheerfulness. Everybody said, chuckling: 'Old Trummy was there. In his usual form. Most amusing.' And those to whom the remark was made chuckled, in return: 'What fun he is! We simply must ask him to dinner.'

The verdict was true, and damning. On that night, he brimmed with information about the United States, its peoples, ways of life, and domestic politics. He passed down the American continent to Mexico, Brazil, and Paraguay; and was excellent in brief spells of nonsense about cannibalism, the treasures of Levantine monasteries, and James the First of England. Being a rattle who never bored, he always kept his audience adroitly in focus.

Clever Lucy! She knew that one detached elderly man, behaving as if he were completely at home, would cover every difficult silence between young strangers, and allow them time for covert mutual examination. She could have made no better choice for her purpose than Trumble, who was already, it was evident, on teasing terms with Adelaide, whom he claimed, untruthfully, to have known since her birth.

Later reflection proved that Adelaide, impressed by Trumble's reputation as a scholar, accepted much from him in the way of ironic compliment that, from another, she would have resented as disrespectful. For the same reason, she enjoyed his digs at Stanhope, listening to them attentively with an unbroken smile. Stanhope also smiled. In the months which had passed since Henrietta's tea-party he had learned much; and with Lucy present as an almost maternal figure he had nothing to fear.

The evening, like all Trumble's evenings, was a success. Only when she next met Stanhope did Lucy say: 'Well, what did you think of my friend Adelaide?' His answer was now forgotten. All he remembered was Lucy's significant after-comment: 'She was charmed with you.'

To one as quick as himself, this was a prompting not to be ignored.

TWENTY-THREE

Warning

HASTE would have been inadvisable. It was not needed. His manner continued discreetly reverent; Adelaide's calmly gracious. He knew that to her wealthy family he might seem an adventurer; but what was more important was his distinction in a kind of work which Curtal called parasitic but which, in Adelaide's world, rated higher, because it was more obviously intellectual, than Curtal's spectacular versatility.

'Such a vulgar little man,' had been Adelaide's laconic comment. 'A sort of Dickens.'

'Oh, a genius!' proclaimed Lucy. 'One forgives vulgarity in a genius.'

'Does one? At least one never forgets it,' sighed Adelaide. 'He doesn't allow one to.'

During this exchange, they had been sitting in Lucy's drawing-room, with its air of the eighteenth century and its prevailing tones of grey and old gold. Lucy was herself grey and old gold, or grey and rose pink; and as she was a little lame she did not move much from her armchair. If she needed anything, she had only to glance at Stanhope, who gracefully brought it at once, a performance which she silently emphasized by glancing again a little later. She spoke no more of Curtal, probably because she had sufficiently contrasted his brassy egotism with the elegance of one who anticipated a woman's every wish.

'And how are you getting on with your book, Graham?' she asked.

He had not gushed. He had not gestured. He had replied, with modesty:

'I've very nearly finished it.'

'What book is that?' came, quite interestedly, from Adelaide.

'A study of Corneille.'

'Oh, *Corneille*.' Her empressement implied: 'Ah, French! A poetic psychologist. And a gentleman!' She would have been bored if the theme had been Colley Cibber, or even Congreve. Her new friend's proper admiration for the rarest kind of French literature gave her cultured pleasure.

Admiration and pleasure were simultaneously welcomed by Lucy Chard.

'You really are our most distinguished critic, Graham!' she cried. 'I feel proud to savour your learning at second-hand.'

'My second-hand learning?' he inquired, archly, thinking, nevertheless, of Curtal's often-expressed scorn for the parasite.

'What rubbish! In a sense, I suppose all learning is second-hand.'

'It's made creative by a first-class mind,' declared Adelaide. This swift defence did not pass unnoticed.

'In my opinion, it's a very good book indeed,' had been her verdict upon the proof-sheets. 'You have a magnificent theme; and you do it justice.'

They were at lunch together in a smart restaurant near St James's Street (he had thought this more appropriate to Adelaide than the haunts of men in Soho); and he was secretly overjoyed by the approval. It showed how shrewd he had been to flatter her by requesting a *candid* judgment. Curtal, immune to flattery, and candid without request, had taken a different line the evening before.

'Your precise lurk, Graham. The man was a damned snob! Classical spouters smacking their chests and bragging. "Moi! Moi! Moi!" You naturally feel snug with them. Snug and smug!'

'No virtue at all?' he had sarcastically asked.

'Oh, the usual artful showing-off. One eye on the aesthetic fleshpots!'

Homely fun! Homely fun! Just what one might expect from a Utilitarian who thought his own raucous vigour the *ne plus ultra* of creative art. Adelaide's consciously measured enthusiasm was preferable. She spoke with the voice of unsullied culture. If he could please her, and her kind, he could ignore the multitude swarming round Curtal, the iconoclast. As Adelaide said, iconoclasm was absolutely third-rate.

She was right. He must aim always at the first-class.

'I'm so glad to hear you say that. It means a great deal to me,' had been his reply, uttered with earnest gravity. Ironic old age saw this gravity as ludicrous; but at the time it had been only half-assumed.

Two serious blue eyes, reminding him of forget-me-nots, were for a moment raised to meet his own. They were as different as could be from the sparkling, bewitching, quickly-shadowed pools which had given vivacity to Sally's baby face. They lacked animation; they were touched with frost. But for once the frost was thawed by esteem, the nearest emotion Adelaide ever felt to enthusiasm.

She ate little, sipped her Rudesheimer with discrimination, refused liqueur and cigarettes, took coffee without sugar. A white ringless left hand rested upon the proof-sheets, as if reluctant to lose contact with something which had made its owner think deeply. She did not say, but she implied, 'I am content to be seen in your company by first-class people in this first-class restaurant. We have established a relation which gratifies me. On the whole, subject to certain other approvals, I should like to develop this agreeable relation.'

The ringless hand was withdrawn. She smiled.

Family inspection followed, all amusingly regal. More amusing now than at the time, when uncertainty and excitement confused him. The mother, a worldly ignoramus, who would have preferred a title, made disconcerting inquiries about his family. The father, a knighted stockbroker, preoccupied with money, was bluffly non-committal, as if he listened to the chink of gold in the next room. Two Etonian brothers, who thought all men not of their College were uneducated, proved unexpectedly friendly. One of them, Everard, who had a passion for motor-racing, took him driving one day, and was impressed by some modest coolness in a number of narrow squeaks. This impression, it seemed, was crucial. Everard's report had been: 'He's got guts.'

Well, that was true. Physical cowardice was not among his failings. Both Everard and Sebastian, the elder, perceived this, and did him manly justice. It was something they understood. Both were afterwards killed in action, a part of the sacrifice made by their class to a rigid sense of duty. They had never reproached

him for failure to die for his country; indeed, the parents sought
his preservation for the sake of their daughter, who became
doubly precious as the survivor. Adelaide herself never spoke
of her brothers without stoical regret. She had not loved them;
but unquestionably she was proud of them.

Love was thinly spread in that family. The children had
spent the greater part of each year at distant schools; the father
and mother, preoccupied with their own concerns, regarded
them as they regarded other family possessions, such as pictures
and jewels, and never wished for their company. There had been
plenty of money; the boys travelled, engaged in various sports,
and when unavoidably at home behaved correctly and un-
emotionally, without any sign of attachment. They would have
despised the Ruddocks' cosy domesticity. It belonged to a lower-
class world which was effectively described in *The Young Visiters*
as 'mere'.

Stanhope, motherless, and with a clerical father, escaped
'mereness'. He had been thankful to meet the family require-
ments. He was still glad to have done so; but in the spiritual
turmoil aroused by Curtal's death he saw the whole affair as the
cause of lost liberty.

'I was never free from that moment,' he reflected. 'She didn't
mean me to be free.'

She didn't mean. . . . The words suggested mathematical
calculation, which would be untrue. She had done no more than
decide upon his marital suitability. They had all—she, her mother,
father, and brothers—so decided. She was twenty-seven, serious,
too intelligent to want a husband who cared only for sport,
dancing, the links, and the moors; and she was quietly complacent
at the thought of marrying into Literature. Distinction was her
aim. Being without artistic ability, as stiff drawings and lifeless
essays (locked in a drawer and discovered after her death)
clearly revealed, she sought it in a partner for life. Lucy Chard
did the rest.

Lucy made their first meeting. She contrived others. It had
been easy to do so. The two quickly dropped into a habit of exchanging quite unimportant opinions in low tones suggestive of
intimacy; they would say, of a new novel or stage comedy: 'Did
you . . . ? I thought *quite* without. . . .' 'Painstaking, of course.'

'I knew you'd agree.' Or they met by designed accident—'Do you expect to be going?' 'I'm not sure. I might go'—and, through Lucy's efforts, at several country houses where walks and talks together were inevitable. She was cool, sisterly, obviously but not demonstratively pleased, in any company, to see him. They were discreetly left by their hosts to settle matters for themselves, which meant, naturally, in accordance with Adelaide's wishes. He was cast in the rôle of Prince Consort. There had been no formal proposal from himself. He couldn't even remember that she had said: 'Aren't you going to ask me something very important?' The speech would have been characteristic; more characteristic, certainly, than the flush or stammer of one more spontaneous. Probably there had been some pressure of the hands, some clear glance of approval, a common movement—while other members of a house party romped within doors—towards the moonlit garden.

They had paused, he believed, in the shadow of a dense yew hedge; where, without speech, they had ended in unexciting embrace the suspense which had become unnecessary. Was that all? Her lips had been pressed to his own, and soon withdrawn, leaving to his dutiful kisses no more than a silken cheek and yet softer hair, while unyielding fingers locked his like those of a tight-fitting new glove. After a slow walk under the moon, they had made a composed return to the noisy company which was swarming out on to the terrace in such high-spirited convulsion that it was easy to join.

He was struck, afterwards, by the advanced readiness of Adelaide's plans for marriage. Short of ordering the wedding-dress, she had arranged practically everything necessary—church, bridesmaids, ideal honeymoon locality, the presents she would receive from her parents. Even a house had been chosen. Was he pleased? Did he agree? Of course he was pleased. Of course he agreed. She was a wonderful young woman.

Wonderful! He remembered speculating once, in the light of their first embrace, upon the quality of her concealed emotion, and the extent to which she would discover herself to him after marriage. Would she, after all, prove amorous?

That question had been answered half-a-century ago; he was no longer interested in it. Small details of the honeymoon, which had been spent in Austria, flickered in memory, and passed into the general chiaroscuro of a marital association rather than a marriage. She was neither coy nor arch, but attentive, experimental, and, as it seemed to him, driven by superlative vanity to hide both desire and satisfaction. He was to give; never to receive.

'An instinctive curmudgeon,' he muttered now, with a hand across his mouth. 'What was I?'

That was too difficult a problem for old age. His attention strayed. It was caught a moment afterwards by a brilliant vignette of Hyde Park two days after the yew-shadowed exchange. No announcement had as yet been made of the betrothal. 'Say nothing to anybody,' she had said. 'Come to dinner at night. We shall be alone—just the family.'

Just the family: how significant!

He saw himself, elegantly-suited, strolling in suppressed excitement along the path by Rotton Row, while young riders, attended by grooms, grouped or cantered near by, and curious bystanders observed what was going on, and listened to the rather loud voices of the children. The sun shone; babies slept in their perambulators; it was high summer. Curtal came marching sturdily from the opposite direction in dark brown tweeds, with—of all things—a bowler hat pressed down upon his head, chin jutting, a scowl darkening his face, so that he looked like an artist's impression of 'Working Man in a Rage'.

That was what Curtal was; an interruption of gentility at play. He did not believe in play. He regarded the genteel as an affront to his uncouth idealism. They should all have been working for the benefit of their fellow-creatures.

At sight of him, Curtal's frown gave place to the usual saturnine grin with which he managed to smirch a friend's elegance. He made no effort to shake hands; but launched straight, as was his habit, into personal statement.

'Did you see what that bloody bishop said about me?' he demanded. 'Wants my book suppressed. He'll sell fifty thousand of it.'

'What did he say? Was this from the pulpit?'

'Called it pernicious rubbish. Unfit for Christian reading. Blasphemous. Ignorant of the Church's history, message, and sanctity. He let himself go.'

'But you don't mind that, if he sells you fifty thousand.'

'I've got a soul above money.'

'Oh, a soul! I thought you and Godwin denied that there was such a thing.'

'Godwin died a hundred years ago. I think for myself. And the bishop calls me a *lost* soul. No, of course there's no such thing. It's a notion vamped up to hoodwink Demos. I think you ought to write to *The Times* about Christian charity, objecting to the man's intemperance—*quis custodiet*, and the rest of it. Will you?'

'Certainly not. The thing will be forgotten in forty-eight hours. You've had your advertisement.'

'Hm. I don't know. No man likes his good name taken away.'

'Have you a good name?'

One would never forget the terrible acuteness of Curtal's retort.

'The truth is, you won't defend a pal for fear of killing the social goose. You're snuggling in too nicely. Lords, ladies, stock-brokers—Graham, you're not, by any chance, thinking of marrying that girl?'

'Which girl is this?'

'Come off it! You know which girl. And I'll give you a bit of advice. Don't do it. Once you're in the grip, you'll be finished.'

Ice had touched his heart. He had answered, with pretended amusement, pretended hauteur:

'Finished? I thought you always said I'd never begun.'

'Oh, I wouldn't say that. You've got plenty of tricks. The right woman would warm your blood. But *she*: you'd be congealed for life.'

'Very kind. Kind and considerate.'

'That's what I am. And I tell you there's more ways of selling your soul than buying a mess of pottage. By soul I mean self-respect.'

'I wondered what you meant. My self-respect is impregnable. As I'm sure yours is.'

'No, mine's uneasy. Always under strain. Yours lives under a top-hat. But Ruddock and I sometimes tip it. Look here, why not have supper with me tonight? I'll get him, too. We'll have this out.'

'I'm sorry I'm engaged for dinner.'

'What, with her?'

'With her, among others.'

'Cut it!' And, at sight of the shaken head: 'I've warned you.'

'You've warned me.'

Their parting had been abrupt, and cordial. After-feelings were less cordial, and disagreeable. So Ruddock was in this, as well. A joint rescue operation! What sauce! And yet, were they right? One didn't marry to please one's friends. The proposed intervention was an absurd piece of impudence. And yet . . . and yet . . . were they right?

Next day the engagement was announced. It was followed by a postcard: *I see my warning came too late. God help you! T.C.*

God help you! His chin sank to his breast. Hadn't Curtal and himself made crass mistakes? He with Adelaide, Curtal with the detestable Cora? Hadn't they illustrated the fatal instinct of mankind, which Curtal denied, to enslave itself for the sake of immediate or ultimate advantage?

The short and long views were both delusive. Why had Curtal suffered himself to be ensnared by Cora? Folly! Folly! . . .

That vision of Hyde Park in summer faded; what remained was the memory of a harsh voice prophesying spiritual death. It sent a chill to his heart.

PART FIVE

Counter-Attack

TWENTY-FOUR

Half-an-hour

'A GENTLEMAN, sir. The gentleman you saw last night. Who tired you. He says he's come to apologize.'

Having been lost in the past, Stanhope could not at first understand what Martin was saying. He opened his eyes to stare at her, and with no difficulty at all he read in that bony face (which surely she had been artificially beautifying, without success?) her view of the caller. It was unfavourable. If Martin did as she wished, she would close the door behind Mr John White for ever. How curious! A sort of unloving loyalty.

'I'm very tired, Martin.'

'I'll tell him that, sir.' She had already turned, rigid with her errand.

'But one moment!'

Now that his mind was free from the clogging of memory, he experienced relief. He had been in danger of sentimentalizing Curtal. Also, previous doubt as to the wisdom of snubbing his caller returned. These poisonous, bitter juniors, morbidly obsessed by the passion of destructiveness, would stop at no slander, for slander was their trade. His physical exhaustion of the night before would be analysed and presented to the world as either a ruse of evasion or an uprising of conscience. He hesitated.

Had he strength enough to face the tough mind and ruthless tongue? He was still disturbed by the emotions caused by Curtal's death and the conflicting views of the man which had poured in upon him, especially as a result of John White's hostile cross-examination. But was he not now newly-armed by knowledge of White's life and character?

Martin was still waiting, attempting by her very silence to influence his decision. He could see the rise and fall of her unrounded breast; almost hear the creak of her old-fashioned corset. Odd creature! She pictured him as helpless; perhaps she pictured herself as a foster-mother. What happened in that crude brain?

'Do you think he really wants to apologize?'

'He says so,' was the ambiguous reply.

'Does he look sorry?'

'No, sir; he doesn't. Quite pleased with himself, I should say. But he was very upset last night, when you . . .' Evidently she could not bring herself to say 'fainted' or 'collapsed'. He ventured a jocularity.

'As baffled as Mephistopheles at the escape of Marguerite! Yes?'

'Rang for me like a madman. I was in the next room, so I came at once. He'd got the door open. Looked like some horrid goblin. Wanted to know if he should fetch a doctor. I said: "No, you'd better clear out." So he went.'

'Hm. Rather crestfallen?'

'Well, he'd been told to go, sir. He just smiled sarcastically, but I think he must have been worried. He telephoned first thing this morning, to inquire; and now he's here.'

'You don't want me to see him, Martin?'

'Please yourself, sir.' Martin was disapprovingly stiff.

'If I don't see him, he may write something unpleasant about me. I don't want that. I'm too old. But if I see him, I'd like you to interrupt us in half-an-hour. Half-an-hour would be enough, don't you think, for courtesy?'

'Five minutes, I should say.'

'Of course, he might not stop so long.'

'Not if he's just come, as he says, to apologize. Shall I tell him "five minutes"?'

'Oh, no, no. One must use finesse with such a . . . gentleman. Has Dr Meredith sent some tablets?'

'Yes, and said I was to get you to bed at once. I told him I couldn't, because of the Miss Ruddocks coming for tea; so he said to let you rest quietly when they'd gone.'

'As I've been doing. Well, then, come up in half-an-hour, and say "doctor's orders". Is that clear? I'd like my supper before going to bed—a glass of wine and a few biscuits will do; just the usual. Oh, yes; and, Martin, will you switch on the

central light? I want to be able to see the gentleman's face
clearly. When I saw him before, he was . . . a little . . . obscure.'

In this way, Stanhope dismissed the charge of hallucination.
Since Martin, by the rustle of her skirt, was evidently no wraith,
he felt insured against dream. Indeed, he was twice the man he
had been overnight. Twice the man!

So believing, he gave his fingers an old man's flamboyant
wave; while Martin, he thought, from the doorway half-smiled
with grim indulgence. He then composed himself for the encounter.

It began almost immediately, so soon that he could imagine
the visitor to have been no farther away than the landing, with
ears attuned for every cadence of the low-toned exchange. John
White came quickly into the room, simulating concern, but in
fact triumphant at having reached him, and with no softening of
vigilance.

Stanhope, however, was almost intrepid. Under a brighter
light he could see the moulding of this young man's face more
exactly than before; the sharpness of the cheekbones, the breadth
of the hair-swept forehead, the curious almost-joined eyebrows,
which curved as if an artist had painted them with two swift
strokes of a fine brush. These eyebrows reminded Stanhope of
others which he could not immediately place. On whose face
had he previously observed such eyebrows?

'I'm glad to see you better, sir.'

Yes, triumph was in the voice, which to an attentive ear said:
'I'm going to have another dig at this evasive piece of wreckage.
I shall keep at him until he's convicted of all I suspect. I vindicate
Curtal by destroying Stanhope.'

'Do you know,' replied Stanhope, with a smile in which
whimsy and defiance of this hateful resolve were mingled, 'I
could say almost the same thing.' He indicated the room's
superior illumination.

'Would you prefer me to switch off that light?'

'On the contrary, I'm all for lucency. Like Goethe, I demand
more of it. I understand you've very kindly called to ask after
my health?'

'To apologize for having *tired* you last night.' The emphasis
was ironic. 'Your female Cerberus was determined that I should
appreciate my sin.'

'You've come to expiate it, I'm sure.'

'To make sure I wasn't, as she hinted, a murderer.'

'I'm fortunate in having some domestic protection. Was Curtal equally lucky? You visited him, I gather, in his last hours.'

The point was taken; the answer snapped.

'For ten years before then. He liked me to go. Strangely enough, I never met you there.'

'No. We made constant efforts to meet, and sometimes did so—at our Club, or a restaurant we liked, the Evergreen. But he was kept busy by his . . . disciples; and since my wife's death I've tended to live very quietly.'

'Less molested by disciples?' The sneer meant that Stanhope was without vital young admirers, a man left high and dry by the new generation.

'I didn't say "molested", Mr White. Nor did I feel envy. As he grows older, every man finds himself taking a smaller place than he once hoped to do in the pattern of his age. I learnt that with resignation many years ago. Curtal didn't. He wanted all his life to change the pattern, as youth does. Hence the disciples! It was necessary to his ego to fight tradition, even when the times reduced him to shadow-boxing. I never fought tradition. I loved it as the child loves his mother. I base myself, politically, on Burke; not, as Curtal did, on the egregious Godwin, or that boresome mountebank, Tom Paine.'

While speaking thus provocatively—a sure sign in him of recovered confidence—Stanhope watched his visitor's face, which thanks to the brilliant light he could perfectly see. Those singular brows ran together in a concentrated frown which again set him groping into the past. This young man, whom he had thought coldly contemptuous of antediluvian humbug, grew madly exasperated at criticism of himself. His mouth became a vengeful line.

'Not everyone will accept your descriptions,' said the hardly-moving line, at last.

'I have no hope of it,' was Stanhope's mild comment. 'But I hope you'll allow me, in charity, to cherish my experience. Old men do that, I know, at their peril.'

White drew a quick breath before replying:

'Curtal was willing to give and take. He enlarged, answered,

encouraged, all the time. Anybody was free to challenge his ideas.
It was a great privilege. It made him very attractive. Hence the
disciples—as you call them—and his influence today, when most
of his contemporaries are dead or moribund.' As Stanhope did
not rise to this affront, he concluded: 'You'd grant the generosity,
the charm, of his personality, I suppose?'

'I remember only his taunts,' murmured Stanhope. 'His
taunts and his assurance.'

There was a stir of interest in John White. He had learned
something authentic at last. He responded to the candour by
retorting:

'Curtal didn't forget yours.'

Stanhope smiled again.

'Was I guilty of any?'

'Weren't you? With extremely adroit malice? He said I
should find you "like the innocent flower".'

Vindictive eyes gleamed from under the black brows. White
knew, and Curtal had known, that Stanhope would be able to
complete the quotation:

> . . . Look like the innocent flower,
> *But be the serpent under it.*

Curtal had improved upon his first political teacher, Godwin,
who believed the millenium would arrive if Kings, governments,
and institutions were swept away, to be replaced by a natural
benevolence of man towards man. One and a half centuries
had passed since the original *naïvetés* were expressed in Godwin's
portentously-named *Enquiry concerning the Principles of Political
Justice, and its Influence on General Virtue and Happiness;* and not
even Curtal, resting upon this counter-Bible, which proposed
to abolish police and priesthood, and set man free for the inevitable dog-fight, would deny that the world was fuller than ever
of dictatorial order.

Bullying, physical, moral, by edict, by restriction, by propa-
ganda, by the *fait accompli*, was universal. Politics had never been
so threatening to the individual. Nevertheless, with a zealot's
self-deception, he preached anarchy as if it were a new and world-
saving gospel. He was lucky in his country. Any other Government would have imprisoned him for sedition; but in England

he enjoyed an immunity that showed how harmless he was thought to be by the bureaucrats.

'It's only Curtal,' they said, laughing at his gibes, and appreciative of his audacity; 'blowing off steam!'

No wonder his army was composed of raw recruits, hot with the sense of being forbidden to do as they pleased in a society regulated to the last pip. John White, cooled by conceit in his intellectual superiority, was such a recruit; but his driving-force was bitterness, instead of Curtal's joy in rant for its own sake. White spread venom. It was the fashion among new intellectuals. He would still be spreading it on his deathbed, with none of Curtal's roaring scandalous mockery. How Curtal had loved scandal! He had never been a prig. And the world, applauding and disregarding its would-be reformers, moved at its own pace towards caducity! 'His influence when other men were seen to be moribund.' His influence! What a farce!

'Only I, and those like me, who keep alight the flame of culture,' thought Stanhope, 'truly serve humankind.'

He said nothing of these reflections. He felt no resentment at Curtal's ribald accusation of cunning. It had been made too often to his face, in unwilling tribute—and with how different a humour! That was the point about Curtal—his humour. This fellow had no humour. He reproduced a statement; but he robbed it of every undertone of . . . yes, of affection. Curtal bragged of outspokenness as the boor boasts of his commonsense, and for the same reason. He had to pretend, for his reassurance, that rudeness was honesty, and that the subtle mind was bound to equivocate.

Oh, but there were a million dishonesties in Curtal. Not merely the noisy misuse of faked figures, the garbling of historical quotations, the pretence to have read books that somebody else had abstracted for him; but the conjuring tricks he did with his own thoughts. You couldn't pin him down. You couldn't correct him. If you produced the correct text he waved it aside, shouting more loudly some tomfoolery about the Papacy or the Normans or the villainies of Canning or Disraeli. But he shouted most loudly of all to drown the promptings of an uncomfortable conscience. His bravado was defiance to generations of chapel-goers, vengeful school-masters aping the Old Testament God, and a childish terror of Hell. . . .

Imagine the effect upon a lad such as Curtal had been, squalid, stinking, he said, of dirty clothes and body, and only half-fed, of the discovery among some cast-out rubbish of two pompous volumes entitled *Political Justice*! Imagine his surreptitious, lip-licking consumption, by the light of a street-lamp outside his window, of those two volumes, in which marriage was denounced, religion arraigned, an earthly paradise of rationality promised! Curtal had once said: 'While other kids were feeding on cowboys and bushrangers, I ate Godwin. He was my prairie, my smut, my desert island, my everything. You're blind, Graham! You, in your pampered childhood!'

Pampered! Good God! That gloomy house; that sadistic old woman; that deadly loneliness. . . .'

'We've said nothing of Key,' suddenly barked John White. 'I know what you thought of Thompson and Ruddock. You under-rated them both. I see why. I've heard from Curtal all I need to know about Holmes, who was obviously a stupid fool—the only one Curtal completely disdained——'

'Did he tell you why?' asked Stanhope, quickly, with the picture of Sally Raikes before his eyes, and memory of Curtal's old despair and the Ruddock girls' encounter.

'Never,' answered White.

'I see. Interesting enough. You were saying?'

There was no hesitation.

'Key: what was *he* like?'

The switch, intended to disconcert, had missed its object. Indeed, Stanhope, much impressed by Curtal's discretion about Sally, was able—Key being dead and forgotten—to be quite bluff. Even as a counter-blow to the inquisitor, he would not betray Curtal's little romance. It too nearly touched himself.

'Key was a disappointment to us,' he answered. 'A charming, delicate boy; slight stammer; fair; slim. . . . At first I thought he had a vein of gold, very small, but genuine. That wasn't so. He took colour from Ruddock, who was his friend; and when Ruddock wasn't there, the colour faded. All he could produce were timid little versicles and satirettes. They were very nearly pointless.'

White nodded.

'That agrees with what Curtal told me. Also, my own opinion.'

'For once, we're all in accord,' said Stanhope, drily. His smile produced punishment.

'You didn't keep up with him?'

Stanhope thought: 'I ought to have helped Key. I'm ashamed of it. The truth is, I couldn't stand him in the rôle of beggar-hero, cheated of his inheritance. That's not fair. I couldn't stand his silent reproach. And I didn't think he was any good. How do you help people you think are no good?' However, he replied, without obvious shame: 'Key married too young. Foolishly. He had a bad war. He was shocked and shaken. And he couldn't get a footing afterwards. It was difficult to do anything for him.'

The following silence made this account seem lame. Evidently White had other information. He presently supplied it.

'Curtal found something. He gave him money.'

'Key wouldn't take it from me.'

'Was it offered?'

'Certainly.'

'That's not what I understood.'

'Nevertheless it is the fact. No doubt he wanted more than I could offer.'

Stanhope felt himself raked by sceptical eyes. He anticipated an allusion to his wealthy wife, or his own earnings, which repute had exaggerated. Well, one couldn't admit that Adelaide, like her father, retained and hoarded her own income, using it for further shrewd investment in non-taxable securities. The allusion did not come; there was a long pause. At last, setting aside the contradiction, White said:

'Curtal and Ruddock bought a little local newspaper. They put Key in charge of it. You didn't know that? You weren't asked to join? Something had happened, hadn't it?'

Stanhope knew very well what had happened. Key, with a nonentity's swelled head, had expected bounty: 'My dear fellow, I've been lucky; you've had the devil's own luck. Take half my all; you'd have done the same for me if our positions had been reversed.' His welcome, on the contrary, had been one of embarrassed distaste. Therefore Key, finding more accommodating friends, took pride in saying: 'I won't have Stanhope in this. I'll take nothing from that . . .'

What if he'd been asked? Adelaide would have said: 'Don't

be a fool, Graham! You can't possibly encourage such a creature.
He'll sponge on you for life.' But he hadn't been asked. He
pictured Curtal and Ruddock with their heads together, discussing the question as they had discussed his marriage. 'Well,
we'll have to leave Graham out of it. The Dragon would never
let him. . . .' Hell! In their eyes he'd been a kept man.

'I can't remember.'

'You admit it was odd, as you were all close friends?' When
Stanhope did not reply, White added: 'The attempt was no
good. Key wanted a quiet life. As you say, he was delicate; he
was also a miserable valetudinarian. At first it was a little nip
of Scotch in his office. Then a bigger nip. Then he began to keep
it beside his bed. No appetite; so a tonic to start the day, something to keep him going, finally a night-cap. Then he didn't get
up. The paper died; Key died, chiefly of Scotch. Sentimentalists
would call it a tragedy. You don't call it that?'

'No, I'm not a sentimentalist,' replied Stanhope, shrinking
from the picture of Key's decline.

'Hm. I understood that. I've seen his children. They live in a
state of grievance. They think the world of Curtal—as a man.' A
turn of the lips, and a sardonic half-glance, conveyed the message:
'Not of you. You weren't asked to the funeral. You wrote nothing
about him, as Curtal did. The children describe you with their
father's one word.' But the speech adhered to Curtal. 'They're
not soo keen on his ideas. Too conventional to understand his
love of the under-dog. You have no such love, I think?'

The question was another quick turn, intended, after what
the speaker believed to have been some unhappy moments, to
disconcert. Stanhope, disgusted by the Keys, but not personally
disconcerted, smiled.

'No, I don't think I can claim that. People in my position,
hedging, or intimidated by Left Wing threats, often profess a
love they don't feel. They're no less selfish or mean or extravagant.
It's an anomaly resulting from rule by votes.'

Impatience showed in the darkened face.

'Your position: you know what Curtal felt?'

'About me? Or about the newly-affluent under-dog?'

'Both.'

'We needn't be abstruse. The explanation's simple enough.

Curtal began as an under-dog himself. My under-doggedness was personal; not, as his was, social. He fought, and went on fighting, in what he felt was his own cause. It wasn't: he died a capitalist, worth a hundred thousand pounds. . . .'

'That's a mere newspaper estimate of the value of his copyrights.'

'It may be so. The point is that he never forgot his back-street childhood; father always drunk and savage at the weekends; mother going the same way when she collapsed; and his own devil-pursued escape to London.'

'You call it "escape"?' asked John White, sharply.

'Oh, yes. Isn't that clear to you? Curtal's whole life was escape. He couldn't bear to be alone, or idle. He had always to be running, the devil at his heels, breathing down his neck.'

'What devil is this?'

'I don't know. It began as poverty and squalor and his father's great fists. It went on as sheer restlessness. People thought of it as "drive"; but it was flight. Call it the devil of character. He'd be described by the new psychology as a manic-depressive; as if that proved anything at all.'

'You don't like the new psychology?'

'I don't see its purpose.'

'Surely its purpose is the healing of the mentally sick!'

'You mean that Curtal, flying from the devil, was mentally sick?'

White's face hardened.

'In the sense that genius is always abnormal, yes. Only mediocrities are sane.'

Stanhope shrugged. He contemplated, and then looked away from, the accuser, without rancour.

All the changes he had noted in this young man's expressions had meaning and deeper meaning, as yet unprobed. Insolent contempt for an old poseur, who was to be deflated by merciless cross-examination, had almost disappeared. Angry disagreement, and the rigidities of social and political fanaticism, were frequent; but these, the least alarming, arose from arrogant youth's dislike of contradiction. White, ever to attack, must himself go free. How like Curtal!

His tragic domestic situation, as reported by Mrs Pinchin,

proved that behind the inquisitor lay another man, in whom
loyalty to a disfigured wife was paramount. Suffering could
pervert any mind, lend acid to any tongue. It might be so here.
Moreover Mrs Pinchin, however ridiculous as the expositor of
insane poets, had testified to her husband's affectionate respect
for White and White's intellect. . . .

How amusing that she, White, and Thomas Pinchin, whom
one admired, should all consider the elegant Lionel a genteel
charlatan. They were serious; Lionel a dilettante; which sufficiently explained the disapproval. But wasn't there something
meretricious, after all, about Lionel? It had seemed so, at
luncheon. And had not Curtal passed on to White a garbled account of charges brought by the Smelfungus Brigade, long ago,
about Graham Stanhope? Or had White formed his own adverse
opinion of one's highly dubious erudition?

Forget such things. White obviously had quality, as man and
critic. His prejudice would have been nourished by Curtal's
ribald tales; but those alone did not account for his harshness.
Curtal never had the instinct to persecute. White must have
derived it from somebody else. From whom? Last night his cry
had been one of almost retributive vindictiveness. 'I am here to
punish? To *punish*!' For what? The malignant disclosure of Curtal's
affair with Hester, and of Curtal's fatal laughter at what was
represented as scatalogical curiosity about that affair, were
sprung with deliberate cruelty. That cruelty was successful. It
had broken an old man's nerve.

If the blow were repeated tonight, and followed by a second
night of hideous dreaming, more than nerve might fail. Sanity
itself.

Damn Meredith, with his carefully nonchalant suggestion of
mental collapse!

The blow could not be repeated. But consider other possible
strains. In eighty years a man might commit a thousand follies.
How many of one's indiscretions and humiliations had Curtal
retailed to White? If these stories, narrated with gusto, had
entered a mind poisoned by hatred, the consequences now and
hereafter could be terrible. The most innocent deeds and sayings,
when twisted, could kill a reputation.

Old fears quickened. White's very silence was threatening.

What was in his mind? Could the key to that attack lie in its association, not with Curtal, but with Hester Thompson?

Stanhope, conscious of a trembling of his hands, looked searchingly into his visitor's clearly-illumined face. It was as intent as that of the famous Notre Dame gargoyle, and as full of evil. Those peculiar brows were laden with sardonic thought. The eyes beneath them shone darkly, as do those of a watching cat.

He had seen that dark glance before. Directed, as this man's was, at himself, and full of hatred. When he shudderingly turned away, the expression was still before him, seeming to glow from each shadowy corner of his room. Thus it had been, unexplained, for many a year; the animal hatred of another person, another person. . . .

Starting with uncontrollable violence, he brought his unsteady hands fast together. He had surprised the likeness which had excited and eluded him from the moment of his first glimpse of John White.

TWENTY-FIVE

Discovery

HESTER THOMPSON! Excitement swept through him like a hot wind. He was again behind a curtain, concealed, while two figures stood in close conversation within his view. He strained his ears to catch their whispers. He imagined anew what he had heard in reality thirty-five years earlier, the searing clangour of an intrusive gong. It tore his nerves; but it produced certainty.

At last he knew why Curtal had stayed away from Thompson's deathbed. It was not because his stomach turned at mortality; it was because, under a dying man's gaze, he could not commit untruth as he had earlier, in secret, committed adultery. The utter deceiver was Hester, smoothing Thompson's sheet, holding Thompson's wasted hand, pretending grief, pretending the unearthly patience of a loving wife; and, across the bed, staring at himself—oh, how brazenly, the loathsome whore! . . .

She knew then that she was three months gone with child; and that Thompson's death, soon, very soon, was necessary to her safety. Had his illness been much longer protracted, even Thompson could not have failed to discover her unfaithfulness, and to die with his final illusion destroyed. She hadn't murdered the poor devil. She had only willed him to go quickly. Willed night and morning and every day. No wonder John White was Curtal's apologist. No wonder he had been free of Curtal's company since Hester's death, ten years ago. No wonder Curtal had so arranged dates that there should be no chance of Stanhope meeting him. White was Curtal's son. There was natural affinity between them.

Nay, in one supreme leap of intuition, Stanhope penetrated Hester's mind. Her stare had been, for once, the open betrayal of long-concealed suspicion and dislike, increased under stress to hatred. Mad with lust for Curtal, who had the raw strength she

191

missed in her husband, she had taken brisk advantage of Thompson's removal to hospital to betray him. She had believed one man, and one man alone, to be privy to the secret of Curtal and herself, and ready at any moment to tell the truth.

Stanhope had never been allowed to visit Thompson unless she was there. And at the very end, when escape from denunciation was secure, she had stared with defiance, as well as bitter animosity.

Here was the same stare.

Thompson, growing weaker every hour, was well-deceived, the soft-hearted fool. He opened his eyes only to smile at her in fondness, closed them more and more wearily as his pallor increased, tried vainly to speak some message which his lips could not form, at last stirred and ceased to breathe. Thus he took his long words and swollen sentences, his platitudes, and bewilderments over events which he could not understand, to oblivion, while Curtal stayed away and Stanhope sat by the bed and Hester feigned sorrow which was at war with the dancing triumph of her thoughts.

That stare had meant: 'Do your worst! You're my enemy! If I could make you suffer, I should do so.'

How melodramatic! How exaggerated her notion had been of his insight! He had not liked her; he had formed some faint suspicion of her; but until last night he had never imagined the depth and long-standing of her passion for Curtal. Curtal had the power to arouse such passion in women, which he never returned in equal measure. By some strange whim of nature, the women never became hostile to him, even when they knew that his pursuit had turned elsewhere.

'Part, I suppose,' thought Stanhope, with sour irony, 'of his genius.'

His mind passed from the hospital bed to the wintry day of Thompson's funeral, when a few people in heavy mourning had gathered to lament the dead man, listened to the dreariness of an agnostic address, and followed the coffin to its resting place. As the ultimate silence fell upon them all, Hester threw into the grave, symbolically, the dictionary which Thompson had carried every day, until sickness made that impossible, in the breast-pocket of his coat.

It was this gesture that made Curtal clutch Stanhope's arm, and turn away, his face distorted and his grip tightening. He had recognized the familiar and often-ridiculed little book. He had known, without doubt, that what others supposed to be an act of loyalty to a beloved husband was in fact a last savage jeer at the good man who for seven years had loved her with his anxious idealism.

'I can't stand this,' Curtal had said. 'I'm not going to face the bloody baked meats. That fearful crowd!—hers and his! Did you see her mother? Come and have a drink, Graham. Stick to me. Stick to me. I'm ill. . . .'

The icy afternoon, already declining towards dusk; the unlighted streets under a canopy of cloud; the feeling, not of bereavement, but of dreary pessimism, were clearly recalled. So was Curtal's maniacal grasp of his arm. Heavy breathing, which resembled a multitude of suppressed sobs, was again audible.

They had walked quickly away into the gloom, both overwhelmed by the apparently impulsive casting of his book after Thompson's lowered coffin. When they were out of the cemetery Curtal exclaimed: 'Why in God's name did she have to do that, the bitch?' Afterwards, under his breath, he muttered: 'Poor bloody fool! He's at peace!'

That was all. They spoke no more of Thompson. Somewhere along the route they found a cab and drove to Curtal's rooms, where with every light blazing they drank red wine, and Curtal's ashen face recovered the tinge of life.

Curtal would not sit down. He stamped restlessly from side to side of his ugly den, with its ragged books and rugs and stupid be-wigged portraits, like an animal in suspense.

'These things always upset me,' he grumbled. 'I ought not to have gone. Damned killing day. Help yourself. Fill up. Fill up. Ever see such a crowd? Numb with cold; respectable black coats and ties; not a decent tally of brains in the lot of them. Good God, how appropriate!'

He had poured and drunk again, for warmth, not savour. His pacing was resumed.

'Ruddock wasn't there. Perhaps he couldn't come. Eh? D'you think he couldn't come? I wish he was here, now. He's straight, is Ruddock. In some ways, blast him, he's the best of us.'

Stanhope could not remember his own share in the conversation. He knew he had been shocked by the dictionary episode. Like Curtal, he had needed the wine, which was again rich upon his palate; but further memory was blurred by the distress of that hour and its association with the present. He must have stayed a long time with Curtal. They had not once referred, he believed, to Thompson. Now that he was buried, the man had seemed forgotten.

He could not have been forgotten by Hester. She did not forget Thompson, or Curtal, or himself. She must have nursed for the rest of her life the feelings she expressed that afternoon. They were loathing of the dead, excitement at being in company with Curtal, whom she hoped to marry, and detestation for the man who, she thought, was her enemy.

What happened after that? He could not recall. In some way he had learned that Hester accused him of dragging Curtal away from the funeral; and he supposed that from a ghastly covetousness of respectability she disappeared into the country until after the child was born. But what was Curtal's action? Some flight, no doubt. Had he then gone upon a mission to the United States? Had there been scenes or letters of upbraiding? Only Curtal could have told. Within six months—it must have been about the time this boy 'John White' was delivered—he married an unknown woman, Cora. Escaping from one harpy, he fell into the clutches of another!

But Hester? She had not sought revenge upon Curtal. It was upon himself that her rage had turned. Why? In his effort to comprehend this puzzle, he loosed his hands, striking one sharply upon the other, and thrust himself lower in his chair, heartsick.

At last he saw that White was watching him. The frown was gone, giving place to sardonic curiosity.

'Are you unwell again?' White asked. 'Has what I said about genius, or Key, or the question of the under-dog, been too much for you?'

His tone was not offensive. It held, apart from possible inquisitiveness, anxiety. Stanhope forced himself to smile.

'Not one word of yours, this evening, has affected me unpleasantly,' he said. 'You mustn't feel guilty.'

'I didn't feel guilty,' was White's retort. 'It's not a habit of mine.'

'Why should it be?' Stanhope was again master of himself, although a little breathless. 'As you know, and naturally I apologize for the trite simile, the bulk of the iceberg is under water. Whatever is said, whatever can be said, except between the rarest of lovers, is unintelligibly superficial. Though modern psychology—didn't we refer to that?—interprets conduct and . . . hallucination . . . by dogmatic formula, the true activity of the mind eludes most formula.'

'Did you say "evades"?' asked John White, with some of the old insolence.

'No, I evade or avoid personal discomfort. There are certain subjects I don't wish to discuss, because another person—let us say, for inoffensive example, my maid, Martin, whom you've seen—would bring preconceptions amounting to appalling misconceptions to bear on them. That would make any discussion meaningless. Like reciting Shelley to a speculative dog. We should both be confounded. You yourself wouldn't be ready, just now, to discuss with me whatever private affairs affect you most strongly.'

'Is this a diversion?' asked White, sharply. 'A parable?'

'You remember I asked if you were happily married. I did that in all innocence; but your answer was abrupt. It indicated that you were to ask all the questions, and that my business was to answer them. I hope you remember, also, that I didn't stand on my dignity, and deny your right to ask questions, even if they were impertinent.'

An expression of anger appeared on White's face. Evidently he had not expected this old man to challenge him directly.

'But I made it clear at the outset that I wanted answers to questions about a particular stage of Curtal's life. However unwillingly, you agreed to answer those questions.'

'However they were put?'

'I'm sorry if I've been too direct for your taste.'

'Not at all. What I'm trying to suggest, very . . . mildly, is that all your questions have a background of preconception; and that all my answers have behind them eighty years of experience different from your own. I'm the older iceberg, in fact. I also have incurable preconceptions. You accuse me of evasiveness.

You've been told that I am an evasive character. I am. But I'm not therefore a negligible character. . . .'

Unmistakably, White had flushed.

'I shouldn't have bothered to ask for these interviews if I'd thought you were.'

'No? That wasn't the impression I'd formed from your manner.'

'My manner——'

Stanhope waved the anger away.

'You speak very vigorously about Curtal's genius. You contrast it with a mediocrity that I'm bound to apply. But you should remember that I was Curtal's close associate—I say nothing, in this connection, of friendship—for more than half a century. As men, whatever you may think of our relative merits as writers, we were on terms of equality. That fact must be set against his jeers to you at my expense—jeers which you yourself have said can be matched by my jeers at him, although I don't remember those.'

Irritation had been busy upon White's face during this quiet statement; and as he heard the words 'whatever you may think of our relative merits as writers' a sarcastic smile pinched the thin lips. But he did not interrupt; perhaps he noted the words for future satirical comment on the delusions of mediocrity? Finding that Stanhope had ended, he said:

'I appreciate all you say, sir. It's my way to speak, even to my elders, with freedom. Your habit, I see, is usually less open; but I think my freedom——'

'Has had a good effect on me?'

'I shouldn't presume to suggest that. You were speaking of the iceberg. I think you meant I hadn't understood your silence just now. That's so. I was afraid I'd tired you. I gather that you were really visiting some lower stratum of the iceberg?'

'I was thinking,' replied Stanhope, 'of your father and mother.'

TWENTY-SIX

Hester

SOME lack of comprehension deepened the watchfulness of that unsmiling face. Probably White, still dwelling on the likelihood of evasive diversion, suspected criticism of himself.

'My father and mother?' he questioned.

'You haven't spoken of your mother this evening.'

The face grew rigid; no longer watchful, but on guard.

'I don't understand you.'

'Come, Mr White; don't fence. You say you want light on one period of Curtal's life; his beginnings as a writer, his early associates, and so on. That's so, isn't it? But having persuaded me, last night, rather disingenuously, to express an opinion of your mother, you sprang on me the story of Curtal's death, and a love-affair I knew nothing about. You remember? I thought she must be one of your trump cards.'

'I have others!' cried White, in imperious anger.

'No doubt. I am ready for them all. But I wonder—a fathom or two below sea-level—why your mother should have poisoned your mind against me. It does her no credit. That was the sort of thing I meant by preconception. As to my life as a whole, that— as you claim to be studying a genius, and not myself—is surely not your business.'

Of course he was less steady than he sounded; but he spoke unemphatically, and he made no plea for mercy. By adroit counter-attack he had removed obstacles to plain-speaking on both sides. At the same time, however, he put extraordinary strain upon his heart, which could no longer bear prolonged effort. He knew this; the fact that he ran a great risk showed how deeply he had been moved in the last forty hours. He had passed from the detachment of venerated age into the warriorship of his first conflicts with Curtal.

197

White had not moved. Stanhope imagined what his impulse must be. Would he leap up, speak bitter words, and go? He did none of these things. He sat absorbing the attack and calculating its implications. Was he resolving to turn it to absurdity? There was neither shame nor regret in his bearing; such emotions had no place in the modern temperament.

What sort of man had he expected to meet? Good God, with his mother's systematic detraction, his father's unscrupulous yarns, and his own scientific contempt for the purely aesthetic viewpoint, he must have pictured a scheming charlatan who would prove as collapsible as Mr Toad! He had promised himself an evening of cruel sport, to furnish material for a subsequent lampoon worthy of Curtal and gratifying to the *manes* of Hester!

But now the view was changed. He·had met, not the simulacrum of a dishonest *littérateur*, but a mind able to counter-attack with spirit. Surprised and angry, being his mother's son, he would be vengeful. All one's strength would be needed to repel his berserk attack.

How long must that attack be endured? The clock! Alas, this brilliant light glittered upon its dial, blurring the hands. Could one last for ten minutes? At the end of them Martin would come to the rescue, a female St George. 'Here are dragons'!

He imagined himself clinging to Martin's roughened hand, crying: 'Save me! Save me!' and in his excitement was caught by a fit of silent laughter.

At last White spoke.

'I begin to understand Curtal's immense admiration for you,' he said, in a cold voice.

Tears sprang to Stanhope's eyes, the tears of a weary, suddenly-moved old man. His unsteady hands crept together again, for strength. He thought, trembling: 'Yes. Admiration. That's true. Immense admiration!'

He was so much affected by this declaration that at first he could make no answer. He saw the cocky little figure, and heard familiar jeering rudeness and blasphemy, as if Curtal exuberantly roved about the room. Simultaneously he felt exquisite delight at having forced a tribute from this young man's ungenerous heart.

Delight passed like the sun-lit flash of a dragon-fly's swoop.

Dread followed. Fear the Greeks when they bring gifts! Neverthe-less, he had won a small victory.

'To understand; not to share,' he at last whispered, a little breathlessly. 'If indeed Curtal felt admiration. He was an in-comprehensible mixture! But that could be said of us all; in spite of the psychologists!' He was teasing; mocking seriousness with the object, not only of concealing emotion, but of disarming the inquisitor.

'I'm not a psychologist,' retorted White.

'Even if you were, you would still be material for the psycholo-gist. Do you think psychologists analyse themselves? Their nights may well be agonizingly sleepless.'

The inadvertent hint was seized.

'Are your nights agonizingly sleepless?'

Stanhope, in alarm, thought again of Meredith. He must not allow any thought of the word hallucination to arise!

'Ah! I see that you *are* a psychologist,' he replied, smiling as he trembled. 'Well, since Curtal's death I've slept less soundly than usual. I mumble old memories; it's the vice of the aged.'

White was suddenly keen.

'You remember very distinctly?'

What was he suggesting? One's reply must be circumspect. One must seem to be as calm as a standing pool.

'Shall we say, sometimes with better understanding? I inter-pret events in ways not possible when they occurred. As links in an invisible, inexorable chain.'

'Are you satisfied, then, with your present interpretations?'

'I'm never satisfied. I'm what's nowadays called a perfec-tionist. These cant terms, such as "perfectionist", don't worry you, I suppose?' Thankful for the passage of time, Stanhope looked again at the clock, without being able to see its hands. 'Tell me, was Curtal a good sleeper, latterly?'

White must have lost sight of his object. He fell victim to the artful question.

'They sometimes drugged him to kill pain. He was in great pain. His courage was incomparable. But he'd fall asleep while we were talking.'

'It was an old habit. He'd spout for hours, and then, all of a sudden, snore. His energy collapsed. I remember that happening in the middle of a fight.'

'I know you once fought. He was surprised at your strength.'

Stanhope, at first startled, recovered at once. Curtal had not mentioned Sally.

'He grumbled at it, I remember. He didn't, I believe, tell you why we fought?'

'Only that he was drunk. You, it appeared, were sober, always sober. He said, "cool-headed, cold-hearted".'

'Yes, he thought that. I meant him to.'

'You were pretending?'

'He had a knife. It was necessary to take it away.'

'Had he attacked you?'

'Oh, people do violent things when they're drunk. Curtal lost his head.'

'He was unhappy, wasn't he? Unhappy about a woman?'

This was very dangerous. It must be blandly smothered, with a steady voice and eye.

'He was over-excited. In youth he was often that.'

'Had you purposely excited him? You had extraordinary power.'

'I? My dear boy, nobody had extraordinary power over Curtal.'

'Influence, then.'

'None.'

'I think you forget. I think you want to forget.'

It was frightening. Drunkenness over a woman, a fight over a woman, extraordinary influence—was that alleged to be in connection with a woman? Some charge must lie behind this!

'Why should I want to forget? I have nothing on my conscience about Curtal.'

'Nothing?' The fierceness suggested daggers, flame, death.

'Neither Curtal nor your mother. Why are you so excited?'

'I'm not excited. I have the best of reasons for demanding an answer.' White's expression was one of repulsive incredulity. He was not excited; he was obsessed.

'You use very strange terms,' said Stanhope, in a clear voice. 'I never at any time whatever did your mother the smallest injury. That's quite certain.'

He lay back in his chair with a tumultuously beating heart. He was suffocating. He saw the brilliant light fading into a

dusk which presaged another fainting fit. This was too much.
It was last night's outrage all over again. He was too old to be a
sadist's knockabout. White must go.

What was the wretch saying? He would refuse to answer. He
was ill. He was old. An old man was entitled to his rest.

'Take your mind back a little more precisely,' came that crow-
like voice. It was uglier than Curtal's. It was as coarse and distasteful as Hester Thompson's heavy black hair. God! What
horrible hair she had! 'Take it back to early days.'

Nonsense! But as he struggled to say 'I shall do nothing of
the kind!' the old timidity checked his tongue. It would be
wiser—more cautious—one never knew what the consequences
of resistance would be—to temporize.

'I've done nothing else since Curtal died. Nothing else. But
I've done it at leisure, meditatively; not with the mortification
you seem to imagine. You're too impatient. You can't understand the vagary of an old man's reminiscence.'

'I understand perfectly,' was the toe-tapping rejoinder.

'I think not. An aphorist I read in my youth—no doubt
Thompson forced him on me—said "We only understand what
already exists within ourselves". That's not true, of course;
everything exists there; but it's half-true. Excuse me! These
events don't frequent your mind; you deduce them, or you rely
on hearsay. I know them at first-hand. That's the contrast I
notice in reading the work of every contemporary historian. . . .'

It was like throwing a stone into a crevasse. Not even echo
followed. After listening awhile, he resumed:

'I've told you about my first meeting with Curtal, about my
grandmother's legacy, and our broadsheet. About Key and
Thompson. Less about Ruddock, because he lived his own
curious detached life, always gay, rather wise, producing what
we thought agreeable trivialities which I'm told are now considered comic masterpieces. . . .'

He had not, while speaking, missed White's irritability. It
indicated dislike of prolixity and evasiveness. Well, prolixity
should be an old man's privilege; to this young man age had no
privileges. Impatience caused a sharp injunction:

'I'm not interested at the moment in Ruddock.'

Ah! He wasn't a Ruddock enthusiast! His preference was for
the abnormal and cloacal. Well, then, what, in those early days,

came next? Great activity, of course. A struggle in the band for supremacy; career preoccupying each one of them; vigorous argument over snatched meals among an ever-widening crowd of youngsters, with Curtal and himself the protagonists, deep in bitter but fraternal rivalry. Young men who slipped out of the circle, into limbo. Young women, from the frivolous to the ravenous, the pretty-pretty versifiers to the be-spectacled earnest, from the intellectually pretentious, to the hot-eyed would-be-free-living. An unholy conglomeration!

Of them all, only Sally Raikes stayed in his mind. Sally, who had all the loveliness in the world. She stood apart in his, as in Curtal's, thoughts. He loved and wrote poems to her, walked beside her, talked, was baffled by her April moods, which he now saw as irreconcilable uncertainties. Curtal was ever with them, a sort of *alter ego*, shouting him down, showing off, rudely bullying Sally because that was the only way he knew of making love, and giving all the signs of preposterous jealousy. Sally must often have laughed and cried, in secret, the little flirt! And yet, was the jealousy so preposterous? Sally had travelled many miles in old age to attend the Service in Curtal's memory. Sally had not made her presence known to himself.

How significant that was! No, no; it meant only that a live dog was more embarrassing to an elderly woman regretting her youth than a dead lion who could not reproach her. She had wept in talking to those girls. She had spoken of Curtal's goodness to her. He was not going to confess an old love to this inquisitor. Curtal had not done so: that was a sign of decency, and a cue.

'I've thought,' murmured Stanhope. 'I did not then know your mother.'

'You met her,' was the frigid reminder.

'Did I? Where was that? Oh, as one of many, perhaps. I never knew her until after she was married to Thompson.'

'You met her long before then. At a house in Hampstead. She said you turned your back on her because she was neither titled nor influential. When you found Curtal was attracted to her, you became actively hostile. You, Curtal, and Thompson were all there. You three, and a girl named Raikes.'

Stanhope's pulse quickened at Sally's name. The rest did not trouble him.

'No recollection,' he calmly replied.

'You forget the party?'

'I vaguely remember that we sometimes went to a house in Hampstead. Possibly lodgings in a house? A flaccid woman poet who wore a sort of medieval costume, and gave us the most abominable coffee I ever tasted. Curtal at that time preferred beer. He was in the beer and elephantine pipe stage. He always whispered to me: "Let's go somewhere and have a real drink: I've poisoned the aspidistra." '

The anecdote was wasted.

'That was the house. The poet was Rosa Channing. My mother was there every time you went. She served the coffee; brought it to you. She didn't make it. You always watched Curtal if he spoke to her; interrupted them; hustled him away. It was because of his friendship for her, which you disapproved, that you fought.'

Stanhope was aghast at this travesty. Did he faintly recall a sullen slouching girl whose hand shook as she forced dripping crockery upon him?

'What a ridiculous story!'

'You say it's untrue?'

'Every word of it.'

'You fought: why, if it wasn't over her?'

Stanhope gave a great sigh.

'Mr White, you've discovered a mare's nest. I'm surprised at you. I've said I don't remember meeting your mother until after her marriage. If she handed round the coffee, I was too much concerned with the danger to my clothes—which in those days were important to me—to look at the bearer. Certainly I never at any time saw Curtal taking notice of a young woman, and I never dissuaded him from speaking to anybody. One didn't. As for the fight, I took a knife from a dangerously drunken man, as you'd have done in my place.'

'You hustled him away at the height of Thompson's funeral. That was a callous and degrading performance.'

Thompson's funeral! Lightning struck Stanhope's memory. He heard Curtal's voice: 'For God's sake, let's get away.' . . . 'Why, in God's name, did she have to do that?' It was a cry of horror at an outrage upon the dead. Curtal had not confessed it at the time; he had not told White about it; but his disgust had been unmistakable. He was done with Hester from that instant.

Stanhope was no longer fainting; no longer old and bewildered; but clear-sighted as an eagle. Everything was in focus. Hester Thompson's distorted vision of himself had been that of insanity.

Ungifted, solitary, unattractive, with swarthy skin and a mass of lank coarse black hair, she must in her teens have written melancholy poems about earth and corpses and lost love, and dreamed of herself as the reincarnation of Emily Brontë. That was why she haunted the lady in Hampstead, whose name, until White pronounced it, he had been unable to recall. The lady wished to establish a *salon*; but, being poor and commonplace, she made her gatherings the most mopish coffee-parties imaginable. She was a bore in search of identity. Oh, terrible! Terrible!

So Hester had been there. He remembered only the urgency of Curtal's appeals to himself to come away. 'I must have a proper drink; this stuff's poison! Come on, Graham! I'm going!'

Naturally, Hester, infatuated by Curtal's rough physical strength, translated crude longing into romantic terms. Curtal was the answer to brooding prayer. 'Send me, O God, a passionate lover!' With such a lover, imprisoned genius would be freed. She would become a great poet, a great novelist, a great and celebrated woman.

'For God's sake let's get away, Graham; or I shall cat all over this greenery-yallery carpet!'

That was Curtal's whisper; she had seen it as his protest against an enemy's effort to separate them. She deepened the impression by self-inflicted torment. 'He didn't look at me this evening. He went without saying goodbye. It's Graham Stanhope. That sneering creature makes him go. I wish I could kill Graham Stanhope, the brute!'

But it was really: 'For God's sake let's go, Graham. Get away from this stink of sour milk and poetic flatulence!'

Neither had noticed the bringer of slop. The noticing was all done by a shy, burning, black-haired mute, in love with the king of beasts.

Then Thompson, looking for somebody to impress with his

long words and marked books, must have advanced upon the
intense and inarticulate coffee-bearer, exhorting, complimenting;
'Without flattery, I must confess . . . noble lines, worthy of our
greatest poetesses, Sappho, Elizabeth Barrett, Ella Wheeler
Wilcox. . . .' How obvious it all was; how close to common
pattern!

At some time she probably despaired of Curtal. Indifference
or distaste had been too evident. Thompson, good-hearted,
ridiculous fellow, offered incense, pomposity, and, as she thought,
solace and a position in the literary world. Perhaps even entry
upon a love-life as grand and squalid—but she wouldn't consider
it squalid—as George Sand's. . . .

The marriage. Disappointment. Thompson probably recited
Emerson and Helps in bed. No greatness. No grand amour. A
weekly struggle with inflated language; enough sense to know that
fustian was Thompson's only wear. Years of boredom and failure
to attract other men; until, as Thompson collapsed and his
friends gathered in loyalty, she made opportunities for being
alone with them and hinting at her sufferings and needs. Precious
moments! Precious half-hours! 'Do tell me . . . I rely so much on
you. . . .' She had used these very words to himself, the liar!

Curtal back again, famous, powerful, at the height of his
sexual prefulgence, none too selective in his amours. Curtal, the
fool, seeing himself as the stallion who gave women what all
women wanted, staying longer than the rest, ranting, being encouraged to do so much more than rant, while she, with Thompson in bed in the room above, desperately wooed.

What point had they reached before that spied-upon interview at which Curtal laughed so much? Was she still struggling
to win him or was she exulting in triumph? Whatever triumph
she had, of which this boy was the living proof, must have been
short. Curtal was never held for long. He'd thrown her over
before the funeral; but the funeral had been the last straw. 'Why,
in God's name, did she have to do that? . . . Let's go, Graham; I
can't stand this!' The appeal, the ejaculation, became in retrospect poignant cries of aversion which no woman can combat.

She hadn't understood. Too stupid. All she knew was that
Curtal had disappeared with Graham Stanhope, shaming her
before the mourners. Therefore Graham Stanhope had destroyed
her happiness, and was a villain.

How odd that she had never, apparently, hated Curtal. What was there in Curtal that made women keep on adoring him in spite of every treachery?

In the seconds of renewed and heightened dislike of Hester, Stanhope had time to indulge in the pity of mental health for mental sickness. The poor she-devil! In imparting to this son of hers a hatred which education had converted into intellectual disdain, she had found relief from misery. Poor creature! What a bore! Had Curtal supported her? Paid the boy's school-fees? It was probable enough. Could one ask such a thing?

With new zest, he sat up in the chair and met White's curious scrutiny almost with radiance. He had been for a long journey into the previously unknown, a journey taken at such speed, and with such conscious insight, that he was greatly stimulated.

'Mr White, I shall say nothing unkind of your mother. She suffered much more than I knew. But when women are unhappy they always look outside themselves for the cause. Sometimes they bring wild charges. Hester did that. She was mistaken in all she told you. In every detail. She built something from—may I use the word again?—misinterpretation. Curtal, the real villain of the piece, escaped. I told you he did so. She couldn't believe he did it from his own impulse. The more she suffered, the more she believed me responsible. I wasn't. I knew nothing about it. Do I really look like Curtal's evil genius, Mr White? Or anybody's evil genius?'

His hands were uplifted and wide apart; his noble head high-lighted and softened by a pale smile.

'You look like an old man skipping for joy, Mr Stanhope,' said White, unmoved.

'Oh, not for joy,' protested Stanhope. 'In conscious innocence. I think I must have convinced you of that.'

'We have different notions of innocence. You deny my mother's story; that's all. I'm not prepared to accept your self-portrait of a benevolent simpleton. Also, you seem so relieved that I suspect you thought I should ask you about something else altogether.'

'I was afraid you might do so,' confessed Stanhope.

'Yet your conscience, you said, was clear.'

'As the day, Mr White. Regarding Curtal. Regarding your unhappy mother, whom I newly see as deserving of pity.'

White's severity did not relax.

'What if I don't accept your clear conscience? What if I put to you other matters that you can't evade?'

'I shall remind you of the time. And that your pretext for calling on me is not the investigation of my sins, but an inquiry into part of Curtal's life. I've answered your questions; I've disposed of a few slanders; that ought to be enough.'

He was not as bold as he pretended to be. The hands were again pressed together before him; the voice was less steady than he could have wished. When he saw John White contemplating him with some of the old derision, he added:

'I've had a long life. My memory is crowded with impressions of men and women. But that memory is a solitary incommunicable feast. I won't share it with you.'

'Women.' White seized the word as a cat seizes a mouse, thereby throwing Stanhope, who was vulnerable on the subject of one woman, into confusion. He waited anxiously.

TWENTY-SEVEN

Curtal's Message

BUT first he attempted mild bluster.

'Women,' he said. 'For example, your friend Mrs Pinchin, who lunched with me today. I liked her. Whether I shall like the manuscript she left with me is another matter. I'd hoped to look at it tonight; but your visit . . .'

He stole a glance at White, quizzical enough, but full of anxiety. Sally, he hoped, was disposed of; she could remain in the recesses of his mind. Gertrude was another matter. He dreaded to hear her name profaned. That, in his present over-excited state, would break his nerve; and because mention of her would break his nerve she now haunted his thoughts.

'Yes,' agreed White, abstractedly. 'She's a good little soul.'

'Curtal didn't greatly care for good little souls,' ventured Stanhope, longing to hear Martin, whom he thought of as Time's wingéd chariot. 'I have a fellow-feeling for them.'

'You imagine they'll give you less trouble,' said White. 'A common error. Curtal was more adventurous.'

Stanhope, having known Curtal, as he believed, through and through, was amused by this further misconception. No man had been more pursued by, and more incessantly in flight from, the predacious female. Sally was an exception. There he was Nimrod, and she the elusive game. Having failed in his one love through too-alarming vigour, he was ever the prey of huntresses. What a ridiculous figure! But it was obvious that colossal vanity would prevent him from confessing his ridiculousness to a son.

John White, meanwhile, added:

'Eliza Pinchin is a very obstinate, tenacious creature who happens to have married a man of extraordinarily strong will.'

'You interest me very much. I should like you to tell me about him. Her ideas on Cowper, most tenaciously held, sounded unconvincing.'

'They're probably absurd. But you won't tell her so.'

'I shouldn't dream of it.'

'That's what I meant.'

The words were aggressive. Stanhope mildly countered them.

'She spoke very kindly of you.'

'She knows nothing about me.'

'Yes? I assume it's not a simple study. She took a sort of potted survey, at lunch, of Lionel Pride, who was here. She had formed some previous impression of him. With help, I understood. He played up to that impression.'

Stanhope, by producing a red-herring, hoped to provoke at least one caustic remark about Lionel; but he was disappointed. White gave him a measuring, cautioning stare, and ignored the herring. This, which could be contrasted with Lionel's reaction, was a sign of quality.

'Women,' repeated White, bringing them back to his own subject. 'We haven't much time; but I wanted to ask you about Curtal's wife. You knew her, I suppose?'

Stanhope shuddered, unseen.

'Cora? Yes, I knew her.' He was cautious. 'What did Curtal tell you?'

'I want your opinion.'

'It's hard to give one in a vacuum, as it were. You never saw her; she made no impact—I think that's the contemporary word?—on her age; she's been dead for many years. If you would tell me what Curtal said of her, I could fill in the gaps. She's not a person I should wish to talk much about.'

'You didn't approve of her,' suggested White.

'She made scenes. I detest scenes. She wanted me to side with her in the rows she started at table. There were violent swearing matches. I could compete with neither of them.'

White seemed to digest the information.

'What was she like to look at?'

'Oh, taller than Curtal. Stout. Florid. Vehemently jealous. A sort of over-sexed hysterical fishwife. An advocate of hanging, shooting, a helot class; and maddened by Curtal's equally violent humanism. Was it humanism? Or inhumanity? I never quite understood.'

'No, you wouldn't be able to understand,' commented John White.

'Do you think Curtal did?'

He was delighted to see his guest flush. That was a score! But again White ignored an inconvenient counter-question.

'I gather you disliked her very much.'

'Disliked? No. I felt absolute horror.'

'Was that simply because Curtal had married her?'

'What?'

The question was exactly repeated. White was harking back to his mother's silly attribution of sinister power. Or was there some strange modern notion behind his resistance? This extraordinary preoccupation with homosexuality? Stanhope, who belonged to a heterosexual generation, laughed.

'Well, no; except that he'd made an obviously grotesque mistake. One of his innumerable grotesque mistakes.'

'You made no grotesque mistakes?'

It was intended as a dagger-thrust; and to a mind already distraught by hidden knowledges it was in fact a sharp and terrible dagger-thrust. Stanhope felt his heart stop beating and then wildly fill his breast.

'We'll stick to Curtal, shall we?' he suggested, very coolly. But the effort to conceal agitation made cruel demands upon both will and body. 'He was trying to domesticate a hyena.'

'Why do you suppose he married her?'

Stanhope believed that he knew the answer. It was: 'To slam the door in your maniacal mother's face!' Should he deliver it? This young man had not spared him. And yet, at a pinch, he had not the courage, or the vindictiveness, to repay evil with evil.

'Something else I never quite understood,' he ironically replied.

White, however suspicious, seemed unable to go farther. His eyes moved in quick thought.

'What was their home like?' he asked. 'Was it the place he had in St John's Wood—where he died?'

'Yes. She chose all that ugly furniture. She wasn't a bad housekeeper. He was better fed than he'd ever been. But his work suffered.'

'The bad middle period, you'd call it? He was reaching after new ideas; grasping the importance of economics and mathematics; but brilliantly adapting them to his own use. . . . You seem amused. Why?'

Stanhope made no attempt to conquer his smile.

'We're far out of my depth, Mr White. The secluded waters of pure Art, you know. I didn't recognize my poor friend. Being familiar with his domestic circumstances—never was the slang "trouble and strife" more apt—I felt he was suffering from strained nerves, and heading for a breakdown. You think he was grappling with the higher abstractions. I won't argue as to that.'

'At the time, you ridiculed him pretty spitefully in various articles. He told me so. He showed me the articles.'

'Ha-ha! He'd kept them, then?'

'As documents. He told me he hadn't minded them.'

'He minded them very much. Adverse criticism made him furious. I have several of his letters——'

'Also kept!' interpolated White, with meaning.

'As documents! They were very violent. I always returned soft answers.'

'Yes, and repeated the offence. Characteristic, wasn't it? You did more than that, I think?'

'I can't remember. When he was at his most acrimonious, we met in the street. Baker Street, I think. Or Bond Street. It was very crowded, I know. He was in a passion. Marched up and said: "Look here, I've a good mind to give you a thrashing!" I said: "Not before all these people, Tom. You'd be run in; and I should have to bail you out. Most ignominious. Think of the headlines!" So he put his great fist away, took my arm, and forgot his passion. The headlines had frightened him. All headlines, you see, had to be flattering.'

'Don't you think he showed great good-nature?'

'He was like a not very well-trained dog. A great deal of barking and stertorous snarling; but he always ran away in the end—still barking.'

'What did you do?'

'Oh, I ran away, too.'

'What a pusillanimous pair!'

'I ran before anything happened. I was very swift. Nobody

noticed. But Curtal, for all his Bobadil swagger, had to bolt in panic, because things had got too hot for him.'

'From women, you mean?' demanded that inexorable crow's voice.

'That would be true of Curtal,' answered Stanhope, smoothly.

'From my mother, for example? That's your story, isn't it?'

'It's one I've never told,' sighed Stanhope, with rampant pulse, 'from chivalry.'

A long time passed. Perhaps it was a minute; but it seemed an hour. Stanhope was taut with anticipation of further attack. He assumed that White was busy adjusting Hester's lessons to another view of his father. At the end of silence, the harsh voice resumed:

'There was another woman I wanted to ask you about.'

Stanhope shivered.

'What woman is this?' he demanded, boldly.

'Somebody he called "Henrietta".'

The name was so unexpected, and in view of his fear caused so great a relief, that Stanhope heard his old legs give an audible crack. His next sensation was one of surprise. Had Curtal known Henrietta? This was something new. How strange that he should have been thinking of her only an hour or two ago. Was it an hour, or a day?

'He wanted me to tell you about her,' continued White. 'He said she'd talked to him about you. "Quite a topic," he told me with immense laughter.'

The mention of laughter made Stanhope wince, as always. The laughter would be diabolic.

'I remember one woman of that name,' he said, carefully. 'Many years ago, when I was young. Not a particularly estimable character; but one of the patrons a young man collects.'

'That would be the woman. He called her a fine lady, as common as dirt, with plenty of money, and a greed for scalps.'

'Yes,' murmured Stanhope, reaching back into antiquity for a forgotten sensation, and using a more discreet euphemism. 'I was once the sort of rising star she cultivated. So, of course, was Curtal. Did she patronize him, too? I'm not surprised. By then, probably, I'd been cast aside as not quite the newest thing. She came back, I remember; but I had my pride, as they say. Also, I'd found other, and stauncher, patrons.'

He thought with tolerance of Henrietta, her sudden frost, her impudent re-summons, and his discovery that her taste, which at first had impressed him, was nine-tenths bogus. She must have heard that he'd been taken up by Lucy Chard, and that Adelaide was not ill-disposed towards him. Such omens would cause her to think again.

'Curtal despised patrons. He called them brain-suckers. They still abound, the hostesses who feed on lions'-flesh. He warned me against them.'

'I do the same. But you already have no need of them.'

'I was warned early. It was one of the things he said the first time we ever talked.'

Stanhope felt strong curiosity. Had Curtal all along acknowledged the paternity? Dodged it? He'd avoid Hester; but wouldn't he feel a ridiculous boyish pride in having a son? The Zoo; Kensington; the British Museum? 'I should have done so!' he whispered to himself. What had Hester's attitude been? Not to speak of the technique of tears and sullenness!

'Ah, yes. When was that?'

'I went to him when my mother died. She told me to go then. I was sixteen. I'd seen him before, heard him lecture, and even met him, though not with her.'

'How interesting,' sighed Stanhope. Had Curtal paid for the boy's schooling? Had there been something every month in Hester's bank? Curtal wasn't stingy. 'How interesting! And that first encounter: how did it go?'

'Wonderfully. I already worshipped him; but to be face to face, talking . . .'

'Yes. Yes?'

Could it be true that the stern face had softened? Stanhope was so eager to know this that he half-turned, jerking his legs again, bringing the knees close together by an abrupt movement. This movement checked whatever White was about to add. There was to be no more about that wonderful meeting. Instead, he asked another question.

'You'd say Henrietta had a lot of affairs?' he demanded abruptly.

Stanhope, sighing in lament, shrugged.

'Quite platonic, I assume,' said he.

'Not in Curtal's case.' Ah! Ah! He was all attention. 'They used to go for walks in the woods and the moonlight.'

'I remember. She enjoyed both. Very charming for her escorts.'

'Whom she tantalized?'

'Whom she tantalized.'

'She accused him of raping her. He was dismissed with a tremendous show of indignation. But the indignation, he said, passed fairly quickly.'

Stanhope was breathless, whispering:

'The braggart! He told you that?'

'She came again. He must promise, she said . . .'

Lost in a dream, Stanhope envisaged a summer night in the woods. A whole situation repeated itself, with the difference that Curtal had presumed farther, more acceptably, than he had done. Yes, she had meant him to be carried away by lust; and, from timidity, he had disappointed her. But she always came again.

'Worthless woman,' he exclaimed. 'I see her now. That must have been great excitement.' Curiosity led him to turn to White. 'Did he go back?'

'No,' said White.

'Good! And yet—poor creature!'

'Why so?'

'The knowledge of contempt. Perhaps not; she was insensitive. There was nothing genuine about her—even indignation.'

'You endorse what Curtal said. He wanted me to ask if your experience was the same as his own. He had some reason; he didn't explain. Superstition? Something she'd said to him.'

Stanhope had been accused by this man, and by Curtal, of salacious inquisitiveness. He could have retorted that, in another, such inquisitiveness was always inexcusable.

'Quite different,' he answered. 'But to a young man with his eyes on the far mountains she had a social use.'

He planned to think of Henrietta when White was gone, to consider her walks with Curtal in the woods and the moonlight, and, of course, her simulated indignation.

The clock chimed. He was suddenly alert. This last period had gone more quickly than its predecessor; more quickly and, on the whole, less alarmingly. He tried to detect his heartbeats.

If he was right, they were more rapid than they should have been, and less regular. He was aware of exhaustion. But, as the hour struck, he could listen for Martin; and after Martin, and Meredith's damnable tablets, he would be done with torment. Pray God he slept quietly!

'No more dreams,' he whispered to himself.

Alas, confidence that he was at the end of an ordeal was un-justified.

'You said your conscience was clear about Curtal,' observed White, as if in afterthought, and with no threat in his tone. 'You also spoke of his angry letters to you. Did you quarrel much?'

'He was always quarrelling.' Stanhope looked at the glowing fire, and began to muse. Yes, he was now very tired indeed, suffering from reaction. There could be no doubt that in the absence of immediate strain his heart was engaged in its own inconsequential gallop. He hoped that Martin would arrive quickly. Listen! Was that the door, and the rustle of her petti-coat?

No; some glowing coal had tumbled like a child's house of cards, making a new pattern amid the red glow. The pattern was beautiful. One could imagine castles and caverns; the inner marvels to be seen in cracks in the outer shell of Vesuvius.

'Always quarrelling. Generally with his own shadow, or the echo of his own voice. It wasn't a sweet voice, you remember. It had an unpleasant vibrance. What Dryden called "the harsh cadence of a rugged line". Part of his maladjustment, I suppose; his crude energy. Did you realise that he had no ear for music? It was so with other famous men—Burke, Fox, Pitt, and Johnson. . . .'

As he spoke, his own soft and tender voice faded. He heard it coming from a great, a weary distance, like the murmur, so much loved in childhood, of a shell. These vagaries of reference were all indications of an over-strained mind.

'You implied that you returned disarming answers,' suggested White. 'You had other weapons, hadn't you?'

'I had the armour of pride,' answered Stanhope, drowsily. 'Curtal had no pride. He was all headlong ambition.'

'A mixture of brain and energy and high motive.'

'What high motive? These leaders of thought are all sustained by egotism.' Stanhope could not repress a yawn. He felt himself gradually sinking into lethargy, and listening for Martin as a sleepy little choirboy listens for the vicar's pause and those blessed words: 'Now to God the Father, God the Son . . .' 'If you read their biographies you find that they were as subject to jealousy and humiliation as the least of so-called lesser men.'

'As subject to jealousy,' agreed White, in a sharper tone.

'To earthly cares. Read the letters of Mozart, whose music is heavenly and whose soul was clay . . .' drowsed Stanhope.

'I can tell you're tired,' exclaimed White. 'You said jealousy. I'm anxious to establish one more point. It's this . . .'

'No point can ever be established beyond cavil.' Stanhope sank lower. His hands crept to his cheeks, to his mouth. He knew that rescue was close at hand. 'If once you could get mankind to accept a single thing as universally true, Curtal's bosh would be justified. But you can't, and his bosh . . .' He found it impossible to complete the sentence, which trailed into inarticulateness.

TWENTY-EIGHT

Rescue

'For you,' White seemed to be saying, 'philosophy has no meaning. We grant that. I'm not proposing to discuss anything abstract. That would be useless at this time.'

'At all times.' He could not positively hear the words he spoke. They were like the oracular mouthings of a drunken man. He was at the end of all intellectual activity. 'As useless as fretwork or serial music. Forgive me if I seem unappreciative of what I am sure is disinterested pursuit of truth. I'm sure of that. But when one is very old, and has had incomprehensible dreams, and a long and tiring day with visitors all the time, Venables and my darlings and Lionel and Mrs . . . But I told you about her, didn't I? Her husband's a friend of yours; and she—was it you or I who called her a good little soul?'

'You told me some of it,' he heard. In spite of illumination, the face of his visitor was now hard to distinguish, and the voice which reached him was distorted. 'Not all. I mustn't tire you with too much . . .'

'Not tire me?' repeated Stanhope. He was extraordinarily amused. 'But you've done it, with your examination and cross-examination, as if I were in the dock for some crime. You've done it.'

'I'm sorry,' said White. He might have used that tone to somebody he'd brushed against on the stairs. 'I'll be very brief. But— *à propos* the question of Curtal's angry letters, and, of course, what you said about jealousy. . . .'

'Did I say anything about jealousy?'

'Curtal's bosh; don't you remember?'

'I couldn't possibly remember all the bosh he wrote and talked in the course of his life. I've tried to tell you about him. . . .'

'You've told me a great deal. I'm grateful. But—*à propos* the question——'

'Yes, you said that.' Stanhope felt naughty satisfaction in pulling his interlocutor up short. 'The question?'

'—I want to show you one letter; to ask what led up to it, and what was in your mind when you wrote it. The letter's no more than forty words. It won't take you——'

'When I wrote? A letter of mine?'

'A letter of yours. About Curtal. Somebody found it among papers belonging to Hugh Babbacombe. . . .'

'Babbacombe? How astonishing! I used to know him. He's dead, isn't he?'

'Stone dead. Dust. Twenty years ago.' The words were uttered with spleen. There was a rustle. A yellow sheet was held, gleaming, towards him.

He thought: 'That's not Curtal's hand, is it?' Something in the colour of it, or in the projection of the knuckles, was extremely like; but he was so tired that he could not answer his own question. Nor could he understand why he should be asked to read what looked like old parchment, when they were supposed to be speaking of Curtal.

'What is it?' he asked, taking the letter. 'I'm afraid I can't read it now. My sight. I find that at night I grow . . . Perhaps you'll leave it with me, to be looked at tomorrow? Not that I expect to have much . . . I have a manuscript by that friend of yours. . . .'

'Fewer than fifty words,' insisted White. 'I want your opinion of them.'

Stanhope looked vainly at the paper.

'Did you say Hugh Babbacombe? I thought he was dead. Did he write this to you?'

'No. You wrote it to him.'

'Oh, yes, I remember you said something of the kind. At one time I knew him rather well. He was senior to me—a scholar . . . At one time I thought he'd be Chancellor; but these things are often bedevilled. I don't know if you've read Mark Pattison's autobiography? You get the whole thing . . . Babbacombe had affinities with Pattison. But he did me a number of good turns. Very loyal, you know, to a man of his own college. A great man in his way. Not your way, of course. His line was classics—not psychology or humanism. Should I say Godwinism? One could say Tolstoyism, or Kropotkinism, I suppose? You don't agree? Babbacombe had a vast contempt for other scholars in his own field. But that's customary, among scholars.'

'You wrote this letter to Babbacombe. It was about Curtal.'

Stanhope attempted to give the letter back to its owner.

'Yes; thank you very much for showing it to me.'

'Read it!'

'Oh, I'm afraid . . . Will you read it?'

White accepted what he was handed. He read with acid distinctness.

'It says: "*My dear Hugh, a menacing rumour reaches me via McComb that there is some thought of giving Curtal an honorary doctorate. Do stop this, if you can. Quite apart from the ephemeral nature of C's work, his moral character is execrable. Yours ever, Graham.*" '

The letter was folded and put away.

'Do you remember writing that?' White asked.

Stanhope could not comprehend the air of triumph. Groping vaguely for an explanation of it, and in the past for the letter's meaning, he did not immediately realize his sin.

'No recollection at all,' he replied.

'It is your letter?'

'You tell me so. It may be.'

White seemed amazed at a criminal indifference.

'You said you had nothing on your conscience about Curtal. You never did him an injury. This is the honour he coveted; and you prevented him from receiving it. Isn't that an injury? Can you wonder that he never forgave the treachery?'

It was terribly difficult to understand such indignation. It was terribly difficult to understand anything at all. There was a letter, apparently written in confidence upon a forgotten occasion; and in some way the letter had come into Curtal's hands. Surely whatever 'treachery' had been committed lay with the person who gave it to Curtal? But had it been given? Or sold? Or stolen? Had one written it? Had Curtal received the degree? All was vague, and the noise in one's ears might have been that of waves splashing in summer upon a sandy coast.

'I don't know,' he slowly murmured. 'I have no power to link the events. Why should you have this letter? Why should Curtal have had it? Why should Babbacombe have shown it, or parted with it? Was the doctorate granted? You see it's all incomprehensible.'

'That won't do,' said White, emphatically. 'You're evading the point. Here was something to be offered; and you, Curtal's friend, did your best to stop the offer. You succeeded. You afterwards received a doctorate yourself. Curtal kept a newspaper cutting with a photograph of you in your robes, walking in procession. He showed it to me. It made him laugh.'

'He always laughed,' agreed Stanhope. 'It was to hide his jealousy.'

'Jealousy!' exclaimed White. 'What is this letter but proof of your own?'

Lethargy had settled upon Stanhope's brain.

'I don't understand,' he muttered. 'I don't understand. Of course one should set the honour of one's University above the accommodation of a friend. It's a question of principle, of a standard . . . a principle . . .' He yawned deeply. His head lolled. He saw the room as the old study in his father's house; and yawned again.

White had risen.

'All this is most unsatisfactory,' he said. 'Of course, if I write the biography, I probably shan't mention it; but I think you owe Curtal's memory some better explanation . . .'

He stopped. Stanhope smiled in the midst of his faintness. Both had heard the door open. Evidently White had seen Martin. . . .

But was it Martin? That couldn't be Martin's voice. It was too clear, too brisk, too authoritative.

'Good evening, Mr White. I'm sorry that you must go now. Mr Stanhope has had a most exhausting day; and this is his bedtime. Doctor's orders.'

White seemed to be petrified. No more an avenger, he was, however irritated, incapable of resistance. He stared. He bowed. He was exactly like Curtal when Curtal was disconcerted. And in that moment of boyishness he became, for the first time, attractive.

'Couldn't I have a few more minutes?' he pleaded.

'No. I've already given you five minutes' grace. This must be the end of your chat. I'm very sorry.'

Who was speaking? It was not Martin, who would have fought in vain against her feeling of respect for a young man of determined bearing. It was somebody courageous and charming. Stanhope, incredulously recognizing the crisp voice and manner, yet marvelled at Jackie's presence in his house at this hour. Hadn't she gone long ago? Why had she not gone? Why was she here? Oh, it didn't matter. Thank God! Thank God!

He lay back, smiling, with his eyes closed.

'I hear an angel!' he whispered to himself. 'A human angel; but with all the appurtenances!'

Whether at sight of that smile or not, White was reanimated by his desire to strike, to wound, to frighten an old man whom he had been taught by his mother to hate.

'Then I must obey,' he said. He bent over Stanhope. 'You understand Curtal's feeling. He didn't forgive that letter; but he treasured it and he laughed with the greatest good-humour at the writer. Not, I assure you, with any jealousy. He was too great a man to feel jealousy. And I must mention, as a last word, that he told me, if I ever saw you, as he urged me to do, to give you his love, and to say that he'd written—I think he said "written"—something you'd never see, that would do you justice with posterity. You don't care for posterity; but it will be here, in time; and Curtal will have helped it. Now I must go. Please forgive me if I've pestered you. It's been most interesting.'

'Most interesting,' echoed Stanhope, in agreement. But he hardly knew what words he used.

There was a movement behind him. They must now be at the door. Straining his ears for the last sound of his visitor, he heard Jackie Boothroyd say, in a low voice:

'You have a heavy responsibility, Mr White.'

To which he believed that John White, quite as low, but more roughly, answered: 'He's perfectly well able to look after himself.'

The door was closed. Only it seemed that there lingered upon the air four other words, whispered so breathlessly that one less acute of hearing than himself would never have caught them ... 'those who love him. . . .'

TWENTY-NINE

The Kiss

ALMOST inanimate, he lay back in the chair with his old thin legs extended, and his hands resting limply upon them. He could not recover from surprise at Jackie's appearance, and several times ejaculated the word 'Well!' in a long-drawn whisper.

'She'll come back, and tell me,' he murmured contentedly, at last. 'They always come back. Who was it said that? Curtal, or myself? It doesn't matter. . . . This wouldn't be a bad way to die, you know. Sitting in front of the fire, very tired, waiting for Jackie's return. Who would be sorry? That word "love" wasn't meant for me to hear. Too low. Perhaps it wasn't said at all? I imagined it, from sentimental longing. The last person to use it sincerely was Gertrude. She was all sincerity.'

Thinking he felt tears upon his cheeks, he fumbled for a handkerchief, and dabbed his face, continuing to hold the handkerchief as something reassuringly tangible. Self-pity for the ordeal he had endured, as well as hunger for affection, was responsible for the tears.

'I don't expect they were tears,' he thought. 'A pricking of dazzled eyes. I must have these lights turned down. But not too far, in case I imagine figures in the shadows. As, last night, I imagined White and dear old Ruddock. I don't want any more . . . hallucinations!'

He then called to mind some of the things he had told White, or learned from White, whose physical presence was forgotten in the wonderful silence of relief. White, sped on his way by the adorable and inexorable Jackie, must have gone out into dark streets, where he belonged, to spread his poison upon the town. The atmosphere of this familiar room was warm with serenity. All around were his beloved books. He did not look above the fire-

place, lest he should meet the cold gaze of one to whom 'love' was
utterly plebeian.

White would never reappear. Wasn't it strange that a man
unknown to him until a few hours ago should dominate thoughts
awhile, and then, abruptly and permanently, fall from his orbit!
That happened throughout life, which was made up of meetings,
brief intimacies, and disappearances. A woman once wrote a
novel, entitling it from lines—were they Tennyson's, or some
lesser poet's?—about 'ships that pass in the night'. Men were like
ships. They were loaded with merchandise; but through them,
also, ran winding corridors which led to cabins where a thousand
selves lurked unseen. Until, of course, they were brought out, like
hideous malformed rats and maggots, by the psychologists. Ha-ha!

He mustn't drool on like this. It suggested that, like so many
who had taxed their brains by too unintermittent use, he was
failing. This had been a long day, beginning, as far as he could
remember, with the Memorial Service to Curtal, which had
induced strange moods; but it was now at an end, and he was safe.
Jackie would be back again in a minute, and tell him why she was
so welcomely here at all, and Martin would bring him a tiny
supper to nibble as a mouse nibbles crumbs. He would go, un-
aided, to bed, and take the tablets Meredith had sent.

The tablets, he was assured, would make him sleep in peace,
and although he was bound to disbelieve in Meredith's skill in
psychiatry the fellow no doubt understood narcotics. Therefore
he would sleep. Tomorrow he would awaken to new strength, and
write another page or two of his *magnum opus* on the aristocratic
element in literature. He had been working on this for thirty
years, and he did not dare to confess how little of it was done.
Meanwhile it was not surprising that numbness should creep into
his legs, which were trembling. There! He had pulled them up;
he could see the pointed knees, like a pair of Matterhorns, sticking
up and, he suspected, still quivering.

There was a slight faintness. It was due to reaction. He had
always been subject to faintness after great strain. He wasn't to
worry about it now. But he wished Jackie would come. What was
keeping her?

'I ought not to be left like this,' he thought, grumblingly, 'in
suspense. . . .'

Just as he was beginning to believe his own grumble, he found her beside him. He hadn't heard her. She was always quick and quiet, there and gone again, leaving him exhilarated; as different as possible from Martin, who crept in at the door, like a cat, slowly rustled across the room, and, as she tended the fire, looked angular and ill-corseted. Jackie, for all her quickness, made no noise. There was beautiful rhythm in her movements; she did not glide, nor, like George Meredith's heroines, 'swim', but walked with perfect balance. As light as a fairy, they would say.

He looked up, smiling.

'I was astonished by your very effective entry,' he drowsily observed. 'I've been waiting for you to come and explain it. I expected Martin, of course. But how Martin was transformed . . .'

'I've got rid of that very conceited young man,' she replied quietly. Was it true, as his imagination suggested, that her cheeks were flushed? 'He wanted to ask all sorts of questions.'

'Very different from Mr Venables!' teased Stanhope.

'He's abler than Mr Venables,' she surprisingly retorted; 'but not as agreeable.'

'Yes, I like good manners,' agreed Stanhope. 'Do tell me how you happened to be here to give him the *coup de grâce*.'

'It was quite simple. Martin's rather afraid of him. She'd worked herself up. She telephoned to ask if I could come and do the job. At least, she asked what I thought she should do.'

'A rescue operation organized!' smiled Stanhope. 'What's called, I believe, "good staff work".'

'She'd had words with him before; and he'd been very rude.'

'The fashionable rudeness, my darling.' Stanhope was unaware that in his murmured response he had used the term of endearment; and Jackie gave no sign of having heard it. 'How kind of you to come. I hope you had a taxi, at this time of night.'

'No, I walked. My father walked with me.'

Stanhope's body jerked in excitement.

'Your father! Is he here? Where is he? How much I should like to see him!'

'He's here, in my room; and you're much too tired to see any more people today.'

'But your father!' protested Stanhope. 'Do let me! Just a peep! A "how d'you do?" A shake of the hand. It would do me good.'

She surveyed him with a little concern.

'I don't think you ought to.'

'Yes. Yes. But first, will you pour me out a glass of brandy? I feel a slight chill.'

'Is it only chill? Not faintness?'

It was faintness; but for that, no doubt trained at school in First Aid, she would have offered him water, while he needed brandy. He therefore lied.

'To warm my legs, which are frozen. Your father will warm my heart—as you do!'

Well, now, what was he like? Was he like Jackie? No; shorter than she, and more stocky. She had the modern slim figure, and youthful verve. Her brightness and fresh colour must be from the mother. But Mr Boothroyd was well enough, well enough, and a man to inspire respect.

He was grey-haired, in his late fifties, thin-cheeked, clean-shaven, and with a straight, blunt-ended nose. He did not smile until one's eyes met his, when they gleamed with responsive intelligence and goodwill. He came forward as quietly as his daughter would have done, but with none of her aplomb, shook hands firmly, and when urged to be seated he sat right back in his chair. There was no obsequiousness; he was, and knew himself to be (except in those moments of regretful monologue described by Jackie), part of the backbone of his country. An excellent country, he thought it.

'This is a great pleasure to me, Mr Boothroyd.' Fortified with a not too copious draught of brandy—she must come from a temperate family!—Stanhope was still slightly breathless and conscious of trembling hands and legs. Bad signs! Bad signs! He must not allow Jackie to see them. If he did, she would take his latest and most welcome visitor away at once. 'Your daughter was speaking to me about you this morning. Was it this morning, Miss Boothroyd?' He thought it best to address her with proper formality in face of so dignified a parent.

'You seemed surprised to know that I had a father, Mr Stanhope.'

'Was I?' He remained the arch old man. 'You should say "delighted". But your daughter's very reserved, Mr Boothroyd. It's a good quality. I wonder whether you would care to join me in a drink? You may have heard that I've had a wearying day. I thought brandy would revive me. But there is sherry in the cabinet there. Sherry, and other less admirable stimulants.' His glance at Jackie herself was answered by a shaken head.

'I thank you; but I won't drink anything, sir,' was Mr Boothroyd's answer. 'I've just had my evening meal. My wife and I both appreciate your great kindness to Jacqueline. We have probably heard more about you, than you've heard about us. I'm glad to have an opportunity of thanking you.'

It was a thin, precise voice, highly suited to a grave and dignified man. Stanhope thought he detected, in the intonation rather than the accent, a trace of Scottish. The hand he had shaken was cool and dry. Mr Boothroyd was one to be trusted.

'Your appreciation can't surpass mine, to you and your wife, for lending me so admirable a protectress. She has just rid me of a very tiresome young man. I've been trying to escape him for what seems like a lifetime. That's a particularly apt expression, because he's been cross-examining me about my youth. The son of an old friend, full of his father's genius and his mother's imaginary wrongs. As I get older, I need peace; he was determined that I should have none of it. Your Jackie, on the contrary, assures it.'

'Only by being what Father would consider rudely stern,' said Jackie, who had remained standing.

'Do, please, sit down, Jackie. If you stand, I feel discourteous.'

'You wanted only to say "Hullo" to Father,' she reminded him.

'I haven't said it yet, have I, Mr Boothroyd?'

The father was smiling; a grave smile.

'No, you haven't said it yet, Mr Stanhope,' he agreed.

'Then I shan't say it for a long time. I must keep my word, and also preserve my independence.'

'I have a difficulty at home with that last, Mr Stanhope.'

'You do? Oh, well, we understand each other at once. I was sure we should do so. But I think her kindness must be derived from you. You have a happy home, I know. Now, what's the secret of happiness?'

'If I knew, I should be a philosopher, sir.'

'But you are one! I can tell!'

'I think you flatter me.' The words were quiet, final. He was not to be affected by flattery. He would go his own way through life, with self-respect, without the vulgarity of ambition; and there was no reproof in his rejection of undeserved compliment. His pride in Jackie would be expressed by the merest word of commendation.

Stanhope glanced, smiling, to see whether she congratulated her father upon his refusal. How protective she looked—of them both. Protective with the touching protectiveness of a little girl in charge of her juniors.

'Your father's company is like balm!' he declared.

But she had noticed the trembling, and was alert to the unsteadiness of his voice.

'The best balm of all will be the supper that Martin's bringing the moment we go,' she answered. 'Then Cox will help you to bed. . . .'

'But I don't need Cox!' he expostulated.

'You may be glad of him. As an adjunct. If not, you can send him away. Then you'll sleep soundly, and I shall be here again at nine o'clock tomorrow morning, to find you refreshed and ready for an easy day. I told Mr White he was on no account to come again until you sent for him. He didn't understand, at first; his defect is want of imagination. But in the end he was almost apologetic. He said that in spite of his manner he really cherished you very much.'

'Hm,' murmured Stanhope. 'You don't impersonate Mr White very convincingly. What did he really say?'

'He said he'd always under-rated you.'

'Very handsome. Very handsome. And you answered?'

'That he was extremely impertinent.'

The father had risen to go. He would not have offered his hand; but Stanhope held out his own in sudden affection.

'Good night, Mr Boothroyd. Do come again, when I'm less tired. Do you know the secret of your home? It's something that has temporarily dropped out of the world. I get its ricochet. It's love. Forgive an old man's appalling banality.' He held and shook the firm hand; and as Mr Boothroyd went from the room took Jackie's hand in both his own. 'You've been very good to me today. Not that you're ever otherwise; but that I . . .' The tears of weakness were running down his cheeks. 'I needed it more today, and am very grateful. Don't forget that I thanked you.'

He felt her impulsive kiss upon his brow, could not see her, looked up, and found himself alone.

Alone; but Martin was quickly there with his supper. She drew forward the adjustable reading-desk which served as a supper table, stood back, addressed him.

'I hope you didn't mind me ringing Miss Boothroyd, sir. I thought somebody more his own style would manage the gentleman better than me. I got worked up about it.'

'You did splendidly, Martin; splendidly. Thank you.'

'Thank you, sir. Now you eat your biscuits; and would you like a little more brandy, or something else to drink? I can easily get it; only I thought you'd rather choose what you wanted. Then Cox and me will see you safe in bed with your tablets.'

He sighed, still tear-stricken.

'So kind, Martin. So kind. I'm overwhelmed.'

Not knowing whether she had understood, Stanhope watched her pass beyond his view. He half-blindly crumbled a biscuit, pondering the curious weakness which he had felt since White's going, and the old man's tears which had beset him in the last ten minutes. Was he becoming ga-ga? He was so much affected that the tears continued to flow, despite the pressure of his handkerchief.

'I mustn't let anybody see me like this,' he muttered. 'I should be a laughing-stock!' Downstairs, Martin, Cox, Cook would all be whispering about him, and sniggering at the knowledge that he, the great Graham Stanhope, had no more self-control than a baby! Boothroyd and Jackie, walking home together in happiness, would be amused by a picture of him in senility. 'I'm afraid, Jacqueline,' Mr Boothroyd would say, 'that the old man's only a snivelling sentimentalist, talking about love like a paper for schoolgirls. You'd better get another job, before he drowns himself in tears!'

'Senile,' repeated Stanhope. 'Senile decay. Southey lived for twenty years with a softened brain. I shan't escape. I'd better have died in my prime, if I'm to be destroyed in my old age by a little kindness!'

He remembered the kindness, however, with affection for Jackie, who was as far as possible from sentimentality; and in remembering Jackie he ceased to cry. After a few minutes he began to look back over the long day, imagining her scathing dismissal of White, and passing to Eliza Pinchin, whose book on Cowper must be such rot; and Lionel (he laughed at Lionel with some malice); Meredith, who made him scowl; Mr Venables, of the B.B.C.; his darlings; and, once more, the Boothroyds. Kind, sweet, *young* Jackie! Lucky Boothroyd, to have such a daughter!

That girl would one day marry—he smiled at his own teasing about the attractive Venables—and have children as honest and beautiful as herself. You couldn't talk of national degeneracy while the Jackie Boothroyds were alive and forward-looking. He must ask Jackie more about her tastes in music, art, books; he must emphasize the necessity for keeping your standards high, so that the third-rate, the *faux bon*, the Curtalian half-baked rubbish, never crept into esteem and vitiated judgment. This was something he could do to show his gratitude.

Thought moved back to White, out there in the darkness. Darkness was his element. He had admitted ungenerosity, and the fact of Curtal's admiration; but with reluctance. In after times he would retract his admissions. His mind was not cool, as he thought, but hysterically partisan. What had he said towards the last, when one was so tired as to be hardly sensible of what passed? Something . . . something . . . something . . . Curtal? Oh, yes, a letter; what was it about?

With a struggle, Stanhope partially recovered the words read aloud to him by White. Their aim had been to prevent an extraordinary error of judgment. What had been the point of that reference to unforgiven treachery?

He caught his breath. To Curtal, the intervention, a matter of principle, was personal treachery. Fantastic! The man had coveted an honorary degree. It would have represented a triumph over vested scholastic interests. The fact that it would have made culture ridiculous was, to him, incomprehensible.

'I couldn't have let that happen. Of course, I'm sorry that Curtal should have felt himself aggrieved. How on earth did the letter fall into his hands? Most unfortunate!'

The weary brain ploughed again through these speculations, touched at times with unease or self-defence, but in general scornful of White's insensate filial loyalty. As it went for the twentieth time over the problem of the letter's discovery and effect, words spoken afterwards flew to his attention. He thrust away the improvised supper table, and staggered to his feet.

Good God! What had White said? Wasn't it a message, a laughing, taunting, message from Curtal? To the effect that Curtal had written something that one would never see? Something for posterity? The lampoon! Treachery! Curtal had been one too many for him! This was what he had dreaded all along. It must be stopped. *It must be stopped.* White must instantly be recalled.

In trying to reach the bell, he lost his balance, stumbled, and fell headlong.

'Martin! Martin!'

PART SIX

The Long Day Ends

THIRTY

The First Dream

BLINDING light was followed by the sound of hurried steps and astonishing assembly of faces, larger than life-size, which advanced and receded like those of silent fish in an aquarium, while water swayed and his ears sang. Two faces in particular became as clear as giant masks in carnival procession. One of them was Meredith's; the other was terrifyingly unknown, grey, and very evil.

Hands were laid upon him. He was being roughly tumbled, as he had seen a drunken man being tumbled after a street accident. His body was being raised, carried. He tried to speak, and could not so do. He tried to say: 'You're strangling me. Put me down. I'm not to be treated in this way, like some old sack. I'm Graham Stanhope, I tell you. I won't have that other man here. He has no business here. I'm perfectly in command of my faculties. It's just this strangling . . .'

Then darkness. Every light, every hope, was extinguished.

All physical pain had ceased. The faces, not now close, were still there, a gathering of dim shapes pricked with gem-like piercing eyes. He thought he was encircled by gigantic bulbous rats, and became again a little boy in his grandmother's garden, watching a family of rat-invaders from a neighbouring field. The rats had seen him; they ran about in little short bursts, as if by clockwork, and approached so near that he was panic-stricken lest they should begin to nibble his toes and fingers, and at last consume him altogether. Phrases from stories had prepared him to be terrified of such creatures. 'Gnawed by rats.' 'The flesh eaten; only the bones remained.' 'Bones lay white in the moonlight.' Screaming, he had run towards the house, unable to feel the ground beneath his feet.

Now he could not run, although the rats stared monstrously. There! More frightened than himself, they were gone. No, they had returned, staring as before. But he was no longer being strangled. He was only incapable of all movement. The face of the second man, Meredith's necessary collaborator in a devilish scheme to declare him insane, was not recognizable. It was horribly intent, like the face of an executioner. And farther away the other shadows whispered together, ready to swarm closer as soon as he relaxed the self-control of desperation.

Darkness returned.

It was broken by a tiny light in the distance, such as he had once seen when peeping into a long railway tunnel. He had been taken there by another boy, who ran into the tunnel, yelling for the sake of the echo, while he, a much smaller boy, screamed to him to come away in case a train rushed up behind them and swept them under its wheels. The other boy then dragged him into the tunnel, giggling, and flung him down upon the line, where he lay bruised until reviving strength enabled him to escape. This was something he had never told anybody. The other boy never took him anywhere again. He was the first of those who disappeared after brief acquaintance. Even the boy's name was forgotten, and what he looked like.

What was the light, now? It was as small and distant as the speck at the other end of the tunnel. It seemed to approach. It was a fairy; a tiny creature no bigger than a man's finger, dressed in shimmering silver, with a diamond crown and a jewel-studded wand; and the fairy said: 'I am the fairy Periwinkle; and I bring you a beautiful white horse to carry you to the world's end, a purse full of gold, and the most beautiful princess ever seen. You shall have a thousand slaves, a hundred palaces, and three exquisite wishes.'

The fairy Periwinkle did not say that the horse would die before it could be ridden, that the gold would prove to be nothing but detestable caraway seeds, and that the princess would turn into a frog as soon as she was touched. She did not say that the slaves were dried leaves and the palaces rotted kennels, nor that the wishes, before they could be formed or granted, would be confiscated by Grandmama.

Hark! What was that?

'Naughty little boy! Naughty little boy!'

The noise roared in his ears like a stage hurricane.

He was again in his grandmother's garden, where he invented lonely games about a desert island. Nobody but himself ever visited the island, which was a dark recess behind the laurels; and he was often afraid and silly, breaking small twigs and tearing the leaves to pretend that he was truly strong. He was very miserable on the island.

But one day Spence, the jobbing gardener who came once a week, brought a little girl of five or six years old, in a blue pinafore and broad-brimmed straw hat, to wait while he dug a vegetable bed and wheeled his barrow here and there. This little girl had evidently been told that she must not be seen by Grandmama; for she lurked behind the broad beans, hiding. But when Graham crept near, dumbly staring, she was not afraid. On the contrary, she sang little songs to herself, and peeped at him over a pair of apple-rosy cheeks.

He did not dare to speak, in case Grandmama should scold and beat him, so he pretended to be busy about something else; but all the time he watched the games she played with scraps of broken china which she found in the earth, and listened to the songs, straining his ears to gather their words. Spence took the child home to dinner at noon, and although as soon as he had finished his own dinner Graham ran back to the place where she had been, he found only the scraps of china. He tried to play with them the games she had played; but he could not do this, and he never saw her again.

She was a very vague memory. He thought she afterwards became an imaginary playmate called Lucy or Catherine, who joined him in games and admired his courage in slashing at pirates and land-crabs amid the hushed shouting in which he specialized. He knew she wasn't really there; he wished she was. His longing for a little girl friend far exceeded his longing for a little boy friend. Little boy friends were stronger than himself, shouted into tunnels, pushed one into ditches, and ran away. A little girl friend would do none of these things. She would admire one's miraculous daring. . . .

A ghostly laugh quivered through his octogenarian body—was his body still there? He could not feel it—as he pictured Adelaide in a little blue pinafore, rosy-cheeked and inquisitive.

Was it possible that Adelaide had ever been a little girl, longing for a little boy friend? No trace of childishness had marred her perfect composure.

Now, was he responsible for that? Assuming—certainly the thought was quite untenable—that she had married Curtal, what would her response to him have been? Curtal's rough, bullying strength, which, when expressed in print, forced readers to throw the books down and bawl disagreement with all the strength of their lungs, would have roused something vehement in her. She would have been compelled to fight, scream, abandon dignity. Whereas, to himself, a closed door was a closed door, and a speechless look of disdain a signal for withdrawal, to Curtal it would have been a summons to battery. Curtal would have scorned her pompous chastity as highfalutin nonsense. He would have seized, bruised, and thrown her aside, insulting her sex, her family, and her outraged dignity.

Of course, she would never have married Curtal. To her, Curtal was a howling vulgarian, with his thick-soled boots and loud ties and his rude assurance. She spoke of him as if he stank. But how far did her contempt arise from discomposure? Humiliation was her bugbear. Let austerity falter, privilege would collapse. Disarmed, she would cease to be Adelaide, and become no more than another of Curtal's draggled doxies. Was it her secret wish to be humbled? No, no, no; that notion was fantastic. Pride was her all. Whatever Curtal's attractiveness, she would never have stooped to a short man.

If love involved abandonment to overwhelming passion, she had not loved himself. But if he had been different? If he had been able to confess to her his longing for the little girl in the garden? For the ecstasy of simultaneous physical and spiritual union? The response would have been distaste. Worse still, an increase of tyranny. Hadn't she always, coldly penetrating his armour of fastidiousness, despised him?

Too late, now, to ask.

So there she was, the alabaster beauty who had been gratified by his appearance, his manner, his success; while he, acknowledging her beauty and social value, lived outside paradise. In the eyes of Ruddock and Curtal he had been a kept man and a fine menial, suffered to enjoy the occasional frigid embrace of a *precieuse.* In Adelaide's eyes, Curtal and Ruddock were common entertainers, devoid of culture, and beneath the notice of any first-class person. At what point did mutual contempt meet a craving for regard? His father had kept *Cora Pearl* behind his books of sermons.

A lovely summer day. The pavements dry and clean after a week of sunshine. Women in the extraordinary bulge and billow of the pre-war fashion; himself, her father, her brothers, and the male guests in grand tails and toppers and spats, or in brilliant naval or military uniforms. A curious smell of new clothes and varnish and High Society. His own small contributions to the gathering, by contrast, very undistinguished in appearance; and even intellectually no match for the great names summoned by wealth and social position.

'Full house,' Curtal whispered in his ear—much too loud for comfort. 'My God, what toffs!'

Crowds outside St George's, gasping and grinning in the sun, armed with symbolic rice, murmuring in admiration of the tall, handsome couple. 'Ain't he lovely!' 'Oo, she's a picture!' A picture; Botticelli's *Primavera.* Himself excited, jubilant, apprehensive; but conscious of his height and carriage, concealing all emotion with smiling dignity. Adelaide as calm and gracious as if she walked into a shop among bowing salesmen to order a new suite of furniture. Had she looked upon him as a handsome piece of furniture?

Her mother's cold eyes suggested as much, damn her!

Adelaide's hand rested lightly upon his arm. She did not otherwise touch him, either then or in the car returning to her father's home; but needed every inch of room for her veil and train. There was nothing in her manner of a bride's tender wooing of a beloved. He thought: 'Good God, she's a stranger!' It was true; her smile at himself, though not forced, was exactly what it had been at their introduction in Lucy Chard's drawing-room.

Yes; but if he had been ardent? Had he cast upon her the chill that she cast upon him? Curtal would have said, roughly: 'Thank God that's over! Come on, girl; show me you love me, or I'll push that bonnet over your eyes!' Brutal dog! He'd been doomed to bitches. Well, she hadn't married Curtal. 'That vulgar little man!'

And he, laughing with Ruddock, 'the Dragon!' A common anti-pathy; Curtal raucously demanding admiration, and supplying it himself; Adelaide insisting upon obeisance, and feeling herself beyond all need for boasting. Was she as sure of that as she seemed?

Curtal wasn't. Yet Curtal, that unquenchable noise, died to a chorus of acclaim, and—according to White—was destined for immortality; while Adelaide passed well-nigh unnoticed from the world. A wretched newspaper, the editor of which had some grievance, headlined the fact that Mrs Graham Stanhope had left only a quarter of her fortune to her husband; but apart from this, and unpublicized votes of thanks from various charities, she was unremembered. None but himself visited her grave; and his own visits were those of duty.

Curtal. Curtal. What the hell was it Curtal had written about him? He was suffocating again; struggling for breath, falling into an abyss.

Were those eyes and bulbous faces nearer? Were they symbols of self-arraignment? Did these thoughts, now first released, reveal the decorous suppressions of a lifetime? The paralysis? 'Come on, girl; show me you love me, or I'll push that bonnet over your eyes!' Never spoken! What had been said was: 'Mind, Graham, you mustn't crush the dress.' 'You're armoured, darling!' 'It all went very well, I think.' 'Perfect, of course.' 'I'm glad you had Everard as best man; he looked excellent.' 'A tower of strength.'

She had meant: 'My brother; not that scruffy little wretch in the hired suit.' He had meant: 'Entirely correct.' She had meant. 'As I wished. I know you wanted the scrubby little wretch.'

Yes, he had wanted either Curtal or Ruddock. Having seen Curtal in church, he knew that Curtal was the friend for a register office, not a fashionable affair. She had been right. He was filled with respect for her sense of the right thing. He also had such a sense.

Discretion continued. With the armour removed, she was elegant in her travelling costume; much too busy and preoccupied with guests and time-table to think of caress. Nor did he wish to caress her. They were the handsome, smiling, unbending pair; quite unimpatient for their honeymoon, but of course keeping their eyes upon the clock, in case the train should be missed.

At last it was time to go. All dignity; hand-shaking, bows, Adelaide kissing her mother and father—both dutiful pecks. Again the waiting carriage; no armour now but reserve and disinclination for any display of amorousness. The train; the carriage to themselves. 'How hot it is! Not together, darling; don't you think?'

'Come on, girl; show me you love me, or I'll fling that hat on the line! And you after it!'

Never spoken. Never in all their lives spoken. If, in some mad moment, the words had been uttered—with, of course, simulated passion—she would have evaded his arms, and looked significantly at whatever bottle or decanter lay within his reach. No reply would have been made; her door that night would have been audibly locked. All as vulgar as a flounce; but highly characteristic. Would her gesture have been meant to repel, or to excite?

Who, then, had been to blame? A rustling as of leaves suggested that every shadow about him was whispering 'you!'

Curtal would have roared with laughter at any recital of these things, afterwards exclaiming with his mixture of cruelty and affection: 'You were a damned fool to let her get away with it. You pruriently thought too much about her chastity and self-respect and the rest of it; the armour she used to raise her value. Women don't understand scruples in a man. I found that out as a lad.'

Useless to retort upon him: 'Yes; and look at the women you got hold of!' Curtal, unabashed, would coarsely have answered: 'Got hold of me, you mean! Not to mention those who failed!' And if you said: 'You always had to bolt from them, remember!' he would have said: 'After a bit, yes. I had a good turn of speed. But what happened to you was a life sentence!'

Vulgar, horrible little brute. They said he was a genius; but what place had genius in that miasma? God! God! What had he written about one—for posterity? The uncertainty heated one's blood to fever; there was nothing he couldn't turn to ridicule. What killed reputation was not attack, but ridicule. It was Curtal's weapon.

He would invent and embroider this story of a chilly marriage until hearers thought he was present all the time. He would bring up the tale of the gardener's grand-daughter, which, when they were exchanging childish impressions, one had stupidly told him. Indecent inferences would be drawn from it. Other stories, equally susceptible of comic treatment, would follow, with appallingly destructive consequences. Graham Stanhope would be drowned in absurdity.

'Ho-ho-ho!' That would be the sound of Curtal's bellowing laughter as he wrote his exposure. In reading what he had written, all mankind would relax, guffawing. 'Ho-ho-ho! This fellow Stanhope must have been a mass of absurdity!'

'Ho-ho-ho!' tittered the shadows. 'He wanted a little girl; and he was carried off by a Dragon! What a sorry story!'

Grinning faces were so close that he could see only gigantic teeth. Dragons' teeth! All despised him, as she had done, as Curtal had done.

THIRTY-ONE

The Second Dream

THE faces reminded him of photographs he had seen of giant crowds in Trafalgar Square, looking up at tiny orators among the lions. They were not individualized; he expected none of them to make any personal communication. 'A sea of faces.' But they watched him, and as he addressed them they nodded or shook their heads, like birch leaves in a storm, without relaxing an attention which because of its extraordinary dead silence was intimidating.

He had addressed many audiences with *sang froid* and observant calculations of the response to his words. Older men and women had listened respectfully to a great man telling them (it was his gift) of fascinating discoveries among classic writers. He had made a point of never condescending; and his audiences went away, he believed, intending to buy and read his books. Whether the intention persisted could not be confirmed, so meagre and disappointing were his royalty accounts. That was the lot of a man who refused to be commercial.

Undergraduate audiences had been, by comparison, more intelligent, better informed, and more captious. They had needed an elaborately circumspect approach, and a note throughout of self-protective irony, because every such audience contained three or four conceited members who sought to disconcert a speaker by politely-couched innuendoes. Those had given him no trouble. He enjoyed public speaking.

These unidentifiable watchers and listeners afforded neither stimulation nor pleasure. He wasn't sure that they would understand what he said, however winningly he conversed with them. One might as well address sheep; sheep, however, which uttered no thirsty 'baas'. A single cry would have been welcome. It would have prevented him from hearing the sound of his own voice, admittedly mellifluous, but at the time curiously flattened.

'I am not here to defend any action of mine,' he cried, opposing defiance to suspected hostility. 'I have been listening very patiently to detraction, and I tell you, here and now, that my deeds, like my judgments, have been in accord with the highest principles. A writer must maintain contact with the best thought of his day. As a poet, he must express that thought in pregnant language; as a critic he must conduct a tightrope walk if he is to represent the fashion. I say, if he is to represent what a great seventeenth-century mystic, whose name, because it was a common name of some sort, Jones, Smith, or Robinson, momentarily escapes me, styled "the climate of opinion". I ought not to have called that climate by its less imposing name, fashion. It was a slip.'

The slip had clearly been unfortunate; for, without ceasing to stare, those nameless ones managed to communicate amusement over it to each other. The crowded faces split into what looked like toothy grins. To a sensitive man, horrible grins.

Such definitions were always dangerous, owing to the arbitrary meanings that words attached to themselves or, by misuse or overuse, developed in the minds of the inexact. Perhaps 'tightrope' was also an unfortunate term. That was the worst of extempore speech; one had no chance to whittle a phrase down to the near meaningless before pronouncing it as a metaphysician's triumph.

However, he could not cancel the words. He must drown memory of them by an excursion.

'Apart from my original work, which has embraced verse and fantasy, and even poetical drama, I have worked hard to maintain the standard of contemporary taste. I have deeply studied all the great critics, from Aristotle to Dryden, from Lessing and Goethe —who, although in action a most repulsive egotist, and as a novelist a crashing bore, was a great poet and critic—to Coleridge, and from Sainte-Beuve to myself. I have lived with these masters, weighed all their views, and offered theirs as my own judgments. You may therefore take it as certain that whatever Curtal may derisively have said of me, with the aim of depressing my reputation, I am a first-class critic.

'Unfortunately, first-class poets and first-class critics can rarely live by their publications in volume-form. I have therefore expressed my views over the years in lectures and weekly contributions—I hope not without distinction—to the Press. I have had, naturally, to animadvert upon certain commercial products. . . .'

A squealing as of a hundred little pigs checked him. It was so violent that he was taken aback. He looked towards a seething corner of the room, where tumult had arisen. Little pigs? Yes, he could see the agitation of their rosy snouts.

'Evidently these are authors whom I have at some time disobliged. That, of course, must happen when men write much —parasitically, as my friend Curtal used to say with cruel humour —about others. The little pigs are quite third-rate authors, I am sure. I have never disobliged anybody first-class, even when, by some freak of Fate, he has seemed to me less first-class than usual. When I couldn't extol, I fell back, as one does, upon ambiguity. Some would call this ambivalence; but I confidently challenge that interpretation.'

The little pigs squealed again; but, as always happens with little pigs, they were driven out of sight, presumably into some sort of literary Dachau, and he was free to proceed.

'If you say that my judgment was ever affected by friendship, I shall deny it. I have had many friends, have known many celebrated people, Cabinet ministers, writers, artists, and men who influenced opinion. Curiously enough, I have forgotten them. They are as faceless to me now as you are. Indeed, you include many of them, and if so you may dimly remember having seen me before. Otherwise, whatever the status and quality of these men when alive. . . .

'I have, as I told you, as a critic, made tightrope adjustments to fashion, so as never to seem behind the times, but always cordially to welcome the new and the young. I did it, as was right, with carefully tempered enthusiasm, in case my words should hereafter be quoted, with derision, as happened with poor old Edmund Gosse over Hall Caine, and has happened since with others about the mis-praised; but I have never been a sycophant. I have always stood for the best, the highest, the purest. . . .'

How strange the silence had become. His heart turned to water. These listeners didn't believe him.

'As a man,' he faltered. 'As a man . . .'

A movement took place among the spectators. The mass, as

before, remained inert; but some few came nearer. At no time were there more than six of them; now and again there were only three; but they unquestionably separated themselves from the rest and, ever more watchful, crowded too close for comfort. He breathed with difficulty, being reminded of the atmosphere of St George's on his wedding-day, when the odour of new clothes, and silks, and top-hats joined with excitement to close his larynx. There was even a passing flash of colour, of sunlight, to recall that embarrassed hour.

He was again kneeling beside Adelaide before the robed clergyman, sitting beside her in the carriage, sleeping beside her in a strange bed, while the noise of horns and cracking whips in a foreign city made him stir with discomfort. He had embraced an unyielding body; his lips had met lips as cold as death which were quickly withdrawn. She had turned away, chill-breasted, how content with him he could not tell then and could never tell. His heart was beating fast as it had done that night; too fast, stiflingly, and with the same bewilderment. Could the body he clasped be her portrait, descended from its frame to chide one who had caused the original pain?

He whispered: 'Adelaide? Is this yourself, Adelaide?'

When no answer was made, he strove to focus the eyes and mouth of a woman with whom he had spent forty years—half his life. They were distinct for a moment; the eyes looking directly into his own, without love, without dislike, like exquisite glass marbles, and the mouth set as it had been in death, when he had shrinkingly kissed her forehead for the last time.

Here, then, was an opportunity to put the questions already posed to himself. If she had—unthinkably—married Curtal, if he himself had been different, what would have been the consequences? No words likely to be pleasant to her seemed possible. Curtal's name could not be pronounced. He must accept her dislike of Curtal as real; and therefore a supposititious case would do nothing but insult her pride. She could never, fastidious as she was, have yielded the smallest part of chastity to a barbarian. But Graham Stanhope, her husband, the man she had preferred to all others; surely he might be allowed to ask that one all-important question?

'Adelaide, in the years we were together, did I fail you? I had my career, of course; you identified yourself with that; you made

opportunities for me, worked very devotedly; succeeded in everything you—we—aimed at. In almost everything. But I, myself,
Graham; did you feel any tenderness, any passion for me? As you
must now know, if you know anything, I wished for your happiness. Did you enjoy any happiness other than social happiness?
Were you ever thankful to be my wife?'

The frost-hardened eyes gazed into his. Adelaide was unmistakably before him. She stood erect, as she had always done,
because she had been taught at school to sit and stand and
walk so; and she folded her arms as he had seen her do in
middle life when, before the fire, she awaited the coming
of guests. The straight lips parted. He heard the familiar even
tones.

'I have nothing to add to what I have already said.'

Another voice followed; not his own, but that of a coroner
long ago.

'Thank you, Mrs Stanhope. Thank you, Mrs Stanhope.
Thank you, Mrs . . .'

The figure was gone. Stanhope's throat was dry. He was to
learn nothing.

When he looked again, Adelaide's place had been taken by a
trio, a very oddly assorted trio in what he realized as the frumpish
costumes of Edwardian England. Hester Thompson, called to
mind by White's description as a young coffee-spilling girl,
drooped in shy sullenness over a tray, her lank dark hair hanging
unkempt about a putty-coloured face, and her eyes averted or cast
down, never once meeting his own. Henrietta, whom he saw with
perceptions clearer than those of their brief acquaintance, as pert,
shallow, and, by Curtal's account, wanton, did not hesitate to
smile, slightly bridle, and reveal herself as a superior slut. Lucy
Chard, a tired old woman, kind, hospitable, disinterested, but
essentially a busybody arranging meetings and matches and
successes for self-gratification's sake, had lost colour, energy, and
charm.

Shallow creatures all. Hester a predestined encumbrance,
unable to express the burning secrets of her heart, because, contrary to her belief, she carried no burning secrets in her heart.
Henrietta a feather-weight, selfish and self-indulgent, laughing in
ridicule at his discretion and acceptance of bogus reproof. Lucy

agedly reproachful because, having owed their marriage to her scheme, he and Adelaide did not, as they advanced to greater attainment, joyously fête their benefactress. He looked with distaste upon the three.

'Not quite the three graces,' he cruelly observed. 'And really, those clothes date you all most distressingly. That doesn't matter with you, Hester, since any sack was good enough for the body of a poet; and I know that you, Lucy, always lived spiritually in the eighteenth century, where you'd have been good company for the Miss Burneys; but Henrietta! You, who prided yourself so much on *chic*! I'm disagreeably surprised!'

What on earth led him to address them so rudely? He could not imagine. To Hester, who had traduced him, he owed no kindness; to Henrietta only a first step into Society; but to a faded Lucy any cruelty was unpardonable. Was he too ill to know what he was saying? He wished he did not feel so ill. He wished these women, whom he wanted to forget, would go.

'I was lonely,' said Lucy Chard. 'I had no hope of further happiness for myself. I had no children, little money. But I took compensatory pleasure in bringing people together for my own and their entertainment, and, being maternally in love with you, I found you a bride. From that moment you were secure from want; and as I admired your talent I thought I had done well. You were very handsome, Graham; but you had no heart. You saw a chance of bettering yourself; and you took it. I never reproached you. If my clothes are dowdy, it is because, growing older, I took less and less interest in society, and at last lived by myself, visited only by the loyal. Not by you. I had served my turn. Tom Curtal was loyal to the last.'

'Oh, don't talk about Tom Curtal!' cried Henrietta, with the drawling laugh he remembered so well. 'Tom was always a fearful bounder. If you showed him the most distant kindness, he jumped to crude conclusions, and behaved like a stag in the rutting season. So primitive. So outrageous. He was the torment of my life. I had great trouble in getting rid of him. In the end I had to tell the servants to shut the door in his face. Men as they grow older always grow indecent. Even old Trummy, always a bore, developed a passion for little girls, and pursued them in the street until the police got interested, and he had to be smuggled abroad. My God, what a bore he was, with his endless anecdotes!

By the way, what did Tom Curtal die of? I should suppose he was cancerous. I know I always found him repulsive.'

'Did you really find him repulsive?' Stanhope asked, with irony, but also with some eagerness.

'Unspeakably. You, naturally, were different.'

'Not repulsive, I gather?'

'But so like a curate! One expected you to kneel in prayer.'

'Possibly in adoration?'

'I wasn't interested in adoration. I should describe myself as a realist.'

'Men would describe you otherwise, Henrietta.'

'That's because for you, dear Graham, the grapes are sour. Such a gentleman! And the grapes so-o-o sour! . . .'

He grasped two suggestions. One of them was that she had been disappointed in himself, the other that she had been disappointed in Trumble, who had preferred little girls. As to Curtal, she was a liar. But then Curtal, too, was a liar. Why should he believe either story?

The three women were dissolving. Lucy—poor Lucy, whom he could never forgive for her meddlesomeness—was already gone; Henrietta, with a tart's last flickering sidelong glance, was returning to limbo. Only Hester Thompson remained, her eyelids lowered. He thought she wished most venomously, as she had done all her life, to wound; but could summon no words. What was it she tried to tell him? He bent forward in distaste.

'You never looked at me,' she whispered. 'You showed you thought me ugly and stupid. I was both, but you were wrong when you dismissed the burning secrets of my heart just now as non-existent. I'd have done *anything* for you. And you knew it!'

The words were barely audible. They passed into the silence. She was no longer to be seen.

THIRTY-TWO

The Defence

Was somebody crying? It sounded as though breath was being
drawn and expelled in sharp jerks. A child playing at trains
made such a noise more loudly. A greyness like that of winter
dawn seemed to be about him, not filled with endless eyes or
with spectres, but for fleeting seconds with two or three realities.

'O-o-oh,' grizzled the one who stood farther away. 'He was
the best, kindest master I ever . . . O-o-oh . . .'

'Martin! You fool, Martin!' he tried to say. 'I was never good
to you. I couldn't have been. It wasn't in my nature. If you
knew as much as I do, you'd know that. Don't be ridiculous!'
He could not frame the words. These stupid people enjoyed
living in a world of falsity. Where no love existed, they introduced
sentimentality. Senti . . .'

That was all. He was back in the atmosphere of attentive
watchfulness. Eyes were everywhere. It was a strange sensation;
but he was beginning to grow used to it, and was not discomposed.
He had some vague recollection of seeing Lucy and Henrietta
and Hester. Had not Adelaide been with them? She couldn't
have been with them. She was always apart. What would have
been her reply to Lucy? 'Well, really, Lucy, this is most un-
reasonable! I did come to see you one day; but you had a
distressingly vulgar creature—another genius, I think you said.
So naturally I soon left! . . .'

The next to appear, he expected, would be Grandmama.
Fine noble woman! What was it Hester had said? Some incredible
lie? He spewed it out of his mouth. No man wanted a whistling
woman. Besides, she was physically repellent. Why must women
have instincts? Adelaide did very well without them. At bottom,
he must have hated Adelaide.

'She wasn't the gardener's child, you see,' he murmured, to

an accompaniment of pale laughter. 'But I was never like old Trumble, chasing little girls. I had no instincts, either. Only burning secrets in my heart. They didn't burn consumingly, I assure you. There was something in what Curtal said. There was always, underneath the rubbish, something in what he said. I shouldn't dream of telling him so, however. Too conceited. He; not I . . .'

While Stanhope thus communed, he was aware of a sweeter warmth and a clearer atmosphere. He looked upon, not three, but four women; and all glowed with the radiance of youth. He heard himself saying, without difficulty, and with a roguish humour: 'I think Grandmama must have been exorcized. Has she? Did you do it, you lovely creatures?

> Weaving spiders come not here;
> Hence you long-legg'd spinners, hence!
> Beetles black approach not near . . .

Do you know, when I first read those words I was reminded of her? She was a long-legg'd spinner; and she was also a beetle, approaching stealthily . . . I was afraid she would come round my bed, now, with her long grabbing fingers. This is a bed, is it? I can't be sure.'

How much his heart had lightened at sight of these four young faces, of which the first was all eyes and apple cheeks, while at one of the others he looked long and quizzically, finding her as fair and delightful as she had always been, although she now roused in his breast no emotion stronger than pleasure. She was very fair; and she laughed. But in the church she had been a little old woman who cried for the death of Curtal and spoke gratefully to strangers of Curtal's goodness to her. She was now both young and old within the blinking of an eyelid, old and young, fair and grey, laughing and crying.

'I see that you're still April, Sally,' he said, with tender kindness. 'Still winning hearts and throwing them away as of no account.'

He was not really upbraiding her. It was easy to tease a child one loved or had ceased to love; and Sally had never minded being teased. What she dreaded was too great seriousness, the little butterfly. But was that the whole truth about her? Clearly it was not.

'Come, Sally, tell me why you broke our hearts?'

What did she say? He had never before been hard of hearing. What was it? What was it? He was attacked by the irascibility of deaf old age.

'Tom . . .' The voice was altogether too low.

'Yes; you told my nieces that he'd been good to you. Did he help you with money? Why did you go to him, and not to me? Why didn't you speak to me in church today—yesterd—when was it? I'm a little confused, you know. I've been so tired . . .'

She smiled, wept, shook her head.

'But I want so much to know why . . . why. . . . You're the only person who can tell me; and you tantalize me by speaking under your breath or shaking your head, instead of answering my questions. Why did you break our hearts? That's the first. Why?'

'I don't know,' was the reply. 'I just ran as fast as I could.'

'Really as fast as you could? Or only to see what we should do?'

'I wanted to escape . . . escape . . . escape finality.'

'No love, then?'

She shook her head again. He thought he heard the whisper, 'Escape, escape, escape'; but it might have come from a chorus amid the assembled faces, and was meaningless to him. To his horror, Sally's face was dimming before his eyes. He cried aloud:

'No consideration for ours? And what about Holmes? That dull-witted fool, whom you also ran away from! Come, Sally, we're old now. The others are dead; we're alive, and capable of communication.

'Escape, escape, escape,' came the whisper.

He turned to the two who were still with him.

'Do you understand that?' he asked, curiously. 'Do you realize that she's the only woman Tom Curtal hadn't to extricate himself from? He was always bolting, you know; but over Sally he was ready to cut his throat.'

'A very drastic form of extrication,' said the second of his remaining charmers, whom he knew to be Jackie Boothroyd. 'Unless he didn't really mean to do it?'

'Oh, I think he meant it. Do you think he didn't?'

'I don't know.' It sounded like a mocking echo of Sally's cry of a moment earlier. 'I never knew Tom Curtal. All I know of him I learnt from the newspapers, and from you, this morning.'

'Was it only this morning? I must tell you all about Tom Curtal. He was a very remarkable character. I doubt if I know all about him, myself. I thought I did; but things have happened today—is it today?—that have given me some new data. I think we'll call them data, at least.'

'By all means call them data,' she answered, laughing. 'I expect they're quite as unreliable as other data, and as your old opinions were, too.'

'You don't believe in data. Nor do I. Most of them are selected. Do you know what that means? Mumbo-jumbo. I could give you data about Sally Raikes; but you could draw any conclusions you liked from them.'

'I should draw the conclusion, *prima facie*, that she was a goose.'

'A goose, eh? That doesn't rank her intelligence very high. I had put it higher. A goose, eh? And I a sentimentalist?'

Jackie Boothroyd laughed. He was quite sure that through the mist of uncertainties he heard her laugh; but she did not otherwise reply. He wished to expostulate, to explain; but the days when he could explain were long over, and he had never seriously expostulated with anyone but Tom Curtal. Adelaide was beyond reach of expostulation; other people were below the level at which expostulation was worth while.

'I am not getting much help from you girls,' he grumbled. 'I think you merely sport with me. I doubt if any woman at all has ever taken me seriously.'

But in uttering these words he felt a colder air arise. He was alone with the last of them, and she was as he had seen her, lying dead, and thus sealing his heart for ever.

'I don't really care to know why Sally left both Curtal and me in the lurch,' he assured this last visible child of his love. And now he was entirely without breath, and his mouth was dry. 'There is only one thing I want to know, and one thing I want to say. You left me desolate. You were my only sweetheart. I have asked myself what Adelaide would have done if I'd been a different man, and, by inference, what I should have done if she had been a different woman. The questions have only an abstract interest: we were what we were, and our relationship was what we both made it. But you and I; that's a different matter.'

A host of old associations took him unawares. He could not stifle a cry of pain. It drowned every whisper, and echoed in his ears like the last trump. He saw Gertrude as she had been at their first meeting, and felt the pang of irresistible desire for her. There, and there only, was his true mate. 'You, you, you, my darling!' He must speak with her, engage her attention, charm her with all the spells at his command. She was not fair as Adelaide was, as Sally had been; she was dark, and she was alone, and, in the theatre *foyer*, she was disappointed.

Ruddock's play, of course, with himself, for friendship's sake, attending a performance in the third week of the run. The play was called—what was it called? some ridiculous title such as *The Better Wife* or *Marriage by Candlelight*; he could not remember and it didn't matter. It was a success. He had gone to the box office to collect two tickets promised to him by Ruddock; and as he entered he heard the box office manager snap: 'Nothing under fifteen shillings.' Was it fifteen shillings? At any rate, it was a sum far beyond the purse of this tall girl, proud in defeat. She turned away, thanking the ungracious fellow with courtesy and unconsciously lifted chin. Only a brave heart could thus respond to impoliteness arising from petty but unconscionable power.

Had the play not been by Ruddock, and had he not known what Ruddock's reaction to such a scene would be, he might have done nothing. 'Not my business. Not my business' was the burden of many of his songs justifying inactivity. But, in this case, he could not let her go.

'Excuse me. One moment,' he said, impulsively. And, in his haughtiest style, to the box-office keeper: 'You have two tickets for Graham Stanhope. Mr Ruddock arranged for me to call for them. Mr Stanhope.'

'Yes, sir.' The wretch's manner changed. He knew the name; the tickets were there; Mr Ruddock had 'arranged'. He was happy to oblige.

'Now.' Stanhope was at his most gracious to the girl. 'You see I have two tickets. It's rank privilege. Did you want two? You wanted one? I want only one. My wife is away; and I couldn't come, as I usually do, to the first night. If you will accept one of my tickets you will honour me very much. It will involve sitting next to me in the theatre; nothing else. My name is Graham Stanhope. I am a friend of the author. And the author himself, who doesn't like empty seats at his plays, would be, I know, as pleased . . . hm, hm . . . as Punch.'

She had not hesitated for a moment. She was interested, even amused—she afterwards told him—by the rather pompous self-introduction, which she saw immediately to be a disclaimer of over-familiar intentions. It was that; but she must have known that if she had not been so pretty, and instantly attractive to him, he would splendidly have ignored her.

'You would have ignored me.'

'I shouldn't. But in fact I had fallen in love with you at sight.'

'As I did, my darling, with you.'

'*My darling*.' Adelaide had never once permitted herself such candour. Her 'darling' was a mechanical, indulgent term, used, he believed, because it gave her less trouble to articulate than 'Graham.'

Of course, they supped after the theatre. Of course, Adelaide being away then and for several weeks thereafter, they met again and again, again and again, falling more in love with each other at every meeting. She was a student, in London on a bursary, knowing nobody, very lonely, and as eager to learn as he was eager to teach all that he had ever discovered in books and among people.

'You remember?' he now said, to the ghost of Gertrude which he had summoned in his dream. 'You remember every meeting, as I do; and all I said, as I remember what you said?'

'As you forget what I said,' was the quiet, unquestionable reply, made with a grave smile.

'Oh, come! I remember the essential things. Not, perhaps, the exact words.'

'I remember the exact words.'

He was choking.

'Those I spoke when I had to tell you that Adelaide found my note?'

'The exact words.'

'You blame me. I felt you blamed me. I've known it ever since. I felt you gave me up.'

'I gave you up. I gave everything up. Life. Hope. Everything. You were finished with me.'

'I came back. I came back.'

'It didn't matter. Your career, your reputation, stood first. You were finished with me.'

'I've never, my darling, been finished with you. Never in all my life. Gertrude! Gertrude!'

He heard his own sobs. He felt detestation for Adelaide. Contempt for himself.

There were no women beside him or before him. He was done with women. But Ruddock and Curtal, for the first time for many years, sat there together, as jovial as a pair of affectionate conspirators. What had they brewed about him? He was not afraid. He had never been afraid of Ruddock, whose slow and drowsy speech concealed the lightest and quickest of comprehensions. He had often been afraid of Curtal, for Curtal had the egotist's unholy insight into the vanities of other men.

Ruddock was fondling the bowl of his pipe, smiling, not at all disposed for loquacity. But Curtal, energetic as ever, sailed straight into the attack.

'Well, my dear Graham, you've had rather tough luck, tonight and formerly, with your womenfolk. They don't seem to have given you a great deal of satisfaction.'

'You, dear Tom, are the last person in the world to taunt me with women.'

'Oh, I've had my days all right. I don't look back on them with chagrin, as you do.'

'That's because of your extraordinary resilience. No credit. You've been humiliated by them a thousand times.'

'I see you've counted rather exactly. Kept data, I gather. I never did.'

'An inexact mind. "There or thereabouts." "Some sort of arrangement." You chanced your arm, Tom.'

'In any case, they're all bitches. Now, that's a singular thing, Graham. You attract women. They think there's something beautifully mysterious about you. There isn't. It's simply that you don't go after them. They hate that. I wonder why it is.

I've had plenty of love-affairs. They're no good. They take up time; and they're always unsatisfactory. What I've wanted all my life is a friend.'

'You've had friends. You've had Ruddock and me.'

'Quite true. Ruddock's a dear old codger, aren't you, my boy?'

Stanhope looked at the spot where he had last seen Ruddock. He thought he could just detect a white plump hand caressing the bowl of a pipe; but of Ruddock's face there was no sign.

'He's gone.'

'He comes and goes like the Cheshire Cat. He'll be back before we've done, I expect. I tell you candidly, my boy; Ruddock's been the wise man. He married a dear wife; he wrote just what he wanted to write; and he didn't care a damn what anybody said or wrote about him.'

'But he's dead.'

'So are we.'

'I'm not.'

'As near as dammit. But in a sense I'm more alive than you are. I'm heading, they tell me, for immortality!' He sniggered. 'The bloody highbrows call me "seminal", whatever that means. Something about seeds, isn't it? Not that I care. I never did care. What I wanted to do was to change the world, kill bureaucracy, and set men free. That was my whole interest.'

'Your whole interest was in yourself. The most complete egotist I ever knew.'

'You say that! What a cheek! Well, I suppose I did talk a bit about myself. Do you know why? I wanted you for a friend, an *alter ego*, Damon and Pythias, the Heavenly Twins; and you funked friendship. I was almost idolatrous of you; the chap who'd been taught all I'd never had a chance to learn. I envied your poise, your refinement, with admiration; you grudgingly envied me my genius. Together we should have made a man. Now it's too late. I got on without you. And you—well, you've had a dismal day, so I won't rub it in.'

'You talk of genius,' cried Stanhope, bitterly. 'Where was it? A silly little man up from the Provinces, who took his ideas second—and third—hand from people like Godwin and Rousseau and Helvétius, whom, because he couldn't read French, he never understood. . . .'

'Why, good God! French! What's French got to do with it? Just because you've poached a few notions about Corneille and Racine! You're nothing but a humbugging highbrow, conceited about his Public School and Varsity education. Pooh! You've got no clothes on at all!'

'All right. All right. You've had your say. Now stop. I understand you've written something about me. Something I shall never see. What is it?'

'Oh, that?' Curtal began to snigger. 'Rather good! It's a secret!'

'Yes!' shouted Stanhope. 'What is it you've said about me? What have you said? He who steals my purse steals trash; but he who robs me of my good name. . . .'

'Oh-ho! Iago! Honest Iago! The sea-green incorruptible! That's prime! Graham Stanhope, incorruptible! The man who kept his finger wet to catch the faintest wind of change! Ho-ho-ho! Ho-ho-ho-ho!'

Curtal began to roar with endless laughter. His laughter was echoed and magnified by a dreadful squealing from the little philistine piglets in the corner of the room, whose rosy snouts, were uplifted in consummate glee. From everywhere else, walls, fireplace, ceiling, came the whisper of general laughter, all provoked by relish of Curtal's cruel lampoon upon one whom, by his own account, he had envied for more than fifty years. The laughter wrought so deeply and fierily upon Stanhope's mind that he was carried to intense excitement. The excitement was greater than any he had ever known. It rose until his head seemed to be bursting with agony; swelling, swelling in an extremity of suffering; and when agony could go no farther something within the brain broke. All was darkness.

This is the B.B.C. Here is the news . . . The death is announced of Graham Stanhope, the poet and critic. He was within a few days of his eightieth birthday; and was taken ill yesterday after attending the Memorial Service to his lifelong friend Thomas Curtal. At the end of this bulletin we shall broadcast a tribute to Stanhope as man and writer, recorded for us before his death a fortnight ago by Thomas Curtal.